STRIKE A MATCH

What Reviewers Say About Fiona Riley's Work

Miss Match

"In this sweet, sensual debut, Riley brings together likable characters, setting them against a colorful supporting cast and exploring their relationship through charming interactions and red-hot erotic scenes. …Rich in characterization and emotional appeal, this one is sure to please."—*Publishers Weekly*

"*Miss Match* by Fiona Riley is an adorable romance with a lot of amazing chemistry, steamy sex scenes, and fun dialogue. I can't believe it's the author's first book, even though she assured me on Twitter that it is."—*The Lesbian Review*

"This was a beautiful love story, chock full of love and emotion and I felt I had a big grin on my face the whole time I was reading it. I adored both main characters as they were strong, independent women with good hearts and were just waiting for the right person to come along and make them whole. I felt I smiled for days after reading this wonderful book."—*Inked Rainbow Reads*

Visit us at www.boldstrokesbooks.com

By the Author

Miss Match

Unlikely Match

Strike a Match

STRIKE A MATCH

by
Fiona Riley

2017

STRIKE A MATCH

ISBN 13: 978-1-62639-999-0

This Trade Paperback Original Is Published By
Bold Strokes Books, Inc.
P.O. Box 249
Valley Falls, NY 12185

First Edition: November 2017

Credits
Editor: Ruth Sternglantz
Production Design: Susan Ramundo
Cover Design By Jeanine Henning

Acknowledgments

It takes a village to write a book. There. I said it.

For this book, my village consisted of my ever-patient wife, my super amazing editor Ruth, team Bold Strokes Books, the world's coolest female firefighter, and a glassblowing studio. Mix them all together and *Strike a Match* was born.

Without the help of Sherri Mullin and her firefighting expertise, Sasha McCray would never have come to life the way she did during the making of this novel. Sherri, your input was invaluable and I appreciate how personal and honest your answers were to my endless questions. Thanks for taking the time (and it was a LOT of time) to reply to my emails. I am especially grateful you explained the equipment and purpose of all the hose thingies and mask do-hickeys to me. I promise to never leave a candle unattended. Ever.

Ruth Sternglantz, I am running out of nice things to say about you in my Acknowledgments section. Just kidding, that's impossible. You're fantastic. And funny. And wise. And just the right amount of teacher-y to not be too preacher-y. I know those aren't real words—I don't care: You're the best.

To the unknowing people at Luke Adam's Glass Studio, thanks for letting me make all kinds of cool glass art in the name of research and for not being mad when I wanted to know the exact temperature of all the things.

Team BSB: Thanks for all of your support. You really fanned the flames and encouraged my creativity to ignite (I literally could not help myself there #sorrynotsorry).

To my wife—I know that you make sacrifices every day to support my, at times, insane writing lifestyle. And I'm sure you've used up all your patience over my looming deadlines, but know that I appreciate you and am in awe of everything that you do. Thank you for reminding me that the cat box isn't going to change itself, deadline or not. You're my rock.

Dedication

For Jenn.

Every love story I write is a reflection of how deeply and passionately I feel loved by you and in love with you, every day of my life. All the moments we share are my *favorite* moments. Thank you for your support and for bringing my newest *Love* into this crazy life of ours. I wouldn't change a thing.

CHAPTER ONE

Sasha McCray watched in disbelief as the entire case of champagne flutes took to the air before crashing to the ground, sending shards of glass in every direction. Never once in all of her years supplementing her firefighting job as a catering waitress had she ever seen glassware defy gravity in such a way. Granted, that clumsy brute Aaron Burger was juggling the dishwashing tray like it was a hot potato, but still, the height he got when he tripped was kind of amazing. Kind of. Except now there was a monstrous mess and the wedding reception was about to start. They had thirty minutes to clean up the glass and get the tables set...assuming they even had extra flutes.

"Burger." Casey Matthews rubbed his forehead and sighed. "You are officially relegated to the coat room. Go find Stefan and get out of my sight."

"The coat room? That sounds so boring." Burger brushed off his knees as he stood from the floor and frowned.

"Really? Because to me it sounds like a safe, enclosed space where you can't break anything. Not that I'm suggesting that you try." Casey warned, "Just go and don't screw anything up."

Burger mumbled something under his breath and Sasha shook her head. He was sweet enough, but tonight was not the night for him to make any more mistakes; Boston's notorious Miss Match was getting married, and it was the job of a lifetime for Casey's catering company.

"He's going to give me an ulcer." Casey pressed his hand to his stomach and dropped his head. "I swear to God, if his brother hadn't saved my ass last month in that fire on Hereford, I never would have hired him to fill in tonight. I'd rather be a man short than try to contain that bull in a china shop."

Sasha walked over to her lieutenant and patted him on the shoulder. "You're doing a good thing. He's new to Engine 28 and he needs to find his own way in the company. You letting him sub in tonight was important to him—it made him feel like one of the guys, you know? I'll keep an eye on him, I promise."

"Sasha, you're good at this. If you ever decide you want to change jobs, I think you'd do well here." Casey gave her a genuine smile. She tried to accept it as a compliment, but she knew her mother had been in his ear again. "I mean it. I could use someone to run the day-to-day operations. This business is doing well—it's gonna be my future. You should think about it some more."

"I'll do that." Casey was her lieutenant and her friend, and she knew that he meant well, but she wasn't in the mood to talk about giving up her firefighting career, not today or ever.

"Well, anyway, I have to get a rush on flutes from the warehouse before the first toast now that we're definitely two dozen short. You're going to man the main floor bars tonight—there are five in total. You're bar supervisor and head floor staff. That cool?" Casey picked up his clipboard and pen and started checking things off.

"Bar service? Yes, sir. I'm down." Sasha fist pumped—it was common knowledge that the bar manager had the best job of the evening. It was fast paced and would make the time fly by, but more than that, it would give her the chance to interact with the wedding guests and see the festivities. She had been looking forward to this night ever since Samantha Monteiro had chosen Casey and his wife Elise's catering company to service her wedding, something that Sasha's involvement with Samantha's matchmaking company had helped to make happen.

Casey gave her a nod and headed back toward the kitchen, dialing his phone as he went. She was glad to have him in her life. He was patient and kind and was an excellent firefighter, and he'd been a great mentor to her over the years. He also had been an absolute saint when Sasha had asked to join his side business to help pay off some of her father's medical debts. Casey didn't even hesitate before he'd agreed; he'd started booking her regularly on her off days from the firehouse, and now she was one of his senior employees.

She looked across the gorgeous dance floor at the maze of tables and sparkling white linens. This was a proud moment for Casey and Elise, and she was happy to do her part. Their company had started out small, doing fundraisers at the firehouse and birthday parties for some of the fire crew; they started with kids' parties and graduations, and then they moved on to weddings and larger events. Elise was the talent behind the operation: she had gone to culinary school and worked at not one but two Michelin starred restaurants before she was thirty. Sasha smiled as she thought about how cute the two of them were together. He might be high ranking at the firehouse, but Elise was definitely in charge at these events.

It had always impressed Sasha how well Casey and Elise got along, even in the toughest of situations. They were high school sweethearts, but fast-forward nineteen years, and now they were catering and staffing the wedding of one of Boston's bold-faced names, Samantha Monteiro, and her soon to be wife, Lucinda Moss.

Sasha grabbed a dustpan and broom and started tackling the mess. Casey had thanked her for the referral nearly a dozen times in private, but putting her in charge of the bar service was the icing on the cake. She swept the shattered stems and larger pieces into one area as Jonah, one of Casey's junior staff, came by with a trash bin.

"Make sure you double line this bag when we clean this up. The last thing we need is someone bleeding on their uniform. Elise will freak." Sasha emptied the dustpan and handed it to Jonah. "I'm going to do a quick count on glasses at the main bar—let me know if you need anything." She started walking away before turning back to add, "You'd better run a mop and a vacuum over this area. Grab someone to help you."

"Sure thing, boss." Jonah gave her a salute and a wink. She bit the inside of her cheek to keep from rolling her eyes. Jonah was probably nineteen years old, twenty at most, but that didn't dissuade him from flirting with her whenever they shared an event. Someone ought to tell him she was into women in addition to being way out of his league.

She jogged over to the large main bar and dug out the clipboard that Casey left under the oak bar top. The front page had a map of the reception area, each bar location marked with a drawing paired with the designated bartender's name, and also designating the area set for dish and glass removal by the kitchen staff. A quick glance told Sasha that Casey had put his most seasoned bartenders at the areas with the highest foot traffic. This would be helpful once the guests starting trickling into the reception. The brides would be taking photos for a while, so the appetizers and cocktails would be the main event for a bit.

"Hey, I heard you're the person I should be thanking for tonight's gig." Shaun ran a cloth over the bar's surface, spraying the organic lemon scented cleaner in between swipes.

"I'm not the one getting married." Sasha shrugged. "Plus, I think you put too much sour mix in the margaritas, so I definitely would have asked for Carmen at the main bar."

"You and I both know that I don't use sour mix in anything. Fresh is best, all the way." Shaun laughed. "And you'd ask for Carmen because she has better cleavage than me, not because she mixes a better drink."

"Well she certainly looks better when she shakes the drinks, I'll give you that." Sasha poked Shaun's rotund belly with her finger before he slapped it away.

"Years of taste-testing Elise's food are catching up to me." Shaun grabbed a fresh glass and poured a dark purple liquid into it, turning toward Sasha and holding it out to her.

"What's this?" Sasha took the glass and sipped it. Shaun had been with the company the longest and he was the best bartender she had ever worked with; his ingenuity with cocktail creations was unmatched. She swirled the slightly sweet liquid around her mouth before swallowing it. It was delicious. Dangerously delicious.

"Tonight's signature cocktail. I'm calling it *Swept Away by Romance*. All local ingredients, a touch of brightly colored liquor, and voilà, signature cocktail to the stars. Well, to the best dressed of Boston anyway." Shaun poured himself a sip and finished it off. "A cocktail worthy of the gorgeous couple, themed to match the event space."

Sasha smiled. "You know, I've never been to the New England Aquarium at night—it's so pretty here."

Shaun stood to his full six-foot-five-inch frame and looked beyond her at the reception area. "They did a really great job decorating the space. This wedding planner is amazing. Hopefully Elise cooks up a storm and we get to work with him again—a guy could get used to this kind of venue."

"I know what you mean." Sasha considered how she got here and almost couldn't believe it. She had gotten involved with Samantha Monteiro's matchmaking company, Perfect Match, Inc., on a dare from some of her firehouse colleagues. There was an ad for eligible bachelorettes in the *Boston Globe*, specifically looking for those that identified as lesbian or bisexual, to meet some of Boston's most eligible lesbians. Although she didn't doubt that the guys had heartily encouraged it for their own perverse reasons, curiosity actually had her walking through the door. It was over a year ago since she had first met Samantha Monteiro.

Samantha had been talking to her admin when Sasha got off the elevator. She was early, more out of nervousness than anything else. Samantha had stopped midsentence and regarded her with a broad smile.

"You must be Sasha." Her voice was like warm honey, matching the rest of her beautiful form. Sasha had to swallow twice to keep herself from drooling. She figured in that moment if Samantha's clients were half as attractive as she was, she was winning. So hard.

"That's me." Sasha had hated herself the moment she opened her mouth, feeling like someone spilled lame-sauce in aisle five.

After a brief exchange, Samantha guided her into her plush, gorgeous office and opened her file. Sasha had been impressed, and also a little freaked out, by the thoroughness of Samantha's preparation for their meeting. She had been searched and re-searched online, her DMV record and professional license obtained, the headshot she'd submitted matched to her license photo, and a copy of her passport sat on top of the neatly arranged file like a prize. Samantha assured her that this was a routine data collection for all of their clients and their prospective dates—Perfect Match wasn't just looking for single ladies, but she and her business partner Andrew Stanley were looking for single women to be paired with some of Boston's best, brightest, and most successful professional women looking for partners in life and love. It had sounded so romantic that she'd nearly zoned out. She couldn't decide if it was Samantha's soothing voice that was having a lulling effect, or that watching Samantha's full pink-glossed lips move was hypnotizing. Either way, her first impression of Samantha Monteiro had been very, very good.

Which was why, a year later, she still had confidence in Samantha's skillset. Sasha had had multiple near matches through Perfect Match. And she had to admit, the matches they had made for her had felt more significant and legitimate than any she had made for herself in the darkened back corner of a dusty bar with a nameless girl. She had felt a genuine connection with both of her matches, most recently, entrepreneurial millionaire tech wiz Shelly White. She'd been disappointed when neither match progressed beyond a few dates. But she knew they were on to something, because for the first time in her life, Sasha had felt a connection with someone that was more than physical. It was as if a stable, loving relationship like her parents had was actually an option for her. She had mentioned that to Samantha on that first day: she wanted to find a love like her parents found, and Samantha had assured her that with time, she would do just that.

So when Samantha announced she was getting married, Sasha had readily suggested her colleague's catering and waitstaff service. She wanted to be there for Samantha's big day.

"Sasha?" Shaun was smirking. "Where the hell did you just go? I asked you like six questions, one of which was sexual in nature, and you just nodded and hummed."

"Oh, my bad. Trip down memory lane—must have taken the scenic route." Sasha shook her head and checked the clipboard again. "What did you ask?"

"A multitude of things, but mainly I asked for more fruit from the kitchen." Shaun pointed toward the oranges, lemons, and limes cut into small starfish shapes on the dish in front of him. "Those float in the signature drink. Imma need about four dozen more."

"On it." Sasha took a quick picture of them and turned toward the kitchen.

"Hey, Sasha?" Shaun called over her shoulder.

"Yeah?"

"Tonight is going to go off without a hitch. I can feel it."

Sasha took a deep breath and walked back toward Jonah to make sure everything sharp was safely stowed away. "I sure hope so."

Chapter Two

Abby Rossmore sighed and checked her phone for the fourth time. They were going to be late if her mother didn't hurry up.

"Mom, at this rate we may as well just mail a gift."

"Abigail, please. It's appropriate to be fashionably late to things," Edie Davenport called from her makeup table across the room of her enormous bedroom suite while Abby lounged on the chaise in the corner.

"Abby," she corrected. *Abigail* was reserved for her strict but dearly departed maternal grandmother. Well her, and when she was in trouble. This was not one of those times. At least, she didn't think so anyway.

Edie made a noise that sounded vaguely like judgment. "Abigail is a beautiful name. I don't understand why you don't use it."

"The same reason I don't use Davenport," Abby said under her breath, deciding not to argue.

"I heard that." Edie turned in her seat and crossed her legs, her elegant gown moving like silk along her seemingly ageless, fit frame—something Abby hoped to emulate someday. "I don't understand why you do that either. There is nothing wrong with being a Davenport, Abigail. Excuse me, *Abby*."

Abby sat up and gave her mother a look.

Edie stood and smoothed out her dress as she reached for her clutch. "You know, most people would kill to have that association, darling. You've spent your whole life running from it. It seems foolish to me."

Abby sighed. This wasn't a fight worth having, again. Tonight, or any night. She knew where her mother stood. She just so happened to stand somewhere else, mostly on solid ground, with her head firmly planted on her shoulders. Something her mother seemed unable to fathom. "Don't you think Mimi would appreciate all the good I do with Rossmore? I think I make Rossmore look good."

Edie laughed that carefree, jovial laugh that Abby adored so much. She loved her mother. They didn't always agree, but Edie was Abby's best friend. They only had each other in this world, after all. She glided across the room and pulled Abby off the chaise, air-kissing her cheek so as not to smudge her lipstick. She cupped Abby's jaw affectionately as she replied, "Yes, bunny. Your grandmother would approve. I'm sure she's in heaven right now beating Mother Teresa's holy heinie at bridge and bragging about her beautiful, smart granddaughter."

"You think she's cheating?" Abby rested her head against her mother's shoulder and thought fondly of her grandmother.

"Without a doubt. I bet she recruited St. Peter to help. That woman had no morals." Edie caressed Abby's hair, careful not to brush any strands out of place.

"See? This is exactly why I repurposed her last name—in an effort to earn her some brownie points doing accounting for the nonprofit. Think of all the people that are benefiting from her bad decisions and questionable legacy."

Edie bopped Abby on the nose and shook her head. "It never ceases to amaze me that my gorgeous, blond daughter never adopted my love of tennis or handsome, dapper men."

"There's nothing wrong with loving numbers, or women, Mom," Abby replied with a laugh. "And if I recall correctly, last time we played, I beat you in singles tennis. I just prefer math to fuzzy yellow balls."

"Or any balls for that matter," Edie deadpanned.

"Edith Augustus Davenport." Abby feigned outrage. "Did you just make a crude joke?"

"It appears I did. Must be time to depart. Mimi must be channeling something in me." Edie winked and tugged Abby toward the bedroom door. "Come now, Abby, you're making us late."

❖

"My, my. Samantha sure knows how to throw a party, doesn't she?" It wasn't often that Abby heard awe in her mother's voice.

Abby could see why her mother sounded so impressed. The reception space was stunning: the tables were lined with glistening fine china and ornate silverware with influences of coral carved into the delicate handles. The centerpieces were flower arrangements overflowing with gorgeous blues and purples, floating in water-filled glass bowls with sparkling crystal rocks at the bottom, reflecting light back onto the seated guests giving the illusion that they were lit from within. The ceiling was glittered in lights and paper-lantern-like globes, mimicking the appearance of the starry night sky above the water, as a faint but ever-present light show cascaded along the dance floor, the calming blues and turquoise shades so subtle you would miss it if you weren't watching closely. Samantha Monteiro had clearly spared no expense at making this night an evening to remember.

"Oh, look. Giovanni is here. Let's say hello before we sit." Edie looped her arm into Abby's elbow and guided her toward the handsomely dressed wedding planner by the entrance of the event space before she had a chance to protest.

"Miss Davenport"—Giovanni smiled broadly and bowed his head—"it's a pleasure to see you this evening." He took Edie's hand and kissed her knuckles.

Edie nodded politely and motioned for Abby to grab two champagne flutes from a passing waiter. "Giovanni, the place looks amazing."

"*Grazie*, Signora Edie, *grazie*." Giovanni puffed out his chest, his mustache twitching. Abby tried not to puke.

Her mother gave a fake, flirtatious laugh, so Abby grabbed three flutes instead, figuring she might need a double.

"Excellent idea, Abigail." Her mother took the extra glass and handed it to Giovanni for a toast. "Another successful event, from the wedding planner of the century."

Abby watched in dismay as Giovanni emptied the contents of her emergency elixir, sighing as she sipped her champagne politely until this exchange was over.

Just when she thought she might be in the clear, he turned his attention to her. "Abigail, it's so nice to see you out of those glasses. You have such beautiful eyes. Did you bring a date tonight?" He looked over her shoulder in search of a phantom.

"I'm my mother's date tonight, Gio." Abby's mother's foundation frequently used Giovanni's services to coordinate events. She'd known him for years, and knew how much he disliked the nickname, but she wasn't exactly in love with his glasses comment so she thought it was a fair trade-off.

Giovanni pursed his lips in a controlled smile. "Ah, well, she's a lucky woman, your mother. Enjoy your night, ladies." He dipped his head and excused himself without another word.

"That was a little rude." Edie gave her an admonishing glance.

"I could say the same thing about his comments regarding my life choice to see." Abby shrugged and finished her champagne.

Edie rolled her eyes and laughed. "You're impossible."

"Impossibly yours." Abby handed her glass off to a young waiter wearing a formal vest.

"I wouldn't have it any other way." Edie adjusted the diamond choker around her neck as the singer of the seven-piece band called the audience's attention to the main doors, signaling the brides' arrival. "See, darling? We're right on time."

Abby guided her mother to the side as the newly married Samantha Monteiro and Lucinda Moss entered the room to thunderous applause. Samantha's designer gown accentuated her bosom with a heart-shaped neckline and a mermaid waist, her train clipped to her bodice, the flowing decorative veil sitting delicately along the back of her immaculately styled raven hair—she was a vision in white. Lucinda clasped Samantha's right hand, her eyes on her bride as they walked through the doors—the adoration loud and clear.

Her own gown was breathtaking, different, understated compared to Samantha's, but with lace and beaded details that from Abby's perspective gave the appearance of a vintage modern reinterpretation of Old Hollywood style. It was very much in character with the Lucinda she had gotten to know over the last few months through her association with Samantha, as a client at Perfect Match.

As they glided past, moving farther into the event space, Abby couldn't help but feel a little envious of their love. She had never seen a more perfectly paired couple in all of her life, including her mother and late father, whose devotion to each other was abundantly obvious in family photos and home movies. No, something about Samantha and Lucinda was positively magical. Their true love match was one of the reasons Abby hadn't given up on her quest to find love through Samantha and Andrew's matchmaking service. But if she was being completely honest with herself, she was losing hope.

"They are a stunning couple, aren't they?" Edie's eyes were tear filled as she clasped her hand over Abby's resting on her arm. "Such a magnificent pair. Imagine the beautiful children they would have together."

Abby looked at her mother, surprised. "I suppose, yes."

"You suppose?" Edie raised her eyebrow as she surveyed Abby. "Abigail, if you brought home either one of those gorgeous creatures, I would do cartwheels. Imagine what the girls at the country club would say." She mused, her lips pressed together in a playful grin, "Let's ask Samantha if she has a sister. I've always pictured you with a tall brunette."

Abby could feel her mouth open, but no matter how much she willed it to close, it wouldn't budge. This was new information—her mother had always accepted her relationships with women, but she'd never weighed in on them. "You pictured me with a…brunette?"

"What? Is that a bad thing?" Edie looked alarmed. "Tall, dark, and handsome can apply to a woman, Abigail. Don't be so closed-minded." She pressed two manicured fingers to Abby's chin and closed her mouth. "You won't bring home any beauties with your mouth open, dear."

"I need a drink." Abby blinked, cataloging her mother's statements for later. "We're going to discuss this further."

Edie clapped with excitement. "Oh, goodie. I wanted to talk to you about Rachel Rabin's daughter, Dianna—she's a lawyer at Brown Brothers Harriman. She played varsity tennis at Yale. I think we should schedule a doubles match for next weekend. She speaks French, Abby. Fluently."

Abby felt her eyes bulge as her mother swooned, her hand over her heart in dramatic fashion that was...Just. So. Edie. She looked around frantically for the nearest escape route—she would not be set up by her mother and her mother's frenemy Rachel Rabin, not now, not ever. She didn't bother telling her mother that she and Dianna had already tested the waters a few times but decided they weren't right for each other. That was something she would take to the grave. "Uh, we can talk about it."

Edie's joyous expression faded. "I know that tone. That means you are taking it off the table. That's the end of joy as we know it."

"That's a little dramatic, Mom." Abby tried to keep a straight face but her mother was all kinds of adorable right now.

"I'm just saying, let's see what Samantha has to say after this wedding is behind her. If she doesn't have a match for you, then let me see what I can do." Edie seemed encouraged, which made Abby nervous.

"If Miss Match herself can't find me a girlfriend, then I'm cashing in my inheritance and moving to an island with feral cats where no one can hear my sobs of loneliness. It's decided." Abby crossed her arms and sighed.

"Now who's being dramatic?" Edie nudged her in the side. "Let's see who's at our table. We can talk about your woeful existence over salad."

"Great." Abby let her mother guide her toward their designated table and tried not to pout as she saw her near match, Shelly White, and her girlfriend step onto the dance floor. Another missed opportunity, another perfect match for someone else.

CHAPTER THREE

Sasha speed-walked toward Shaun's bar and dropped off another plate of fruit stars. The rate at which the guests were consuming the signature cocktail was almost alarming. Well, considering the degree to which they were also draining the champagne reserve, it *was* alarming. She hadn't had a chance to check on the wine inventory yet, but she was willing to bet it was taking a serious hit.

"Queen of the Fruit! Thanks." Shaun grabbed a few stars and dropped them into the three glasses waiting on the bar top.

"Funny." Sasha snagged a cocktail shrimp off Jonah's serving tray as he walked by. Shaun gave her a look. "What?"

"You're supposed to eat out back where no one can see you—you know that." He sipped a glass of water and wiped his brow. The cocktail hour had been as busy as they expected and it didn't look like it would slow down much. That happened when there was an open bar the entire wedding—lots of foot traffic and lots of snacks to keep the wolverines at bay.

"I promise you no one will notice a missing shrimp. But yeah, I hear ya. It's been insane and it's only the cocktail hour." Sasha leaned against the bar and looked out at the reception hall. They were still walking appetizers around for another fifteen minutes. Soon the first course would come out and most of the crowd would take a seat for a longer period of time, which was good because two of the less experienced servers had already collided with guests and dumped the contents of their trays.

"It sure has. Everyone is pretty nice though, so that's good." Shaun smiled and took the order of two attractive gay men at the bar. Sasha recognized Andrew Stanley right away.

"Hey, Andrew."

"Sasha—oh, that's right, I forgot you were our catering connection. You look great in a tuxedo. Well, you look great in just about anything, I bet. How are you?" Andrew had a perma-smile on his face, Sasha figured it was because his best friend and business partner was finally tying the knot. His smile was infectious.

"I'm good. You know, staying out of trouble." Sasha reached past him and extended her hand to his date. "I'm Sasha."

"Ben. It's nice to meet you." Ben was about an inch shorter than Andrew. He was clean shaven and wore a tux complementing Andrew's best man attire. They were a handsome couple.

Andrew took the drink Shaun handed him and turned his attention back to Sasha. "Don't stay out of too much trouble—it's a party after all. And Samantha's paying, so bottoms up." He raised his glass in a mock toast and took a sip.

"Will do." Sasha squeezed his elbow and waved as he and Ben retreated into the crowd.

"He seems nice." Shaun held a martini glass up to the light, appearing to inspect it.

"He is. Funny as fuck, too." She looked to her right just in time to see Jonah nearly knocked off his feet by a guest abruptly sliding out their chair. "Shit. I'll be right back."

She ran to Jonah's side, catching the tray of cocktail shrimp before it tipped too far to the right, and grabbed his elbow with her left hand, to help him retain his balance.

"Jesus Christ. That lady came out of nowhere." Jonah looked a little frazzled. He adjusted his suit jacket and cracked his neck before reaching to take the tray back from Sasha.

"Lower your voice, Jonah," Sasha said behind a fake smile, painfully aware of the proximity to the woman in question. "That's the bride's mother."

Jonah blinked and snapped his mouth shut, looking a little pale. Sasha motioned for him to join her a few feet away before she spoke again.

"Why don't I finish this tray off for you? Head back and grab another one, then hit the east side and clear off the dish tray behind Carmen's bar—it's looking a little precarious." He nodded and turned to go before she stopped him. "You'd better get the dish tray first. I don't trust that guy with the cane over there."

Jonah looked toward the smaller bar on the right and nodded, disappearing into the throng of guests standing around the dance floor watching the brides as they continued to dance for a few songs after their first dance.

She watched them for a moment with a warmth in her chest, happy to see them both so content, before she refocused on the cocktail shrimp task she had just signed herself up for. She turned to the right and addressed the first two people standing there. "Cocktail shrimp?"

The dark-haired woman turned at the sound of her voice. It was her near match, Shelly White. "Sasha?"

"Oh, hey, Shel. Shrimp?" Sasha shouldn't be surprised to see her; Shelly had mentioned she would be at the wedding when they had had dinner last month. That was something new to Sasha. She and Shelly had gone on half a dozen dates and things were really progressing between them, when Sasha had an accident at work with Casey and was supposed to be out of town for a training as she recovered. But everything sort of fell to shit after that, and she and Shelly lost touch. Sasha wasn't used to maintaining friendships with her exes. Truthfully, she'd never had a connection with anyone before Shelly that she'd want to continue a friendly relationship with after the romantic or sexual side fizzled out.

That was how she had realized that she was looking for a change. Something was different in her now. She wanted more. But seeing Shelly happy with someone else was still a little difficult—it still felt fresh even though it had been a few months now.

"These are huge." Shelly's girlfriend Claire took one and reached out to squeeze Sasha's elbow. "How are you?"

"Good." Sasha kissed Claire on the cheek, careful not to drop her tray. Claire was perfect for Shelly, even if at times she hated to admit it. They just seemed to get each other. Shelly seemed to be comfortable around her in a way that she hadn't quite achieved with Sasha. They were cute together, and recognizing that helped Sasha move on.

"What are you doing here?" Shelly declined the shellfish Claire offered her, sipping her drink instead.

Sasha shrugged. "Picking up a few catering shifts here and there for some extra money. I jumped at the chance to be a part of Samantha's big day. She's the best."

Claire nodded. "She is."

Sasha bit back a laugh—Shelly had confided in her that Claire had been totally anti-matchmaker from the moment they'd met, even though their entire first meeting was choreographed by Samantha, unbeknownst to them at the time. Sasha wondered how many of this evening's attendees were Samantha's clients, or possible matches for said clients. One never could know with Samantha—she was wily like that.

Applause from the surrounding crowd interrupted their conversation as Samantha and Lucinda playfully danced in the center of a larger forming circle. Sasha looked at her tray and glanced at her watch. "I've got to get these little guys to the masses before the first course comes out. It was great seeing you. Game night soon?"

"Definitely." Shelly raised her glass toward Sasha and smiled. "You're on my team this time though. Jamie totally cheated last time."

Sasha laughed as Claire rolled her eyes and blew her a kiss. The last time she had dinner with them, Claire's brother Jamie had come over to play video games with Shelly and a pretty heated Mario Kart tournament was born. Jamie and Claire dominated the first and second place spots of every race—it was a total ambush. Sasha had really enjoyed herself, even though she was easily the least skilled gamer there.

"Bye, Sash." Claire waved as she and Shelly headed toward their table. Sasha watched them get comfortably seated, making a mental note to pop by their table later to check in on them.

When she glanced back toward the center of the room, she noticed a woman looking frustrated, staring down the front of her expensive dress. The woman turned and Sasha could see why: there was a red wine mark in a streak on her lap. She looked up to grab Jonah's attention and motion for him to bring some seltzer water before she realized why the woman looked familiar—that was Marisol Monteiro, Samantha's mother, and she was willing to bet that the wine stain was the result of Jonah's ineptitude.

She hurried over to Marisol, handing off her shrimp tray to Jonah and shoving him out of sight before the older woman noticed. "Can I help you, ma'am?"

Marisol glanced up, appearing surprised by Sasha's presence. "That server spilled wine on my dress." She pointed toward Jonah's back and her forehead creased in annoyance.

"I can get someone to help you get that out before it ruins the dress, ma'am. Give me one second, okay?" Sasha went into crisis management mode—there was nothing worse than a red wine stain on the mother of the bride's dress before pictures were taken. This was a code red if there was one. Before Marisol had a chance to reply, Sasha jogged to the main bar and grabbed Shaun's walkie-talkie.

"Casey?" Sasha waited for his reply.

"What's up, Sasha?" Casey's voice was muffled; Sasha could hear the loud noises of the kitchen staff hustling behind him.

"Is Elise there?" She didn't have the time to try and explain the importance of this to Casey. It would be a lost cause.

"She's busy, what's up?" He sounded annoyed.

"Put her on, it's important."

The line went quiet for a moment before Elise's voice chimed in. "Everything okay, Sash?"

"Negative. Red wine spill on the mother of the bride, totally our fault. How do we fix it?"

"Oh, crap. Depends on the material of the dress." Sasha heard Elise tell someone near her to stir something while it was simmering. "Is it in a noticeable place?"

"Oh, yeah, big time." Sasha was starting to sweat; this felt unreasonably more stressful than firefighting.

Shaun pulled out some lemons and seltzer and pushed them toward Sasha with a shrug. She frowned and tried Elise again. "So, anything?"

"Well the usual routine won't resolve the stain if the material is too fine. Does Shaun have salt?"

Shaun nodded and poured some into a small bowl for Sasha.

"Affirmative, salt is available."

A few people approached the bar and ordered drinks, so Sasha stepped to the side. Elise continued to think out loud on the line. "Okay, gather the supplies and call Giovanni."

"Giovanni?" Sasha had zero desire to engage with the eccentric wedding planner any more than was absolutely necessary. Yes, he was a great contact for Casey and Elise, but the guy was kind of a whackadoo if you asked her.

"Something I can help with?" A female voice from behind her caused her to turn. An attractive older woman decked out in diamonds and pearls smiled at her kindly as she motioned toward the stain supplies.

"Maybe." Sasha turned off the radio and shoved it into her back pocket. "Any tips on how to get red wine out of what appears to be a designer gown?"

"Oh, darling, of course. Who's the unlucky victim?" The woman followed Sasha's gaze toward Marisol, who appeared to be chastising Jonah. "Gotcha. I'll handle this, dear." She took the collection of items Shaun and Sasha had assembled and headed toward the unfolding scene with a gracefulness that made her appear to almost be floating.

"Who was that magical creature?" Sasha said to no one in particular, amazed at how quickly the woman deescalated the scene. Jonah slinked away looked thoroughly reprimanded and Sasha hoped he stayed in the kitchen for a while, or at least swapped his serving section with someone else. She reached for her walkie-talkie to suggest that to Casey when someone next to her answered her question.

"That is Edie Davenport. She's a wiz at stain removal, so you're in luck."

Sasha looked up and locked eyes with the beautiful blonde speaking, her hazel eyes twinkling as she smiled. She looked so…"I know you. Abby, right?"

Abby nodded and accepted the drink Shaun held out to her. "I wasn't sure if you would recognize me. How are you, Sasha?"

Sasha dropped her gaze to the glass at Abby's lips as she considered how she knew this woman. Had they dated? No, she would remember those lips. Had they slept together? She studied the delicately manicured hand holding the glass and mulled that over. No. She looked back at Abby's eyes and let herself get lost for a moment—her name had come to her instantly, but she couldn't recall from where. Then it occurred to her. "The mixer. We met at one of Samantha's mixers."

Abby raised her eyebrow. "We met at more than one. I'm glad to see I made an impression."

Sasha felt her face warm at her reply. She had met many of the eligible bachelorettes at those mixers. They were all attractive and funny, but her focus had been on…"Shelly. I was sort of laser focused on Shelly. Sorry, I…Sorry." She wasn't sure what else to say so she fell back on the advice her father always told her: when in doubt, listen before you speak.

Abby shrugged and looked out at the dance floor with a frown. "It's okay. I was in the same boat."

Sasha turned with her and saw Shelly and Claire dancing and laughing. She looked back at Abby and found Abby watching her. "Yeah. That's kinda—"

"Sucky," Abby supplied with a laugh.

"Totally sucky." Sasha shook her head as she considered the irony of the situation. She was standing at the bar watching her near perfect match dance with her girlfriend, while commiserating with another near perfect match at the wedding of their shared matchmaker. It was kind of ridiculous. She decided to run with it. "So, clearly I'm working at this event." She motioned toward her uniform. "Woefully still single and in a unisex tuxedo. What about you?"

"Well, although I'm not a fan of the term *woeful*, I, too, am single. But I am decidedly better dressed." Abby sipped her drink and did a curtsy.

"You've definitely got me there." Sasha took a moment to appreciate the emerald cocktail dress Abby wore. It pulled out the green in her hazel eyes. Plus, it was very figure flattering, which Sasha also noticed. "You look great."

"Thanks." Abby looked back to the dance floor and chuckled. "I think the stain debacle has been resolved. I see hugging."

Sasha let out a sigh and leaned against the bar in relief. "Oh, thank God." Marisol was embracing Edie, her expression markedly improved from earlier. "Crisis averted. I would offer to buy this Edie Davenport a drink, but the cocktails are free, so I don't want to come across as cheap."

Abby leaned against the bar next to her and nodded. "Yup, that would totally seem like a cheap thing to do. You'll have to come up with something more creative."

Sasha considered this. "Yeah, I'm pretty sure her necklace is worth more than my life. I'll see if I can't convince the kitchen to whip her up something special."

"I have it on good authority that her favorite after-dinner drink is cappuccino and that she has a soft spot for lemon meringue."

"You're a valuable information resource." Sasha turned, leaning on her elbow to face Abby more fully. "I'd better keep you around."

Abby gave her a curious look. "I'm not really one to be *kept*."

"I didn't—I mean, I'm not suggesting—"

"Relax." Abby briefly placed her hand on Sasha's forearm. "I'm kidding."

Sasha blew a wisp of her dark hair out of her eyes, looking for a segue. "So, tell me, how did you get invited to the biggest wedding of the year?"

Abby paused, sipping her drink before she replied. "I work at a nonprofit that does a lot of work with Samantha and Andrew."

"Oh? What do you do there?" Sasha ignored the crackle of the walkie-talkie in her pocket. Abby was intriguing. She was gorgeous and flirtatious, but a little sassy, too. It wasn't often that Sasha was caught off guard by a pretty woman—but twice now, Abby had made her stutter or blush.

"I'm an accountant." Abby shocked her once again.

"An accountant?" Sasha couldn't help the once over she gave Abby and, to her horror, her mouth began saying things that her brain was screaming to keep to herself. "There is no way someone as gorgeous as you fools around with numbers all day."

"Is that so?" Abby blinked, a small smile settling on her face as she placed the now empty cocktail glass on the bar. Sasha was aware of Shaun trying to stifle a laugh behind them. She swallowed, waiting for what would be a totally deserved tongue lashing for her forwardness.

"Does it bother you? That I prefer the company of numbers to people with limited filters, such as yourself?" Abby's lips shined as her tongue slid along them. "Contrary to what your skewed opinion may be, one can be both gorgeous and into math."

Sasha wasn't sure what to say, but her father's advice was clearly trodden on now. Abby saved her from making any more of a fool of herself as she turned to leave.

"But thanks for the compliment." Abby reached into her purse and slid a tip across the bar top toward Shaun, who was now shaking with laughter. She gave Sasha one last glance before she walked away. "Your back pocket is squeaking."

Sasha's hand went to the walkie-talkie as a muted squeal came from it, masked only by Shaun's uncontrollable laughter. She watched Abby stride away, her dress shifting seamlessly with every move, a beautiful, delicate creature disappearing into the crowd as the dance floor began to empty. She sighed. She had royally fucked that up.

"Smooth, Romeo." Shaun was wiping tears from his eyes as he attempted to pour drinks, a small line having gathered to the right of Sasha.

"Shut up, Shaun," Sasha said under her breath as she stepped away, turning up the volume on the walkie-talkie and checking in with Casey. "What?"

"Sasha," Casey huffed, "I've been trying to reach you for like five minutes. Did the stain thing get resolved?"

"Yeah, sorry. It's all good." Sasha couldn't make eye contact with Shaun because every time she did, he just snorted and got a little redder from laughing.

"Good. I need you to pop in here. The first course is almost ready and we have a little backup—" The sound of something breaking in the kitchen cut off the rest of his sentence.

She quickly turned down the volume in case swearing followed the unmistakable sound of dishes smashing and dropped her head, trying not to pout. This was definitely not how she had anticipated her night going.

"Don't worry, Sash." Shaun pursed his lips, his face still flushed from chuckling. "I'll hold down the fort. Think you can bring me a few more stars, Fruit Queen?"

Shaun giggled uncontrollably as Sasha tossed a crumpled cocktail napkin in his direction as she headed for the kitchen. Fruit Queen, indeed.

CHAPTER FOUR

S amantha." Lucinda's tone was playful but warning.

"Yes, my dearest wife?" Samantha loved the sound of that. Saying it aloud felt like a dream come true—she and Lucinda had been through a lot in their relatively short time together, and this was easily the happiest day of her life. Well, maybe after Lucinda accepting her proposal, and the night of unbridled passion that followed it. Maybe.

Lucinda laughed and spun Samantha, kissing her softly and holding her close. "I don't think I will ever get tired of hearing that."

"Well that's good because I'm pretty sure that's the only way I will address you from now on."

"With the *dearest* part?" Lucinda's hand settled at the middle of her back, guiding her into the next turn.

"I'm sure I'll substitute other words on occasion. Like *beautiful* or *sexy* or *wonderful...*" Samantha followed Lucinda's lead and stepped into the turn confidently. Dancing with Lucinda Moss was as easy as breathing these days. They had some of their best conversations during these moments—it was like time froze outside of their little bubble. She was still on her high after finishing their first dance as a married couple, thrilled at their perfect execution, glowing at how proud Lucinda was that all their practice had paid off. The whole thing made Samantha feel very emotional. And surprisingly charged.

"I know that look, Samantha." Lucinda's arms were wrapped around her, and they swayed with the music, taking a few more minutes to themselves before they would start to mingle with their guests. They had agreed to enjoy tonight with each other as much as possible. Samantha had been the one to suggest it. In all her years of matchmaking the biggest complaint she heard from her married clients was that the night became more of a meet-and-greet than a celebration of their love. Samantha was determined not to let that happen to them, which was precisely why their vow exchange was a private affair with their immediate friends and family. The reception was a time of partying and joy—but they intended to share that with each other as much as possible. Which was another reason why Lucinda noticing that look made Samantha feel like kind of a hypocrite.

"Tell me, love. What does *that look* mean?" Samantha wrapped her arms around Lucinda's neck and brought their lips close. Being able to say that Lucinda was hers forever was doing all kinds of things to the butterflies in her stomach.

"That look usually means you're up to something. I think, considering our recent exchange of promises to each other, that we ought to have a clean slate, no secrets. What's up?" Lucinda's blue eyes twinkled. Samantha loved her a little more.

"Well, I was thinking…"

"Mm-hmm, told ya." Lucinda tightened her arms around Samantha's waist, pulling them closer together as the crowd around them danced to the music in the background.

Samantha wrinkled her nose and laughed. "I was thinking that once we got back from the Italian Riviera…"

"And the villa in Sardinia." Lucinda kissed her.

"And after the villa."

"Where we'll have no cell phone reception, no internet, no distractions, and I'm hoping, no clothes." Lucinda's hands wandered off her hips ever so slightly, sending a shiver up her spine.

"Precisely. After all of that…" Samantha could taste the promises of sleepless nights and lounging, nap-filled days on the lips of her bride. Her stomach tightened in response.

"Do you really want to think about *after that*, Samantha?" Lucinda's lips were by her ear as she continued to dance them slowly. "Don't you think you might be rushing past the best part of this wedding—the honeymoon? I'd hate to think your attentions were elsewhere. I have a feeling you're going to need all the focus you can muster for the things I have planned for you."

Samantha felt faint. Lucinda ran her hand up Samantha's back and along her side, brushing the side of her breast before settling at her ribcage. Samantha closed her eyes at the contact, willing herself to breathe, her ribs expanding and the pressure of Lucinda's hand becoming more obvious. This plan was backfiring. "Shit."

Lucinda laughed and slid her hand back to the comfortably PG position at Samantha's hip. "You were saying?"

Samantha opened her eyes to find Lucinda's knowing smile greeting her. "You're the worst."

Lucinda merely shrugged, leaning forward to press a lingering kiss to Samantha's lips. She breathed out slowly. "Just reminding you to enjoy the moment, like we agreed."

Samantha nodded, keeping their lips together as she snuggled closer to Lucinda. "Right."

"So." Lucinda kissed her forehead as the next song began. "Obviously, you have something on your mind that needs discussing. Do tell."

Samantha pulled back and gave Lucinda a broad smile. Lucinda just got her. It was magical. "Well, I was thinking, don't you think Abby and Sasha are a good-looking couple?"

Lucinda's brow wrinkled in confusion. "Abby? Cardigan, accountant Abby? The one that Shelly was matched to?"

"That's the one." Samantha nodded with excitement. She couldn't wait for Lucinda to catch on so they could discuss it. "And Sasha..." She tried to hurry this realization along.

"The firefighter?"

"Right. Her mother was a dancer remember?" Samantha tried to jog Lucinda's memory.

"Ah, yes. The Russian ballerina. How could I forget? What about her?"

"Well, I think she'd be a good match for Abby."

"Sasha's mother? Don't you think she's a little old for Abby? Plus, I think she's married. And straight."

"What? No." Samantha huffed when she realized Lucinda was teasing her. "Ugh. You—"

"Are the most loving and caring wife, ever?" Lucinda supplied as she turned them.

"Yeah, that." Samantha rolled her eyes and laughed. "Anyway, look over at the main bar." Samantha turned them again, so Lucinda had a clear sight toward the bar.

"Okay, wow, that bartender is tall," Lucinda marveled.

Samantha turned to look and sighed. "That's Shaun. He's the primary intoxicologist. I'm talking about the people at the bar, Luce, focus."

"Andrew and Ben? They *are* awfully cute together."

"Lucy," Samantha whined. "The women at the bar, next to them."

Lucinda pretended to squint and gave Samantha a dramatic, playful nod. "Oh, you mean Abby talking to Sasha. Abby looks great—green is a good color on her. That's a nice upgrade from the cardigan."

"Finally." Samantha turned them so they both had an unobstructed view. "See how Abby touched Sasha's arm just then. She's flirting. This is good."

"Why is that good?" Lucinda paused. "I mean, I know why that's good, but more specifically, why is that good at this exact moment in time, such that you feel the need to discuss it during our wedding reception?"

"It's good because I haven't been able to find either of them a match since Shelly and Claire got together. And earlier I saw Sasha looking a little sad as she watched them dance."

Lucinda leaned back and cast a suspicious glance toward Samantha. "You're watching the guests watching the other guests? Samantha, I thought we agreed you wouldn't work at our wedding."

"I can't help that I'm naturally observant, Luce." Samantha shrugged. "It's a gift."

"Mm-hmm." Lucinda laughed. "Okay, let's say I humor you and agree that they would be an attractive couple, because, undoubtedly, they are each beautiful and smart and funny."

"Yes?" Samantha loved when Lucinda entertained her wild matchmaking mania.

"But what do they even have in common?"

"Shelly." Samantha replied as though it was as clear as day.

"Who is with Claire," Lucinda added.

"Right. But that's what they have in common. Shelly. They were both supposed to be matched to Shelly. Clearly, Shelly was better suited to be with Claire. But what if Sasha and Abby are actually a match for each other? I mean, I think it's kind of genius."

"It's kind of *something*, that's for sure." Lucinda teased her and twirled her on the dance floor.

"Rude." Samantha shook her head and pointed back toward the bar. "I'm just saying, I think it's something to consider."

Lucinda's gaze followed her gesture and she frowned. "Maybe. But if the way Shaun the giant is laughing and Sasha is blushing while Abby walks away is any indication at all, you may have missed the mark on that one."

Samantha watched Abby roll her eyes as she walked past them, sitting at the table with her mother, Edie, in a huff. "Crap."

"Okay, let's make a deal." Lucinda slowed their movements and cupped her jaw, directing her attention to Lucinda's face. "When we get back, after we thoroughly enjoy ourselves and have really embraced the awesomeness of married life, I promise to entertain your theory on Abby and Sasha. But after we get back. Fair?"

Samantha let herself get lost in the blue eyes looking back at her with adoration. She was so looking forward to their time together— this wedding had been a dream to plan because, in truth, her match to Lucinda was a dream come true. But Lucinda was right, like always—this moment was about them. Not about Abby or Sasha or Perfect Match, Inc. "Fair."

"Good. Let's grab a snack before the toasts. Too much champagne on an empty stomach makes you frisky, and I'm just as eager as you are to start the honeymoon, but maybe not in front of Marisol."

Samantha laughed. "Party pooper." As Lucinda led her off the floor toward their sweetheart table, she glanced back at Sasha just in time to see Sasha watching Abby sip her water a few tables away. She was on to something; she could feel it in her bones.

CHAPTER FIVE

All the lobster bisque shooters went out. The general opinion was a home run." Elise high-fived her sous-chef. "Salads are being circulated and a confirmation on the plated dinners has been completed. We are cruisin'!"

It never ceased to amaze Sasha how the behind the scenes chaos of the kitchen never seemed to effect Elise. She was cool as a cuke all the time, no matter the circumstance. Especially considering Casey called her back here to help clean up the entire vat of spilled lobster bisque. It was unbelievable how quickly a new batch was whipped up on the spot, like the entire dish hadn't been ruined. It was a little freaky.

"How are those fruit stars going?" Sasha asked over Casey's shoulder. He'd been relegated to the fruit sculpting once the first course went out.

"Fine. These things are harder to cut than you'd think." He held up a bandaged thumb. "I've changed that dressing twice."

"Good thing you're trained in first aid, Lieutenant." She reached past him and picked up a butchered orange slice, slipping it into her mouth and savoring the sweetness. "I'll help with the fallen soldiers."

"You're a peach." Casey returned his attention to the slippery fruit in front of him.

"An orange, actually, but who's counting?" Sasha grabbed another slice and headed toward the floor.

"Hey, Sash?" Elise's voice halted her progress.

"What's shakin', Chef?" Sasha looked in the reflective surface of a huge walk-in freezer and adjusted her ponytail, paying close attention to the way her layered hair fell across her shoulders. She had every intention of popping by Abby's table later and trying to save face from their conversation earlier. She could redeem herself, for sure, but if her hair was perfect, that would only help the cause.

"There's a food allergy at table twenty-four. I think that's near the bride's family's table. Can you double-check on the stain issue and bring the plate out personally? I don't need anyone going into anaphylaxis out there."

"Sure thing, Chef-y." Sasha reached for the dish but Elise pulled it away at the last second.

"Shaun told Casey that you totally screwed up a come-on. True?"

"That guy's got a huge mouth to match his huge head." Sasha pouted and frowned. "It wasn't that bad."

"Okay, whatever you say." Elise shrugged and pointed toward Sasha's mouth. "Your lip gloss wore off. Try this, maybe it'll help." Elise reached into her pocket and tossed a dark red lipstick in her general direction.

Sasha reached for it, nearly knocking one of the simmering pans from the stovetop. She juggled it twice before catching it just as it was about to land in the green substance bubbling in front of her.

"Jesus, Sasha. You're nearly as bad as Burger. Don't make me have to put you in the coat room, too." Casey stood behind her with a plate of nearly perfect fruit stars. "Drop these off with Shaun on your way to the allergy table."

Sasha's heart was in her throat after the circus maneuvers she'd had to do to keep the lipstick from ruining Elise's food. She glared at them both as they began laughing before she turned to leave once again.

"Sasha—don't forget about the lipstick," Elise called with a wink.

"Fine." Sasha put down the two dishes and walked back to the refrigerator, applying the dark color carefully and evenly along her full lips. She smiled as her mother's Russian heritage was reflected back at her, her dark hair and dark eyes some of her best assets. She usually used a lighter lip color to offset her features, but Elise was right, if she had any hopes of salvaging her interaction with Abby, she'd have to pull out all the stops. And her childhood on the pageant circuit had proved that the combo of dark red lips on her pale, smooth complexion was a definite showstopper. She turned back toward Elise. "How do I look?"

Elise looked up from the pan she was tending to and nodded. "Like the lady-killer you are. Go get 'em, tiger."

Casey catcalled as she stepped out into the reception area, fruit stars and allergy plate in hand.

❖

"So, you two looked cozy," Edie said between delicate bites of the salad that she cut the moment it arrived at the table. Her mother was always following those charm school rules.

"Me and who?" Abby knew what her mother was getting at, but she wasn't going to make it that easy. She poked at the crouton, feigning interest.

"You and the tall, dark brunette." Edie smiled to herself and nodded her head, "I noticed you two talking. She's stunning."

"You saw what you wanted to." Abby reached for her water glass and took a sip.

"So, what's her name?" Edie tried again, Abby realized that her mother's interest wasn't a passing one—she was doomed. Better she cut this one off at the pass, otherwise the rest of her night was going to be ruined.

"Sasha."

"That's a great name, strong." Edie nodded to herself as she chewed. "What does she do?"

"Womanize." Abby hadn't meant to say that out loud. She looked up at her mother anxiously, hoping she'd missed it.

Edie stopped midbite, the fork paused in front of her lips. Nope. She definitely didn't miss that. "That came up in conversation at the bar? You were there for about fifteen minutes."

Abby felt bad. It wasn't that she didn't believe what she'd said. It's just that she hadn't meant to give it any credit. She knew it was deeply rooted in her own insecurities. Well, that and she had seen how Sasha was with the other women at the mixers. She was a clear and blatant flirt. "I know her. We've met before. She was a client of Samantha's—ironically, she was matched to Shelly as well. So I was at a couple of mixers with her."

Edie's eyebrows rose at this new information. "She's a client of Samantha's? Does she own the catering company?"

"What? No, I don't think so. I think she's just working the event." Abby didn't understand her mother's thought processes sometimes. She had just told her she felt like Sasha was a womanizer and yet her mother was more concerned about what she did for work.

"Oh." Edie looked disappointed. "She's a professional waitress?"

"No. I don't know. Maybe. What does that matter?" Abby chased a tomato around her plate.

"It doesn't, I guess." Edie sipped her champagne flute. "Why is she a womanizer?"

And they were full circle. "Uh, I guess I don't know that she is. It's just, she's very flirtatious and outgoing. The other women at the mixers were always talking about her and oohing and aahing her, you know? Like she was some magical hot unicorn." When her mother didn't reply she looked up at her again. Edie was smiling. "What?"

"You called her a magical hot unicorn." Edie pointed her fork in Abby's direction. "You think she's attractive."

"Of course I think she's attractive—I have eyes." Abby bristled. "I mean, she's tall and has those perfect cheekbones and looks surprisingly good in that tuxedo suit thingy. Like it's kind of a crime. They're meant to be unisex. But she's clearly very much in the sexy female department." Abby stopped, she was rambling. Shit.

"Oh no, don't let me stop you. Go on, please." Edie's hands were folded neatly in front of her, her rapt attention directed at Abby. "Tell me more."

Abby sighed. "There isn't any more to tell. That's it."

"So Sasha is attractive and flirty and looks good in her nondescript waiter outfit and you're mad about it because you noticed."

"Right." Abby paused. "Wait, that's not what I—" She took a breath. "I'm mad because she called me gorgeous and in the same breath told me I was too attractive to be an accountant. As if one thing has anything to do with the other."

"She used the word gorgeous?" Edie leaned closer, her excitement palpable.

"Yes. *So* not the point though." Abby tried to redirect. "The point is—"

"Excuse me, Abby and Madame Stain Saver." Sasha appeared behind her mother, interrupting them. "I've been sent by the kitchen to bring a special plate for a guest with a shellfish allergy. Is there any chance it's one of you lovely ladies?"

"Oh, that's me, dear." Edie moved her salad plate aside for Sasha to place the new plate in front of her. "You can call me Edie. How's our friend with the stain?"

"I just checked in with her, and she's enjoying another glass of red wine, sans stain. All seems well. You're a lifesaver." Sasha playfully wiped her brow and Edie laughed. Abby hoped she was invisible.

"That's an overstatement. I was just in the right place at the right time." Edie gestured with her hand in Abby's direction. Abby swallowed thickly. "Have you met my—"

"Coworker," Abby supplied when Sasha looked in her direction. "We, uh, work together at the nonprofit."

Edie gave Abby an admonishing look and Abby hoped Sasha didn't notice. It was sort of true. Sort of. Kinda. A little.

"We've met. Abby tells me she's an accountant. Are you as well?" Sasha's smile was genuine. Abby's attention was drawn to the deep red lip color she had on. She didn't remember that from before. It was hypnotizing.

"I'm more of the philanthropic type," Edie responded diplomatically and Abby was relieved. Or would have been relieved if she could force herself to stop staring at Sasha's lips.

She became aware of both sets of eyes on her. "I'm sorry, did you say something?"

Edie raised her eyebrow and leaned back, sipping her champagne, looking amused.

Sasha spoke first. "I asked if you'd like to dance later. I was hoping to make up for my verbal misstep before."

Abby was so shocked by the directness of the comment that she didn't reply right away. To Sasha's credit, she didn't look shy or backtrack; she merely maintained eye contact and waited. The forwardness of it all was a little hot. "Uh, sure."

"I think she means to say she'd be delighted," Edie added with a playful slap to Abby's hand.

Sasha's red lips curled into a warm smile. "Great. I'm looking forward to it."

A young waiter arrived behind Sasha, balancing a tray of entrees for the remaining guests at the table. Sasha introduced Jonah and helped him unload. Before she stepped away she leaned over Abby's shoulder and whispered, "I meant what I said before I stuck my foot in my mouth. I really do think you're gorgeous. Enjoy your meal."

Abby watched Sasha walk away, still in disbelief at what had transpired. She reached for her champagne flute, nearly knocking it over.

"You ought to pay attention to where you put those hands, Abigail." Edie looked smitten.

Abby bit her lip and tried to focus. Sasha had definitely asked her to dance, apologized, and called her gorgeous in the span of a few minutes. She couldn't remember the last time something like that had happened to her. If ever.

"I like her. She's brazen. And beautiful. That red lipstick looks great on her." Edie bobbed her head side to side as she hummed to herself. After a moment, she paused. "Why didn't you want her to know that you're my daughter?"

"I'm not sure." That was true—it was reflexive. She wasn't ashamed to be her mother's guest at the wedding. But then again, she wasn't exactly advertising that either. No, it was something Sasha had said earlier—the necklace comment. It had made her a little embarrassed. The choker Edie wore tonight was definitively glamorous, but it was nowhere near her nicest or most expensive piece. "I guess I just wanted to—"

"Make your own way. A little mystery is a good thing at the beginning of a relationship. It keeps the passion burning hot."

"I don't think we're at the relationship phase, Mom. We just met. Well, sort of." She rolled her eyes and turned her attention to the gourmet entrée in front of her.

"But you like her. So it's only a matter of time." Edie was confident, too confident for Abby's liking.

"We'll see."

"What do you have to lose? An island of feral cats and the *Beaches* soundtrack on loop?" Edie nudged her with her elbow and tapped her nose.

"Nothing I guess." Abby sighed. As much as she hated to admit it, her mother was right. She had nothing to lose.

❖

Abby distractedly stirred the cappuccino in front of her as she watched Sasha handle the shaker behind the main bar. She'd had a hard time ignoring Sasha after she'd dropped her mother's plate off at the table and whispered in her ear. In fact, she'd found herself watching her for most of the night. Much to her mother's enjoyment. That woman missed nothing. Not. A. Thing.

Her mother's hand closed on her own. "Abby, you're pulverizing that cup with your spoon. I guarantee you that if it's not stirred by now, it will never be to your standards. Let's give the fine china a break, okay?" She took the spoon out of Abby's hand and placed it delicately on the folded white dessert napkin between them.

"Sorry." Abby wasn't sure why she was apologizing, because her mother's tone wasn't sore.

She figured it had more to do with getting caught.

The wedding had been perfect. The toasts were sincere and honest with just the right amount of humor. The music and dancing had been fantastic; watching Samantha and Lucinda glide across the floor so effortlessly was envy inducing. All in all, it had been one of the most fun and love-filled weddings Abby had ever attended, and yet, she was unhappy. Or, rather, she was distracted.

"You've been watching her for hours, Abigail," Edie pointed out. "Take back some of that control and ask her to dance."

"What control?"

"The control that Sasha took when she asked you to dance. The ball is in her court, so to speak, right? That must be a little maddening." Edie traced her fingers along her choker. "I didn't raise you to sit back and wait, Abby. Get that dance on your own terms. Go."

Abby was out of her seat before her mother's words had settled in. She wasn't one to back down from a challenge, and her mother was right—she had been watching Sasha for most of the night. What bothered her wasn't that she was captivated by Sasha. It had more to do with the combination of interest and anxiety that swirled around her, waiting to be asked to dance. She wanted to dance with Sasha. She wasn't going to wait all night for nothing.

Her surge of confidence lasted all of five seconds when something at the bar caught her attention. Sasha appeared to be flirting with an attractive red-haired woman. She stopped in her tracks—the response was automatic—and considered the womanizing comment she had made to her mother earlier. It lingered in her subconscious and she couldn't shake it. Was this really a road she wanted to go down? Desperate and single, accompanying her mother to a wedding, only to lust after the charming waitress/bartender at the event?

She jolted in place, ashamed that the pretense she usually assigned to her mother reared its ugly head in her own thought process. *This is why you're alone, Abby,* she thought. *Because part of you thinks you're better than everyone else.* Just as she turned to head back to the table, Sasha looked up at her and smiled. She took a deep breath and decided to be brave. It was now or never.

Chapter Six

Sasha did a mental tally of the things she had to get done in the next few minutes. She was filling in at the main bar for Shaun while he took his fifteen-minute break, but the steady flow of people to the bar hadn't given her the chance to go over Casey's to-do list. She gave the shaker one last hard agitation before pouring the contents into the three martini glasses she had lined along the bar. Her shoulders ached from the endless cocktails she had mixed and the countless trays she had carried throughout the night. The wedding never quite slowed down; it seemed as though everyone was everywhere at once. It was clear the guests were enjoying themselves, and the part of her that enjoyed people watching was thriving. Still, she was getting tired.

Her back pocket squawked as she drained the last of the shaker into the third glass and garnished it with fruit stars from the bowl. She wiped her hands and reached for the walkie-talkie. "Can you repeat that?"

"You're supposed to end all conversation with *over*." Elise's voice was playful on the other end.

"Sorry. Over." Sasha smiled as she wiped down the bar top.

"I said, your special dessert is ready. I'll have Jonah walk it out. How's it going?"

"Over."

"What?" Elise sounded confused.

"You didn't end with *over*. I was just helping you out. Over." Sasha winked at the attractive woman waiting at the bar and nodded as she pointed to a cosmo on the bar list. She started gathering the ingredients when Elise's voice crackled over the speaker again.

"Did you dance yet with that woman who's far too smart and beautiful for you?"

Sasha reached back to turn down the volume but it was too late—the cute redhead in front of her was already giving her a raised eyebrow. She bit the inside of her cheek and slid the completed cocktail across the bar with a shrug. Once the guest walked away she turned her back to the bar and spoke softly into the receiver.

"Seriously, Elise? Your timing could not be worse."

"I'm just trying to keep your eye on the prize, Sasha. Over."

Sasha spun around and looked toward the back of the venue at the kitchen entrance and caught sight of Elise waving with a smirk. "You're watching me?"

"I got bored. Your life is more exciting than mine. Anyway, I think that woman you like has been watching you. Over."

"You need to stop meddling and keep stirring, or whatever you do back there." Sasha huffed and shook her head. "Over."

Elise laughed. "I'm pretty much done for the night. The desserts are already out and the after-dinner coffees are being dispersed. Now it's just clean up and catch a breath."

"And meddle. Don't forget the meddling part. And you forgot to say *over*," Sasha added as Shaun approached to relieve her.

"Right, right. Okay, I'll let you focus on what you're doing. Keep me posted. See ya, Sash."

Sasha leaned toward the receiver to reply when Elise's voice taunted, "*Over.*"

"What are you two up to?" Shaun stretched and eyed the walkie-talkie.

"Nothing. She's bugging me." Sasha slipped the radio under the bar as she noticed Abby approaching. "I'll get this one."

Shaun snorted and made a show of wiping down the bar, as if she didn't notice him priming himself to eavesdrop.

Sasha redirected her attention to Abby. "Hey, I was just going to pop by your table."

"Oh, really?" Sasha thought she sounded hopeful. As if Abby could read her mind, she cleared her throat and spoke again, lower this time. "I thought I'd come by and chat with you."

Sasha was about to reply when she noticed someone approaching in her periphery.

"Special dessert plate from the chef." Jonah gave her an exaggerated nod and blew a kiss to no one in particular.

She wondered if she could subtly throttle him. Instead she took the plate and dismissed him after he lingered, staring. "Go away."

Jonah looked between Abby and Sasha with a huff. "Fine. I'm going on break." He punctuated his statement by untying his apron and tossing it at Shaun, who continued to inspect the cleanliness of the glasses in a ridiculous way. He looked like a giant handling a child's tea set. Worst. Spy. Ever.

She looked back to Abby. "Sorry. What was it you wanted to talk to me about?"

Abby made eye contact with her briefly before looking over her shoulder at Shaun. Sasha wondered if she could tell he was trying to listen in. These guys were totally killing her game tonight. She had to put some space between Shaun and Abby, or nothing good would come of it. She walked around to Abby's side of the bar, attempting to block Abby's sightline of Shaun.

Abby raised an eyebrow at her and said, "I was going to ask you about that dance. Assuming you're still interested, that is."

"Of course I'm still interested." She hadn't expected Abby to say that. Abby blinked at her and she realized that she was still holding the plate of lemon meringue like a fool. She glanced over her shoulder and handed the plate to Shaun. "Make sure Ms. Davenport at table twenty-four gets this. Tell her it's from me and thank her for her stain help. I'm taking my break."

Shaun was leaning so close to hear them that he nearly fell over when she addressed him directly. What an ass. He cleared his throat and nodded, but not before giving her a broad, knowing smile. She would catch hell for this later, she could count on it.

"So, about that dance…" Sasha reached out and took Abby's hand, guiding her toward the dance floor. Abby stopped abruptly and the force caused Sasha to stumble a bit, her hand anchored in Abby's.

Abby answered her perplexed look with a smile. "You *can* dance, right?"

Sasha grinned. Her mother had been a professional dancer in Russia before emigrating to Boston in the seventies. Of course she could dance—it was in her blood. "I can. Can you?"

Abby shrugged. "I've been on a dance floor or two in my life— you know, when I find the time to step away from my calculator and abacus."

"Well then, it sounds like we'll do just fine." Sasha took the dig in stride and decided she liked Abby even more when she was a little feisty. Sasha pulled Abby toward the dance floor, weaving them between couples until they were just to the right of the center. She settled into the lead position and waited for Abby to adjust.

"You're leading?" Abby's tone was playful. Her eyes flickered to Sasha's lips and she made a mental note to thank Elise later. Sasha took the opportunity to appreciate the beautiful blond shades of Abby's hair. Why hadn't she noticed how captivating Abby was before? She assumed it was because she had been so focused on Shelly at those mixers, but still…there was something intriguing about Abby—she was just the right amount of sexy and sassy. She was hot.

"Right now, I am," Sasha replied, sliding a little closer, deciding to see if Abby was as attracted to her as she was to Abby. "But I'm not someone who always needs to be in control."

Abby laughed and took the initiative this time, guiding Sasha's other hand to her hip. "That's good to know. I'd hate to think you had the wrong impression of me—I'm no pushover."

"I'm game to get *all* the impressions of you." Sasha pulled Abby close, inviting herself into Abby's personal space. When Abby didn't protest, her confidence ignited. They were definitely on the same page here. She didn't bother trying to be discreet about the way she stared at Abby's lips. She wanted to make sure Abby knew what she had meant earlier—she was gorgeous and she wanted to get to know her better.

"And what if you don't like what you find?" Abby inched closer, her hand encouraging Sasha to hold her tighter. Sasha wondered how much closer they could get before they were breathing the same air. Her stomach tightened at the thought.

"I doubt that very much." Sasha turned them slowly and massaged Abby's lower back through her dress. "If anything, I bet the more I know of you, the more I'd want to know." The truth in that statement surprised her—she wasn't used to being so candid. She was notorious for being cool and noncommittal when it came to women. This was something that Samantha and her matchmaking ways had helped Sasha understand was a defense mechanism, and she wondered why this interaction was so different.

Abby's eye contact seemed to intensify and Sasha couldn't tell who was in control of this conversation anymore. Abby moved against her so sensually, so confidently, Sasha began to wonder if she was ever actually leading or if she was in fact being led all along. When Abby's hand slid from her midback to dance along her hairline, the tightening in her stomach moved lower. It was decided—Abby was clearly in charge of this interaction and Sasha loved it.

They were so close that when Abby spoke, she could feel the breath along her lips. "It sounds as though you may be the one that's impressionable."

Sasha felt wet. This banter was giving her all kinds of delicious sensations. "I'd let you make an impression on me. I'd like it to be a lasting one. Maybe we could…"

"We could what?" Abby's eyes traced over her lips again and Sasha's body hummed at the warmth of Abby pressed against her. She was only vaguely aware of the happenings around her, but it didn't matter. Her closeness to Abby mattered.

"Maybe we could—" The sound of a room full of glasses being tapped by the wedding guests to signal a kiss between the brides felt serendipitous. She decided it was now or never. "Kiss."

Abby's lips parted in response but Sasha didn't wait for her to reply. She leaned forward and closed the gap, placing a soft, lingering kiss to Abby's lips. She held her close and sucked on Abby's bottom lip as the guests around her cheered in the background. She momentarily considered how it might be inappropriate to kiss a guest at a wedding she was working at, but all those thoughts faded away when Abby's tongue entered the equation. She made no attempt to stifle the moan Abby stirred up with the intensity of her matched kiss.

"Hey, Sash—whoa." Jonah's voice behind her shattered the moment into a million pieces. Abby pulled back with a surprised gasp and Sasha groaned at the abruptness of it all.

As Abby tried to step back, Sasha held her close, willing Jonah to disappear into thin air. When he awkwardly cleared his throat indicating he hadn't indeed evaporated, her shoulders drooped. "What, Jonah?"

"Casey needs you. Burger lost someone's something in the coat closet or broke something, I'm not sure. Casey looks so mad—you should probably talk him off the ledge." Sasha didn't bother turning to face Jonah. She had never hated that clumsy kid Burger more in her life.

She sighed. Abby had stepped out of her grasp and looked a little dazed. She only nodded in agreement—that dazed feeling was mutual. "Okay, Jonah. I'll be right there, thanks."

"Well that was unexpected." Abby ran her thumb under her bottom lip and Sasha had to root herself in place to keep herself from reattaching her mouth to Abby's.

"The kissing or the interruption?" Sasha ran her hand through her ponytail, more for something to do than anything else.

"Both, I suppose." Abby's expression was unreadable. Sasha took comfort in the fact that Abby didn't sound disappointed. Even if Sasha felt disappointed that the kiss was over.

"I have to—"

"Go. Yeah, I got that." Abby gave her a small smile.

"Can we, I want to…Maybe we can do this again sometime?" As soon as the words came out, Sasha regretted them. What a moron.

"Uh, sure." Abby reached out and took her hand before placing a kiss to Sasha's cheek. "It was nice catching up with you, Sasha."

"You, too." Sasha felt like all the confidence and game she'd had moments ago had gotten up and gone without her. As Abby walked away, she finally found her voice. "I'll catch up with you later."

Abby looked back over her shoulder and gave her a small wave. Something told Sasha that that was her ship sailing away. Never had she been more sorry about being right.

CHAPTER SEVEN

Abby hated waiting. The only thing she hated more than waiting was waiting for her mother. That was a special kind of annoyance that had only gotten worse the older they both got. Her mother was destined to be late for her own funeral, it was decided. But she couldn't really fault her mother this time around. She *had* kind of sprung this on her.

"I'll be out in a second," her mother called from her massive walk-in closet.

"I'm sure that's not even remotely true," Abby said under her breath.

"Don't mumble—it's impolite." Edie Davenport emerged from the closet with the grandeur of an Oscar winner on the red carpet. She was ageless, but more from good genes and a life of wealth than plastic surgery. Aside from that tiny eyelift and some Botox she had four years ago, she was basically untouched. "How do I look?"

"Expensive." It was true. She was dressed in a pantsuit that flattered every curve of that ageless frame. And there were diamonds, lots of shiny diamonds. Everywhere.

"The necklace is too much?" Edie looked in the mirror and touched the three-carat diamond solitaire floating above her collarbone.

"No, no. Far from it. I think the Liberace look you have going with the giant diamond encrusted brooch and three flashy rings is what puts you over the top." Edie gave her a face. "But the necklace is fine."

"Never change, Abby. Your sense of humor and superiority are your best assets." Edie grabbed a scarf from the neatly organized rack on the back of her closet door and looped it around her neck. It was perfect. It quieted the loudness of her displays of wealth while somehow completing the outfit in the most amazing way.

"Har, har." Abby laughed and pointed to the clock. "We have to go. Samantha is a busy woman."

"I still don't understand why we're doing this. I mean, don't get me wrong, I love any opportunity to spend time with Samantha— she's a doll—but still, this seems ridiculous." Edie was contemplating a few purses as she spoke.

"The cream one, it goes well with your scarf," Abby supplied as she stood. "And I told you before—it's time for you to meet someone your own age to terrorize. It's been long enough since Daddy died. You're not getting any younger."

Her mother gave her the same sad smile she always did when Abby brought up her father. He had truly been the love of her mother's life, and she had made no attempts at dating or meeting anyone since he'd passed five years ago. But it was a waste—her mother was a fantastic person and she deserved to continue to live a long and happy life with someone who could help her realize the potential that awaited her out there. At least, that's what all the romance novels Abby read for leisure had taught her over the years.

"You do have excellent taste. At least you got something from me." Edie picked up the cream purse and nodded toward the door, saying nothing as she walked by. Abby knew she was hesitant about this meeting, but she just needed a push, that was all. That's what she was telling herself anyway.

As they drove to Samantha's office, she let her mind wander. This had all started after Samantha and Lucinda's wedding last month. She had embarrassingly fallen for Sasha's flirtations and entirely blamed the bottomless champagne for the mind-numbing kiss that she'd participated in. That's what annoyed her about it— without even hesitating she had deepened the kiss and dragged it well past the PG-zone when her tongue got a mind of its own and ventured into Sasha's mouth. She shook her head at the memory and tried to refocus on the task at hand: finding her mother a life partner.

The night after the wedding she had found her mother passed out on the couch in her living room, exhausted from crying herself to sleep while watching old home videos of Abby with her father. She helped her mother to bed and put the movies back on their shelf, wondering how many more times she would find her mother living in the past. Edie had been a little sad after the wedding had ended the night before, but Abby hadn't understood why until that night. Her mother had been so moved by the passion evident between Samantha and Lucinda, that she was reminded of the love she had lost. It was a low she hadn't seen her mother reach in a very long time. And it wasn't a place she wanted to revisit anytime soon.

She had made up her mind at that moment that once Samantha was back from her honeymoon, she would sign her mother up for Samantha's service, while quietly taking a break from the matchmaking process herself. Her interaction with Sasha and how quickly she had lost control was enough to make her pump the brakes; she had a lot to figure out before opening herself up to someone again. She didn't want to be another notch on the belt of someone like Sasha, and yet, embarrassingly, that's exactly what she had done at the wedding. No, it was time to step back and let someone take a chance at love who was capable of truly finding it. She had to get her mother on track, and she'd worry about herself later.

❖

"So, let me get this straight." Samantha paused after hearing Abby's request. "You want to abandon your own search for a perfect match in favor of pursuing one for your mother?"

"Yes." Abby thought she had made herself abundantly clear and yet Samantha was looking back and forth between her and her mother from the other side of her enormous desk with a look of extreme confusion.

"Why?" Samantha leaned back and touched the tips of her fingers together. Her skin was more tanned than usual. Abby assumed it was from her honeymoon on the Riviera. She wanted to ask about the trip, but now didn't seem like the time.

Abby huffed. "I don't see what the big deal is. It's simple—my mother needs a companion in life. You're the best person for that job. I'd take it as a compliment. Clearly I trust the process and your magical skills. I don't lend my mother out to just anyone."

"I'm sitting right here, Abigail. And you make it seem like I should be adopting a dog from a shelter for *companionship*." The use of air quotes by Edie was not lost on Abby. "I'm perfectly fine on my own—there are lots of women of a certain age that live out their glamorous lives without any need for a man, or a *companion*, as it were."

"Okay, okay. I've heard enough." Samantha stood and smoothed out her skirt before walking to the front of the desk and leaning against it. "There is no reason why both of these things can't happen at the same time, in tandem. My concern, Abby, is why all of a sudden have you given up on the process?"

"I'm not giving up—I'm immersing my mother in the process because I believe it'll work. I'm just taking a break."

"Again, I'm sitting right here." Edie looked amused. She crossed her legs and leaned forward. "I have a feeling this has something to do with that tall, dark brunette."

"Ooh, that sounds promising." Samantha smiled. "Tell me all the things."

"It's nothing." Abby addressed Samantha before turning to her mother and repeating the phrase with a little more conviction, "It's *nothing*. Not a thing. No big deal. Drop it."

Edie let out a dramatic sigh and fanned herself. "That's not true. It was definitely something. I saw it with my own two eyes—there was flirting and kissing and I dare say groping."

"Mom!" Abby thought she might die on the spot.

"Groping? When did I miss the part about groping?" Samantha questioned in that honey voice that always made Abby spill more than she wanted to. "No one likes to miss the juicy bits, Abby. Who were you groping? And why was your mother a witness?"

Before Abby could reply, Edie took the floor. "It was at your wedding, I'm sure the whole guest list got an eyeful. She was a waitress there, tall, attractive—"

"Sasha?" Abby's head whipped toward Samantha. "You kissed and groped Sasha at my wedding? How did I miss that?"

Abby was confused as to why Samantha looked so disappointed. "Probably because you were getting married. And it wasn't as big a deal as my mother is making it out to be."

"Yes, it was. You were all dreamy eyed for hours. And you had her lipstick on for the rest of the day." Edie was positively glowing as she relayed the goings-on to Samantha. Abby felt a little ganged up on.

"Hey. I thought we were talking about my mother becoming a client here. How did this become a bash session on me?" Abby hated the whine in her voice but she couldn't stop it either.

Samantha stood and crossed her arms. "This is what's going to happen. I'm going to add Edie as a client and see if we can't find her a good match and introduce her to the process—you know, get her feet wet a bit." She moved to the other side of her desk and pulled out a paper. "I'm going to have my admin Sarah organize all the forms I need you to fill out in order to get you into the system. Can you bring this to her and get it started? I'd like to talk to Abby alone."

Edie raised an eyebrow but didn't argue. "Is Andrew here today? I wanted to ask him about the museum exhibition next month. He mentioned wanting to host a mixer there one or two nights."

Samantha glanced at the clock. "He had a conference call about twenty minutes ago. Have Sarah interrupt him if he's still on it."

"It's always a pleasure, darling." Edie took the paper from Samantha and gave her the standard Edie air kiss good-bye. "We'll see you next month."

"You'll see me before that." Samantha winked. "But yes, art exhibition, possible mixer, got it."

Abby watched her mother leave and close the door behind her and suddenly her throat felt dry. Why did Samantha want to talk to her alone?

Samantha's dark brown eyes looked back at her expectantly. When Abby didn't say anything, Samantha began, "Abby. What's going on? Really—spill."

Abby sighed. "Nothing. Nothing is going on. That's the problem. I think I need to get out of my own way and step back. My mother—"

"Leave your mother out of this. We both know there's plenty of money between the two of you that one of you doesn't have to stop being a client for the other to become one. Stop that nonsense right now. Your mother will begin her own path if she so chooses. We're talking about you right now, and I have to be frank, the reason we haven't found you a match is because you're foundationally dishonest with these women."

Abby was shocked. Did Samantha just call her a liar? "What are you trying to say?"

"I think I was perfectly clear with my word choice. You haven't been successful because you're keeping too much of yourself a secret. It doesn't give the women I've paired you with the chance to get to know you. They can tell you're hiding something—that's why it doesn't get anywhere."

"Not true. Things with Shelly were going really well. I thought we had a real connection," Abby argued.

"Oh, you did. The connection was that you're both stinking filthy rich." Samantha laughed. "When will you let me put you front and center like I did for Shelly? You're the big fish here, Abby, and by asking me to hide you into the wallflower background as an anonymous eligible bachelorette, you're selling yourself short. And misrepresenting yourself in the process. You have no reason to be ashamed of your family name or legacy. This backdoor dating approach isn't helping you, and you know it."

The words stung more than Abby wanted to admit. It had been her idea all along to date incognito. Samantha had resisted it from the start but Abby had been adamant. She wanted to find love with someone through her interactions with them on a candid, genuine basis—her wealth had netted her nothing but trouble in the not-so-distant romantic past. Time and time again, Samantha had tried to reassure her that her company, her process, helped to thin out the crazies and would match her with someone who would be her emotional and physical ideal, not just someone looking for a sugar mama. And she'd thought she finally found that in Shelly. But something hadn't quite felt right. She knew it after the first date. There was a spark missing. She just didn't want to admit it.

"Listen." Samantha's tone was soft, encouraging. "Let me change some things on my end and see what I can come up with for you. We were on the right path with Shelly—that's clear. I will dedicate my time and focus to finding your mother a match if she agrees to the process. But I am not giving up on you, and I am not taking you out of the rotation. Just let me retool our approach a bit. Fair?"

Abby didn't like the compromise Samantha was proposing, but she knew if she was going to get Samantha on board to help keep her mother from crying herself to sleep watching old family movies, she had to meet her halfway. "Deal."

"Good." Samantha walked around to embrace her. "I meant no offense by what I said. On the contrary, I think you're amazing and beautiful and smart and funny. I don't want to cloak all your awesome just to separate you from your family name. If you untie my hands, I can do so much more for you. Let me try, unrestricted, to work my magic. Just once. One chance. I can do it, I promise."

"One try," Abby conceded and sank into Samantha's embrace, hoping she hadn't just made a deal with the Devil.

Chapter Eight

Sasha leaned back in her chair with her feet propped up on the common area table as she tried desperately to stay awake. It had been a long twenty-four-hour shift at the firehouse. There had been call after call from the moment she laced up her standard issue uniform boots yesterday morning. She couldn't remember if she had even managed a shower today—the day and night had blurred together.

The soreness in her neck increased and she sighed, sliding her feet off the table and unceremoniously dropping them to the floor with a thud. She was in desperate need of a nap and some of her mother's pork pie, stat. The thought awoke a resting anxiety in her, making her feel much more alert all of a sudden. Her mother. Ugh. What day was it?

She looked past that snoring Burger buffoon on the couch to the bulletin board across the common room. The calendar was obscured by about a dozen flyers; she couldn't see it from her vantage point. She stood with a groan. That last medical call at six in the morning involved a lot of heavy lifting to get the patient out of the fourth floor and down to the ambulance. Chair lifts were some of her least favorite rescues. Her shoulders still ached in protest.

She was careful to walk as quietly as possible past Burger— he had been more annoying than usual, and she was hoping to end her shift without incident. Ever since Casey fired him on the spot after Samantha Monteiro's wedding for screwing up his coat check job, Burger had been way more enthusiastic and helpful around the firehouse. Like he was trying to get back on Casey's good graces or something. All that meant was that he was a million times more annoying and underfoot than he used to be. Worst. Probie. Ever.

Sasha knew why he was so desperate though. Working for Casey outside of the firehouse was fun, profitable, and exciting, in a different way than firefighting. But more than that, it meant working alongside your firefighting brothers and sisters and helped nurture the all-important bond they needed—to trust each other. Firefighting was a dangerous job. You had to know your peers had your back, at all times. But besides all that, Casey's catering company paid very, very well. It was an easy gig to pick up on your off days at the firehouse, and she had overheard Burger talking about getting a new car, which required extra cash. Cash he was no longer getting on the side since he ruined that lady's mink coat. Casey was still trying to pay off the repairs.

Money. That's what motivated them all at the end of the day, it seemed. And she was no different. As she moved the dog walking flyer and the push-pin littered packet for upcoming training dates to uncover the wall calendar, her fears were confirmed: it was nearly the end of the month. Somehow, no matter how many shifts she worked, how many catering jobs she picked up, how many lunches and dinners she made at home, she was still just barely above water in the money department. And the end of the month meant it was going to be that much harder to see her mother later on today. Pork pie with a side of *I can't pay all your father's medical bills*. Joy. Try as she might to help dig her parents out of debt, she never seemed to be able to get ahead of her father's worsening health. They were always racing against something, time or debt collectors.

"Hey, Sasha." Samantha's voice jarred her from her impending panic attack.

"Samantha, hey. What are you doing here?" She smiled and took in Samantha's tight dress and tall heels. She was carrying something. "Are those cookies?"

"Nothing gets past you, does it, Sash?" Samantha teased as she cracked the lid of the gourmet cookie tray. "I may have had one or five on the ride over. They're amazing."

"They look it." Sasha craved the sugar rush and increased energy the cookies promised, but Samantha's presence here was more exciting. "What's up?"

"I was in the neighborhood. Thought I might stop by and see if Casey was working—I may have a new catering opportunity for him." Samantha looked past Sasha and waved. "Looks like I'm in luck."

Casey jogged over, smiling broadly. "Samantha! What brings you by?"

"I was just telling Sasha that I may have a catering opportunity for you—a new connection at the Isabella Stewart Gardner Museum. They're opening a new exhibit and Andrew and I will be attending an award ceremony for a local philanthropist in addition to hosting a mixer or two there at some point. I think you'd be perfect for the job—I'd like to talk to Elise about some passed hors d'oeuvres ideas I had to complement the theme of the night. This is a close family friend of mine. If it goes well at the venue, we'd like to contract you for the mixers after the fact."

Casey beamed. "She'll be ecstatic—this is great news. Thanks, Samantha."

"I'm still getting rave reviews of the wedding. You and Elise make a great team." Samantha seemed so genuinely appreciative, Sasha's heart swelled, glad for her lieutenant and for the connection she had helped to foster. "Oh, before I eat these, please, take them away."

Casey thanked her again before he took the cookies to the common area table and whistled for the guys to come check out the snacks. Burger jarred from the couch and nearly fell to the floor at the high-pitched noise. Sasha barely had time to step in front of Samantha to protect her from Burger's stumbling, disoriented shuffle.

"Chill, Burgertime. There's a lady on the premises. They're only cookies—no fire here."

Burger only grunted in response, his tune changing abruptly when he noticed Samantha. "I don't think we've met, I'm—"

"Leaving. You're leaving," Sasha supplied as she ushered him toward the growing crowd around Samantha's cookie tray.

Samantha laughed and looped her arm in Sasha's. "You're my hero. Say, any chance a girl can get a tour?"

"For you, Madame? Anything." Sasha patted her hand and led her away from the brewing fight over the last chocolate chip cookie. "They are such animals." Sasha shook her head.

"They're really good cookies. Sometimes injuries happen in the name of dessert," Samantha said.

"I can see that." Sasha's fatigue from earlier felt like it was diminishing, and she was glad for the distraction. "Anyway, this is the bunk room, these are the showers..."

Sasha enjoyed sharing this part of her life with someone. Her mother had refused to step foot on site since Sasha was injured a while back. It was a regular point of contention for them lately. Valeria McCray wanted her daughter to do something safer. Sasha wanted to live her life by her own rules. It seemed like her father Duncan was the only one who could calm Valeria's wrath. But her father's health was fading by the moment and soon it would only be the two of them, and that thought scared Sasha more than living a life without her best friend—her father—by her side. She wasn't sure she was strong enough to lose him and face off against her mother alone, forever.

"What's in here?" Samantha peered into the short hallway toward the main office.

"That's the office. The administrator is in there, the schedule sheets, the chief's office, training manuals, boring stuff."

"What's so boring about being prepared?" The gruff voice of her chief caught her off guard.

"Nothing, sir. Training keeps us sharp, keeps us safe." Sasha stood a little taller, reciting the company motto with ease.

"Mm-hmm." Chief Luke Herrman appraised her with a small smile. "Who's your guest, McCray?"

"Samantha Monteiro," Samantha replied as she extended her hand to him. "Sasha was giving me a little tour—you have a wonderful station, Chief."

"Luke, you can call me Luke." He smiled broadly and squared his shoulders as he shook her hand. "Thank you."

The sound of a machine groaning in defiance from the office behind them broke up the introduction.

Luke frowned. "That sounds expensive." He strode in the direction of the noise and Sasha attempted to direct Samantha elsewhere, not wanting to get into any trouble with her shift nearly ending. A loud shriek halted her retreat and soon she and Samantha were following the captain into the office space.

The scene unfolding in front of her would have been comical if she didn't already know that this would exponentially increase her cleaning regimen before the shift ended. The temporary administrator was frantically picking up pieces of copy paper that seemed to have been exorcized from the copy machine, shooting out at a feverish pace. Streaks of black ink and toner covered the exposed parts of the floor not littered with piles of ruined paper. Chief Herrman was grumbling something that sounded like swearing as he tried to shield the ever-expanding ink spill from reaching his office door.

Before Sasha could even begin to process how to help, Samantha was unplugging the copier from the wall, stopping the paper hurricane in its tracks.

The admin sputtered, "Chief, I'm sorry—I don't know what happened."

The chief's expression was a mix of annoyance and disbelief as he looked around the room. "What is it exactly that you were trying to do?"

"Make a copy?" The young temp swallowed loudly. "I think I pressed the wrong button."

"I'd say that's an understatement." Sasha couldn't help herself.

The chief sighed, "Okay. Clean up this mess. And I mean *clean* it. No ink on the floor, no streaks. I don't even want to find a paper clip out of place, Bernard. Do you hear me?"

"Yes, sir—uh, Chief." Bernard saluted but then thought better of it before nodding and scurrying out of the room.

"Rosa needs to be back ASAP." The chief frowned and looked forlornly at Rosa's desk.

"Who's Rosa?" Samantha asked.

Sasha had almost forgotten she was with her. She answered, "She's the senior administrator. Total phenom in the scheduling and organizational department. A little tight with the social funds, but—"

"That's enough, McCray." The chief cleared his throat. "Rosa is out on maternity leave with twin boys. Try as we might to stay on top of things, we just can't seem to get everything done without her."

Samantha reached down and picked up one of the copies on the floor. "A fundraiser? You're organizing a fundraiser?"

"Trying and failing to, yes." Chief Herrman looked depressed. "We do one major fundraiser every year to help cover some of the travel costs for training sessions, get supplies for the firehouse, put on some local education sessions, etcetera. But without Rosa to help collect funds or organize a raffle of some sort, we're drowning. Bernard means well, but he's just—"

"Incompetent," Sasha said.

The chief looked like he was going to respond but Samantha interjected, "I'll do it. Let me help. I have a knack for these kinds of things."

"What? Really?" Sasha had never seen the chief look so hopeful. It made him seem almost...personable.

"Really." Samantha reached out and touched the chief's hand, melting him a little more right before Sasha's eyes. "Tell me, Chief, how do you feel about dating auctions...?"

❖

"Why are you rubbing your shoulders like that? What happened? Something is wrong, I know it." Valeria McCray's eagle eye never missed a thing. Even after all these years of trying to keep things from her mother, Sasha never seemed very successful.

"It's nothing, Mom. Just a long shift." Sasha tried to downplay her aching shoulders. That chair lift had really done a number on her. What she wanted right now was a warm meal, a hot bath, and a fist full of Tylenol to soothe her aching everything.

Her mother regarded her with her usual suspicious glare, only grunting in reply. Then the English/Russian muttering began.

"Not tonight, Ma. Please." Sasha didn't think she had it in her tonight.

"You can make better money doing something less dangerous, Sasha. Your beauty is wasted under all those smoky, dusty clothes. It's only a matter of time before something like last time happens again—"

"Enough, Mom. Enough." Sasha was tired of hearing about the Hereford fire. There was a four-alarm fire on Hereford Street in Downtown Boston, and the roof had caved in while her squad was inside. Casey had been knocked sideways and Sasha was concussed. She'd suffered two bruised ribs and a superficial burn on her leg. It had scared her mother. And if she was being honest, it had scared her, too. But she would never verbalize that, definitely not to her mom. She didn't need to give her mother any more ammunition. This was part of the job—the danger was part of what kept it interesting. At least, usually that was the case. "I'm plenty beautiful in my bunker gear. Not that that is even remotely important. There's more to life than being beautiful."

Her mother frowned and furrowed her brow. "Of course you're still beautiful in those filthy trash bags and oversized boots, that's not the point. The point is that you have the luxury to also be gorgeous in addition to being smart and talented. It's a waste to be hiding that good-looking face under that ventilator thing."

"Stop arguing with your mother. She's right. Your face is too good-looking to hide it under that oxygen mask thingy. I can say that because you look just like me, thankfully." Her father appeared in the doorway. His sideways grin and wink melted her heart as usual; also as usual, he was leaning against the doorframe trying to keep his balance and catch his breath. The nasal cannula providing him with the continuous oxygen he needed to survive was slightly askew, and he looked a little gray. Her heart sank—he was fading more and more each day.

Sasha forced a laugh as she walked over to adjust his oxygen line. "The only part of me that looks like you are the five random freckles on my nose." It was true—she was the picture of her mother.

"Not true." Her father took in a labored breath. "Those are clearly my eyes."

"Last time I checked, they were *my* eyes, but I won't argue with you because you're—"

"Old, feeble, and your father?"

The truth in that jest hurt Sasha more than comforted her. "I was going to say senile. But those work, too."

He laughed but it quickly became a cough and Sasha immediately regretted teasing him. She missed their easy, playful banter the most. Some days were better than others, but today was clearly not one of those days.

"Duncan, sit. Breathe through your nose. Drink this water." Her mother was at his side with a chair and room temperature water faster than she could even process what she was saying. It was like she was anticipating this type of reaction. It occurred to her that she should check in with her mother as to how the day to day had been going. She had been mostly absent of late, working hard to put away some money to help them get out from under her father's growing medical debt. Her mother was his full-time caregiver, and yet she still found ways to make money on the side with her seamstress work and the Russian language lessons she did online after her father went to sleep at night. Which seemed to get earlier and earlier as time went on. He just didn't have the endurance he used to.

Her father sang "Valerie" to her mother, as he always did when he was trying to make her smile. Once upon a time he had a beautiful voice. Sasha remembered all the times she'd caught them slow dancing in the kitchen when they thought no one was looking—her father serenading her mother the entire time. The love her parents had for each other was what had inspired her to join Samantha's matchmaking business to begin with; she wanted a love like theirs. She just hoped it would happen in her father's lifetime so he could see it—Sasha settling down with a nice girl was her father's only wish. And she felt like her time was running out.

Her mother smiled and stroked the side of her father's face as his breathing became labored. He paused at the first verse and took a slow, steadying breath. Her mother kissed him then, probably to let him know she got the point, and he didn't need to go on anymore. He smiled, the message clearly received.

Sasha took the opportunity to turn away, deciding now was the time to set the table and help her mother serve dinner. The sweet expressions of affection between them made her heart hurt these days. Her father's now slim frame and heaving chest made him look much older than his fifty-six years. And her mother, her beautiful ballerina mother, although still statuesque and stunning, her posture still perfect and her build exquisite, but her mother was aging as well. Her father's illness had caused the appearance of gray in her mother's raven-dark hair, light purple circles had formed under her eyes, and her brow creased with stress wrinkles. They had all aged much too fast since that fateful night when everything changed.

"Sash, how was your shift?" Her father motioned for her mother to turn up the dial on the oxygen concentrator just beyond the kitchen in the den. Her mother had already been en route. The way they read each other had always amazed Sasha.

"It was good. Long. But good." She served her mother's pork pie to each of them, her father's portion smaller than the others. He didn't have much of an appetite, even with all the steroids he was on to help him breathe.

"Tell me something exciting. Old lady with a cat in a tree? Frat party pig roast disaster?" Her father's eyes twinkled—he loved the fact that she was a firefighter. He told her often that she was his hero. The sad irony was she had become a firefighter as a result of her father's sickness, and for no other reason. He had been her hero her whole life, but sometimes his words felt like a burden. Some hero she was—she couldn't save him from this disease, no matter what she did for a living.

"Nothing quite that exciting, Pop." Sasha poured more water into his glass. "Although, I did have a guest at the station today…"

"A guest. What kind of a guest? A lady guest?" Her mother was just as hell-bent on getting her to settle down as her father was.

"Actually, yes."

"You got 'em coming to your work now, Sash? That's my girl—beating 'em off with a stick." Her father beamed. Her mother swatted his arm.

"Trust me—I'd be more than happy to wife up with this woman, but unfortunately, she's already married." That was true. Sasha had always been attracted to Samantha. Who wasn't?

"Speed bump, not stop sign." Her father narrowly missed her mother's swipe this time around. "What?"

"Duncan. You're incorrigible." Her mother pointed her fork at him. "This is the kind of talk that has kept your daughter free and single all these years."

"Yeah, Dad. You're a terrible influence on me." Sasha rolled her eyes at her mother for dramatic effect. "If only I had a better role model in my life, I might have turned out differently."

"Unlikely," her father replied matter-of-factly. "I knew I was destined to have a lady-killer as a daughter on your first day of kindergarten when you came home with three different girls' favorite toys, claiming they were gifted to you by your new girlfriends. Imagine my surprise when I found out they *had* been given to you and you hadn't just stolen them."

"Oh, I did steal something...I stole their hearts." Sasha laughed as her mother tossed a dinner roll in her direction—her father snatching it out of the air before impact.

"Exactly. Lady-killer." He bit the roll and tossed his hands up in the shape of a goal post. "No one is going to comment on the catlike reflexes of the old man?"

"We're just waiting to see if you pass out first, no reason wasting our zeal for nothing," Sasha teased and her father cough-laughed. She got more than just her rogue freckles from her fair-skinned Irish father—she also got his sense of humor, his charm, and his extroverted nature. She'd learned quick wit and her ease in social situations from her father. Although her mother was no introvert by any extreme, she was much less of a presence in a room than her father used to be. He was like the sun on the darkest day—he lit up their home with his carefree belly laugh and ridiculous lame dad humor, his corny jokes never falling flat when paired with his perfect comedic timing and exaggerated gregariousness. He was the best storyteller she had ever known. She wondered how many more of his stories she had yet to hear. And how much time she'd have to hear them.

"Anyway. You were saying. Pretty lady, work visit. Go on." Her father took a recovery breath and motioned for her to continue.

"Right. So, Samantha came by the firehouse today."

"The matchmaker?" In addition to never missing anything, her mother never forgot a name.

"One and the same." Sasha savored her last bite of pork pie, enjoying her father's favorite dish.

"And?" her father asked.

"Well, she stopped by because she was in the neighborhood. She came with cookies, so she was quickly voted most popular at the station. I gave her a tour—"

"A literal one or a figurative one?" Her father wiggled his eyebrows suggestively.

"Duncan." When her mother chastised, her accent flared. It was something Sasha and her father had joked about for as long as she could remember. Her father chuckled—clearly now was no different.

"Literal." Sasha scrunched her nose and giggled. "But we ran into the chief."

"Dun, dun, *dun*." Her father added the background sound of an evil villain before wheezing with laughter. "How is old Crabby Pants?"

"He's a nice man, Duncan." Her mother gathered the plates and began serving dessert.

"Says the woman he hit on." He gave her mother a look of mock annoyance.

That had easily been one of the most awkward moments of Sasha's adult life: her mother at the bar of the Fireman's Award dinner, getting her father a cocktail, when the newly divorced chief tried to put the moves on her. Had Sasha not been up for an award later that night, she would have fled the banquet hall immediately. She was beyond grossed out—her gruff, often grouchy, and unapproachable stiff of a chief was trying to mack it to her mom. The horror. Luckily, the chief had been mostly discreet about it. Mostly. It only followed her through two shifts at the firehouse before he squashed it with extra toilet cleaning duty to anyone who breathed a word about it.

Her mother shook her head in reply and spooned the whipped cream on her father's strawberry shortcake with extra vigor. "You were saying, Sash?"

Sasha nudged him with her elbow and clinked her glass against his conspiratorially. "Oh, nothing really. She popped by and I introduced her to the chief and she volunteered to help out with the fundraiser this year since Rosa is out."

"When is Rosa due? I want to send a card." Her mother walked toward the wall calendar and pointed to a few dates at the end of the month. "A guesstimate is fine."

"Eenie, meenie, miney, Tuesday the twentieth." She took a shot in the dark.

"Ten bucks says you're wrong." Her father extended his hand in wager.

"Twenty bucks says I'm right and it happens during the middle of the night." She took his hand and countered.

"Deal." He nodded and thumb wrestled her like they always did when they made a bet, and like always, he beat her.

"Sasha, this is the longest story ever." Her mother crossed her arms in annoyance and motioned for her to get on with it.

"Fine, Ma. Just trample all over my buildup." Sasha took a bite of strawberry and was reminded of her childhood—she loved this dessert as much as her father did. It was her favorite. "So anyway, Samantha offered to help the chief plan the fundraiser and suggested doing something a little different this year."

"Which is?" Her father was on the edge of his seat.

"A dating auction. She had the idea of putting up the eligible firefighters at the company and some other local singles up for a dating auction to raise money for the charities we support and to help fund some of our training courses this year. The chief was a little hesitant at first, but the guys loved the idea. It's going to be a whole event—an emcee, passed hors d'oeuvres, those little bidding signs, and swanky prize packages to sweeten the deal."

"Well, I'll be…" Her father looked like a kid in a candy store. "Tell me you're doing it, Sash."

"Well, I wasn't going to, but Samantha kinda made it sound like it wasn't negotiable. I think it'll be fun." Sasha shrugged. The guys at the house had been pumped from the get go, and it was a little contagious.

"And how will she ensure it's a success? Does she even know anyone who would want to attend this sort of thing?" Her mother supplied her usual amount of realism and doubt.

"Samantha assured the chief she had plenty of wealthy clients that were looking for a man, or woman, in uniform. She said she could fill the audience with her eyes closed and one hand tied behind her back. There's a little photo shoot scheduled next shift for all the guys and girls participating—she's having a professional photographer take action shots to put in the auction catalog to enhance the bids. We have to write little blurbs about ourselves. Actual blurbs. Can you imagine?" The more she talked about it, the more excited she got—this was going to be a blast.

Her father wolf whistled as best he could with the oxygen on. "Any chance that girl from the wedding will be in the crowd? You know, the sexy blonde with the hot lips?"

"Dad," she whined and immediately regretted telling her father about the kiss she'd shared with Abby the night of the wedding. She regretted it almost as much as she regretted not getting Abby's phone number—by the time she had gotten back from the fur coat debacle, Abby and her friend Edie were long gone. She had been kicking herself ever since.

"Those were your words, not mine." He scooped up the last bit of whipped cream and finished it off with a happy sigh.

"Truth." There was no point in denying it. That kiss was something she'd revisited often in the weeks since that night—there was just something about Abby and those *lips*. She would be over the moon if she had a chance to meet up with her again. Samantha clearly knew her if she was at the wedding. Why hadn't she thought to ask Samantha to put her in touch with Abby before? "Here's hoping she makes an appearance. I'll work on my single lady strut just in case. Wanna help me pick a song to walk out to?"

"Obviously." Her father nodded and gave her a high five before coughing briefly.

"Best. Wingman. Ever." She smiled at his enthusiasm even as his frailty kicked her in the bottom of her stomach. She wondered how many more of these moments she would have with him. As she reached for her phone to pull up potential entrance music options, she decided to live in the moment and let those feelings haunt her another day. After all, there was important work to be done.

CHAPTER NINE

Abby hadn't seen the new addition to Lucinda Moss's dance studio before tonight; in fact, she had only been to the original location once. But from what she remembered, this side was entirely different. For tonight, Samantha had transformed it into a burlesque-show-like venue. And in true Samantha fashion, she had spared no expense.

A stage draped in lush red curtains filled the largest wall of the room with an ornate and colorful emcee podium set off to the side. Bright lights bordered the stage and framed a runway that extended out about twenty feet into what she assumed was the audience section—lines of neatly arranged chairs filled the floor, with tiny tables placed throughout adorned with votive candles and small flower arrangements. It was like a fancy, high-end dinner theater setup with the most elite patrons. From what Abby could see, the crowd was chock-full of some of Boston's wealthiest and most eligible bachelorettes, with a few handsome eligible bachelors also holding auction books. She noticed Samantha's business partner Andrew Stanley handing out the books by one of the bars off to the side, and it occurred to her that she should get one.

When she scanned the crowd more carefully, she recognized a few familiar faces, people who contributed to her mother's foundation or regulars on the art scene—philanthropist types. Her mother would be right at home here. She looked around and found her at the bar Andrew stood near, chatting with her frenemy Rachel

Rabin. A sinking sensation settled in her gut when she realized that she had never seen Rachel without her eligible and gay daughter, Dianna, the woman her mother was determined to hook her up with if this matchmaker thing didn't work out. As if she could read her thoughts, Dianna appeared at her side with a glass of champagne.

"Hey, Abby. I'm surprised to see you here—pleasantly surprised—but surprised nonetheless." Dianna handed her the glass and added, "You look great."

"Thanks." She accepted the compliment and the flute, figuring there was no harm in either. Dianna was plenty attractive. It wasn't that she wasn't physically attracted to her, just she oozed money and privilege, so Abby had never really been interested in the romantic connection that her mother was constantly trying to promote. More, she wasn't interested in the hours Dianna kept as a high-priced defense attorney. They had dated a few times and slept together a few more times—but Dianna worked long nights and attended lots of fancy galas, and Dianna loved that life. Abby had had her fill of galas and society obligations, even if she had to attend them from time to time; that was one of the reasons she went by her middle name, Rossmore. But she was still a Davenport, and she was deeply entrenched in the family nonprofit. It was why she got into accounting to begin with—well, that and the love of math that no one seemed to understand. She and Dianna wanted different things, and that was fine.

"So, what brings you to the auction tonight?" Dianna's gaze was intense. Everything about her was intense. Her tall and tight physique, the severity of her angled haircut, the way she pursued women, the way she was in bed…not exactly unappealing. But it was intense.

"I'm here as moral support for my mother." That was true. Mostly. She was also here because Samantha had told her that she had a few women she wanted her to meet tonight—a sort of mixer within a mixer thing. But mostly she was here because Samantha had found someone she wanted her mother to meet, someone she was confident was a perfect match in the waiting.

"She's getting back into the dating game?" Dianna's smile was warm. Their families had been in the same social circles for decades, and she knew Abby's father's death had hit her mother hard. "Good for her. This is a big step."

"Yeah, I'm proud of her." Abby meant that. She was proud her mother agreed to this.

"Is she working with Samantha?" Dianna pried a little. Abby contemplated whether or not to deflect it.

"She is." She decided to be honest.

"Samantha's the best." Dianna sipped her own glass and looked toward the stage.

That got Abby's attention. "Have you worked with Perfect Match before?"

Dianna's intense eye contact returned to her own. "Mm-hmm. Dating is hard these days. One can use all the help one can get."

Abby mulled that over as Dianna added, "I hear there are a few eligible women on auction tonight. Samantha does a lot of charitable work with my family's scholarship foundation and her wife Lucinda hosts a free dance class at the studio once a month for my alma mater's 1Ls as a favor to me. So we came to support Samantha, but I'd be lying if I said I wasn't a little curious about bachelorette number twenty-seven."

Abby regretted not getting an auction book when she first walked in. Who was number twenty-seven? And why was Dianna interested in her? "Oh?"

Dianna gave her a once-over in that sexy, take-control kind of way that reminded Abby of the passion they'd shared between the sheets. "She's beautiful. But we could both save ourselves a lot of money and time if we tried our luck with each other again. She might take a nice head shot, but she's got nothing on you."

Dianna's hand grazed along Abby's holding the champagne flute and Abby shuddered. Her forwardness had always ignited things between them—it was what made Abby want to fuck her but not date her. She laughed to distract the other parts of her that Dianna revved up, reminding herself of the reasons she didn't think they were a good fit. "You always did have a way with words."

Dianna looked emboldened. "That's not a no."

"That's not a yes, either." Abby finished her glass and squeezed Dianna's hand. "Thank you for the drink and the kind words."

"They aren't just words, Abby." Dianna held her hand briefly before letting go. "And you're welcome. I'm sure I'll see you throughout the night. It was good catching up with you."

Abby smiled and nodded, deciding she might give Dianna's proposition further consideration. It had been a while since she'd had the opportunity to be topped. And Dianna was certainly a competent top.

"I see you and Dianna have gotten acquainted." Samantha spoke from behind her. She wore a tight red dress, her cleavage and jewelry on display, Abby noticed.

"Reacquainted," Abby corrected, before a thought occurred to her. "Is she one of the women you were hoping to introduce me to tonight? Because I can save you the trouble. Our families are friendly. We've been introduced. A few times."

"Yeah, I got that from the little bit of your exchange I observed." Samantha appraised her with a smile. "So, sex only or did you try dating?"

"Is it that obvious?" Abby felt like she should be embarrassed, but she wasn't.

"To me it is." Samantha shrugged. "But that's kind of my thing, seeing what other people don't."

"It was a little of both. More sex than dating."

Samantha nodded. "I figured. The way she looks at you implies she wants more of that."

"The sex or the dating?"

"Both," Samantha replied. "And to answer your question, no. She wasn't the one I had in mind. Although I can see how you two would be drawn to each other. But I don't see her as your perfect match."

"Why's that?" That was a bold statement. Abby wanted clarification.

"Why didn't it work out between you two outside of the bedroom?" Samantha countered.

"She's too—"

"Intense." Samantha finished her sentence. "That's what I thought, too."

Abby nudged Samantha. "You're pretty good at this stuff, huh?"

"They don't call me Miss Match for nothing." Samantha looked in the direction of Edie at the bar. "I'm glad you came, Abby. And I'm proud of your mother for taking a chance."

"Me, too." She meant it on both counts, but didn't feel like elaborating. "Tell me about this guy you want to hook my mother up with."

"Ah, yes. He's charming, handsome, debonair, brave, a real life hero..." Samantha's voice trailed off as she got Andrew's attention and waved him over.

"He sounds like a dream come true." Abby smiled as Andrew approached. She didn't know him as well as Samantha, but she could see why they were successful—they were great together.

"You beckoned, darling?" Andrew slid his arm around Samantha's waist and appraised Abby. "You look great, Abs. Really. That dress is a knockout."

That was two compliments tonight. She mentally high-fived herself for going back to the closet and changing again before she left home. This dress was going to get a front-of-the-closet rotation, stat.

Samantha air-kissed Andrew on the cheek and took an auction booklet from his hand. "I love you—truly—but I just wanted a catalog."

Andrew scoffed and dusted off the shoulder of his tux. "Fine. I'll just go hang out with your old lady. Talk about spectacular— Lucinda looks like a tall glass of water in that blue dress. She's giving me the gay vapors." He fanned himself for effect.

"Ooh, tell her to save me a seat up front. Do you have everything you need to emcee?"

"I've had three martinis and a handful of pretzels—I'm sufficiently lubed up." Andrew winked at Abby as Samantha shoved him playfully. "I gotta go review my intros and double-check with the sound crew so we don't have any weird mic issues or missed cues. I'll see you ladies later."

Abby waved good-bye but was anxiously awaiting the auction catalog Samantha continued to hold in her hand, just out of Abby's reach. She looked at it longingly.

"Eager much?" Samantha teased.

"I'm dying to know all about this Prince Charming you've mapped out for my mother." Abby nodded excitedly and reached for the booklet.

"Manners, Abby." Edie walked up and fanned herself with her own catalog. "Samantha, you have outdone yourself. Some of these men are positively edible looking."

"If someone doesn't give me a catalog, I'm going to lose my mind." It was true. Abby was excited to see Samantha's prospect for her mother, but more, she wanted to see who Dianna was interested in, lucky bachelorette number twenty-seven.

Samantha handed over her copy with a laugh and Abby started thumbing through it. Each page was dedicated to one eligible man or woman. There was an action shot of them doing their day job or a recreational activity they enjoyed. Each photo was accompanied by a self-written blurb that talked about the person's interests and so on. At the bottom of each page were the general stats: age, height, favorite food, ideal date, something quirky about themselves.

As Edie and Samantha chatted by her side, Abby scanned the faces and first names provided. A quick skim of the cheat sheet at the front revealed thirty auction participants, eighteen men and twelve women. Their careers included nurse, dog walker, lawyer, doctor, artist, mathematician, sommelier, EMT, and police officer. It was quite the list. They varied in ages and, in an interesting twist that she appreciated greatly, sexual orientation and preferred dating partner were listed as well. So far, she was pleased to see at least three women identified as bisexual, queer, or lesbian on the docket for the evening. Now, on to mystery girl twenty-seven…

Samantha's hand covered the page before she could read it. "Okay. So, about the person I think will be a good match for your mother."

Abby used all of her patience and forced charm school training not to slap Samantha's hand off the page. "Yes?"

"His name is Luke. He's a divorced fire chief in Boston. A real man's man—likes rugged outdoorsy things but has great taste in wine and loves to cook. He takes cooking classes twice a month and is working on a recipe book of his favorite meals. He's handsome and sweet and everything"—she turned to Edie—"you asked for."

"A man in uniform? I like it." Edie was always game for an adventure. Tonight was clearly no different. If she had any hesitation, she wasn't showing it. "A firefighter. Wow. That's such a brave career choice. And a chief, no less. I'm intrigued."

Samantha gave her a broad smile. "You told me you wanted someone to travel with, someone to take the time out of their days to appreciate the little things. You wanted a gentleman with a strong jawline who believes in chivalry and isn't afraid to watch chick flicks. Luke is that man. He's equal parts adorable and delicious. You'll see."

Edie nodded along to Samantha's words and Abby felt a little left out. Had her mother really asked for those qualities in a partner? It surprised her to think that her mother might be committed to this. Of course, she was proud of her for coming tonight, but half of her thought she was going through the motions because Samantha had suggested it. Abby was starting to realize that maybe her mother was more on board than she had thought. It made her feel a little guilty. Why hadn't her mother told her these things?

Before she had a chance to give it more thought, the lights flashed and people started to take their seats. Samantha excused herself, and Edie pulled Abby toward a reserved table right next to the stage—the show was about to begin. Out of the corner of her eye, she noticed someone approaching. It was Sasha.

"Sasha. Hi. What are you doing here?" Abby found herself standing awkwardly by the table as her mother took her seat.

"Abby. Hey. I'm so glad you're here." Sasha was wearing that deep red lipstick again; her eyes were drawn to it. The lights flashed around her a second time in warning.

"Sure. I mean, no. Wait. What are you doing here? Are you working the event?" As soon as she said that she regretted it—Sasha was not wearing a catering uniform. Quite the contrary, actually. She was wearing a firefighting jacket that was open, exposing a black push-up bra with suspenders holding up the uniform trousers that hung loosely over her boots. How had she neglected to notice Sasha didn't have a shirt on? And why was she dressed like a firefighter?

Sasha must have caught her staring because she dipped her head to make eye contact before replying. "I'm on the auction block."

An announcement went out for all participants to head backstage and Sasha turned to leave. She paused and looked back at Abby. "Don't leave tonight before I have a chance to get your number—I think we have some unfinished business to attend to."

Before Abby could think of a charming or flirty response, Sasha had disappeared. Her mother cleared her throat next to her. "That's the pretty girl from the wedding, isn't it?" Her mother craned in her seat to try to see Sasha's already disappeared form. "I feel like she had more clothes on the last time we saw her."

"Uh-huh," she replied dumbly, letting herself revisit the defined lines of Sasha's exposed abdomen—that was a pleasant surprise. All of it. The near-naked Sasha part especially.

"Close your mouth, dear. People are staring." Edie pulled her by her hand into the seat next to hers and offered her a glass of whatever the waiter had just dropped off. "You'd better drink this. I have a feeling you'll need the hydration."

Abby sipped the contents of the glass and tried to ignore the giggle her mother used to punctuate her statement. Sasha was on the auction block tonight. Sasha wanted to get her number before the night was over. She felt they had unfinished business to attend to.

Abby swallowed hard. Her mother was right: she was going to need all the hydration she could get.

The evening was a blast. Abby couldn't remember the last time she'd seen her mother belly laugh in public. Andrew was the perfect emcee, delivering cheeky monologues and playful introductions, driving up the bidding for the eligible bachelors and bachelorettes by sweetening the deals—adding free concert tickets, limo rides, museum passes, and the like to breathe life into the already exciting prospect of getting a date with a dreamboat. It was a masterful performance and the waiters kept the booze pouring, the appetizers rotating, and, more importantly, the money flowing. Samantha's fundraiser was on fire and it was just getting started.

Abby fanned herself with the auction catalog as she tried to catch her breath—her mother had gotten into a rather heated bidding war over that Luke fellow with the woman who always attended the private museum showings and ate all the cocktail shrimp. Like, all of it. It was a miracle she wasn't flamingo pink.

Her mother and the shrimp woman volleyed bid after bid back and forth—it made Abby dizzy. Things got a little wild when Samantha came onstage and took the mic from Andrew, spicing up the date with Luke by offering a sunset hot air balloon ride with bottomless top shelf champagne. Her mother was on her feet before the word *champagne* even passed Samantha's lips. Her taste was too rich for the Crawfish Queen and the audience cheered when Luke jogged off the stage in his formal dress uniform and scooped Edie up, easily transporting her to the rear bar through a sea of applause.

It was romance novel perfection and Abby loved every second of it. This was exactly the type of distraction she needed before the inevitable happened: the mystery woman, bachelorette number twenty-seven, would take the stage any minute now, except she wasn't a mystery anymore. According to the catalog, twenty-seven was no other than looks-amazing-in-her-unisex-waiter-outfit Sasha. And the word on the street was the firefighting getup wasn't just a costume for the auction block—it was her full-time job. Talk about hot.

"Are you enjoying yourself?" Samantha took the seat next to Abby as Andrew introduced the next bachelorette—a pretty blond lawyer from Harvard.

"I am." Abby accepted the cocktail the waiter for her section dropped off, and she turned toward Samantha and motioned to her drink. "Would you like one? I'm buying."

Samantha shook her head. "I'm all set. No drinking on the job. Besides, you should save your money for more important things."

"Like what?" Abby had no intention of bidding on anyone tonight. She had already seen Sasha and was planning on exchanging numbers with her later—there didn't seem a point to also buying a date with her if she was basically guaranteed one.

Andrew cued up the music for the next suitor and the unmistakable sound of Right Said Fred filled the room. "You're kidding me, "I'm Too Sexy"? Who has the balls to come out to that song?" Abby scoffed.

"I think you mean *lady* balls." Samantha laughed when Abby's jaw dropped.

"No way."

"Oh, yes. In many ways, yes." Samantha cheered and stood as Sasha sauntered out on stage in a choreographed dance, slowly strutting along the runway, her head down and a fire helmet obscuring her eyes until the chorus started up, at which time the helmet was tossed to a cheering woman in the crowd and she started shrugging off her jacket. Abby tried to concentrate on what Andrew was saying, but she was distracted by Sasha's thumbs sliding up and down the suspenders. The jacket long forgotten, she was in just a black bra and pants now.

"Let's start the bidding at two hundred and fifty dollars. Ladies, who wants a chance to let Sasha put out that fire for you?"

A slew of auction catalogs went up, the fluorescent numbers on the back signaling the enthusiastic interest of multiple women in the crowd. At each increasing bid, Sasha walked toward the bidder and gave them a little show—a kiss on the cheek, a playful wink, she even sat on one older woman's lap and let her smack her ass. The whole time Abby watched in shock, unmoving, at what was unfolding in front of her. As the numbers climbed, the bidding started to slow down. And then Dianna Rabin's hand went up in the air. She doubled the largest bid and raised her martini glass in Sasha's direction.

"Dianna," Abby cursed under her breath. She had forgotten how interested Dianna had mentioned she was in *her* mystery girl. Her blood boiled.

"Now, now, Abby. This is what I was talking about—saving those pennies for the right moment. This is that moment." Samantha leaned across the table between them and motioned back to the stage. Sasha was standing in front of Dianna and Dianna reached out and snapped one of Sasha's suspenders to the adoration of the crowd.

"You can't be seri—" Before Abby could finish her sentence, Samantha grabbed her elbow and thrust the hand clutching her auction catalog into the air.

"We have a challenging bid!" Andrew cheered and both Dianna and Sasha looked over in surprise. But no one was more surprised than Abby.

"Samantha, what the hell?"

Samantha merely shrugged. "Whoops."

Before Abby could decide whether she was angry or not, Dianna called out another bid, grabbing Sasha by the suspenders when she moved toward Abby's direction.

"You're not going to let Sasha get scooped up by Dianna, are you?" Samantha teased in response to Abby's annoyed grunt.

Abby wasn't the jealous type, typically. But this wasn't a typical situation, was it? She watched as Dianna looked back at her with a wink before grabbing the front of Sasha's pants and tugging her closer. Sasha's elevated height on the runway paired with Dianna's tall frame put Dianna's mouth right in line with Sasha's—

Before she knew what she was doing, she was out of her seat with the catalog high in the air. Andrew called out her bid and Dianna looked back over her shoulder, her expression wicked. That was a look Abby was all too familiar with—this was about to get interesting. She took a deep breath.

"Do we have a challenging bid?" Andrew sounded almost giddy, but Abby didn't dare take her eyes off of Dianna and Sasha.

Dianna took a sip from her martini glass before setting it aside. She picked up her bidding sheet and pressed her palm flat to Sasha's abdomen, leaning forward to lick a line across Sasha's stomach, her bid sheet waving like a victory flag. The crowd roared, and Abby saw red.

"Well, now. This is getting a little X-rated." Andrew fanned himself before looking toward Abby. "Shall we let these ladies have a room or does anyone care to—"

"I'll triple it." Abby was convinced she was possessed. Someone was definitely controlling her from outside her body. There was no way she just bid over three months' mortgage payments for a date with a woman she was most likely already going on a date with anyway.

"Sold!" Sasha yelled from the stage, cutting the bidding war short. She kissed Dianna on the cheek before she bounded off in Abby's direction. To Dianna's credit, she applauded and gave Abby a friendly nod. Abby wondered—if she ever did take Dianna up on her proposal, would this little bidding war come back to haunt her?

"Well done, Abs." Samantha patted her on the back and disappeared just as Sasha walked up.

"You know, I was going to take you out for dinner regardless of whether or not you bid on me, right?" Sasha was standing close to her. Close and still not wearing a shirt.

"I was hoping." Abby decided trying to maintain eye contact was an impossible feat.

Sasha smiled and ran her hand along the back of her neck, looking almost shy—that was something Abby had never seen from her before. "That's kind of a lot of money though, Abby. I'm feeling a little insecure—I mean, you just bought yourself one hell of a date. I don't want to disappoint."

Abby blinked. "Then don't."

Sasha laughed. "Well, that settles that."

Abby nodded, not sure what to say next. She had just spent an exorbitant amount of money buying a date with a woman she barely knew, but had already kissed. A woman she feared had some serious womanizing tendencies, a fear not quelled by her flirtatious striptease just moments ago. She had clearly lost her damn mind. Clearly.

"Can I buy you a drink?" Sasha's lips parted and the contrast of her white teeth on that deep red lip color was mesmerizing.

"I think it's the least you could do," Abby teased. "But first, can you do me a favor?"

"Anything." Sasha gave her a serious, focused look.

"Can you put on a shirt? I'm having a really hard time not having a conversation with your breasts." Abby figured at this point just owning up to the distraction that was Sasha's perfectly toned and cut body was the best thing to do here.

"Oh, sure." Sasha looked momentarily modest before that façade quickly faded. "But you know, Abby. I have a feeling we have great potential to be breast friends."

Abby laughed and wondered just how true that statement would become.

CHAPTER TEN

Sasha examined her makeup in the mirror in the front foyer of her parents' home and second-guessed her decision to wear her hair down.

"You look great—stop fussing." Her mother's image appeared over her shoulder. Their similarities were striking: she had her mother's milky white skin, strong jaw, and dark eyes, although the shape was more her Irish father's than her Russian mother's. She had a light dusting of freckles on her nose and across her shoulders; she burned in the sun like her father. Even with his fair skin and complexion, he still managed to keep a darker tan than Sasha had ever achieved—he credited it to the lifetime of outdoor construction work he did before the accident. His farmer's tan had never faded, even as his health did. Their only child, when she stood side by side with them, together, it was clear she was equal parts each.

Her mother looked tired. The bags under her eyes were particularly dark today. "Have you slept, Ma?"

Her mother met her gaze in the mirror and sighed. "Your father's nights have been getting worse. He has more mucus. It's harder to breathe. The machines are only doing so much."

Sasha felt herself deflate.

"Don't worry, Sash. Focus on your big date. There will be more worries tomorrow and the next day. No point in spoiling a good time in the present." Her mother swept a mass of dark hair off Sasha's shoulder. "I like it down. You are stunning."

"Thanks, Ma." She leaned into her mother's touch and let herself be held for a moment. Some of the physical affection had faded from their relationship over the years—she assumed it was from the strain of her father's health needs. But she missed it, nonetheless. Sometimes she just wanted to be held by her mom. "Oh, before I forget…"

Sasha walked toward the front door and opened her purse. She pulled out the small manila envelope and handed it to her mother. "Last month was a good month. I had a couple great catering jobs and worked a few double shifts at the firehouse. This should help put a dent in things."

Her mother's face was grateful, but she only nodded as she took the envelope and put it in her pocket, not bothering to look inside. Sasha knew it pained her to take Sasha's money, but she also knew that without all the overtime and extra catering jobs she did, her parents would have to sell the house, and even that might not keep them afloat. She couldn't undo the damage to her father's body, but she could at least help lessen the burden financially.

"Thank you, Sasha."

"Sure thing, Ma." She didn't make a big deal out of it, ever. She was their only child and her parents had sacrificed everything to make sure she had the best education and life money could buy. They had never lived grandly, but they loved fully. And she wanted to make sure that same standard was afforded to her father for the rest of his life, no matter how short that might be. It didn't matter if she worked more hours than not. If he was cared for and didn't have to worry, it was all worth it. They were worth it. He was worth it.

"Did you get her flowers?" Duncan's voice was raspier than usual, and he balanced against the door frame of the kitchen to talk to her.

"Flowers? We're not going steady, Dad. It's a first date." Sasha watched her mother back out of the room, careful not to let her father see the envelope in her pocket. She and her mom both worked hard to keep the debt and debt collectors from him—he needed to focus on his health, not on the endless pile of medical bills.

"Sasha. This woman literally paid for you. As in *you were bought*. Owned. Belong to her for one night." Duncan shook his head. "The least you could've done was get her flowers."

"She didn't purchase me as a sex slave off the black market, Dad. It was a charity fundraising auction—I'm just a really hot tax write-off." She blew him a kiss and he laughed. "And obviously I bought her flowers—they're in the car. Back off my game, Old Man."

"Just remember to pack protection." Her father's attempts at keeping a straight face were thwarted when her mother hissed in his direction.

"Duncan, enough." Her mother looked scandalized. "Have a good time, love. Feel free to leave me in the dark about the details."

Sasha saluted her and stage-whispered to her father, "Make sure the warden lets you have that extra dessert I brought by."

"Operation Macaron is already under way." He reached into his pocket and pulled out a half-eaten cookie he had clearly hidden. Her dad was the best.

❖

Sasha wasn't used to so many rules. The truth was that she was more of a rule breaker than a follower. But when Abby had requested they meet at their date destination instead of Sasha picking her up, she decided to go with it. That's when Abby added her other stipulation—she would pick the date venue and the time. Sasha wasn't sure how to feel about that. She was more comfortable with a little more control, especially since she was planning to show Abby the best first date of her life.

She had thought of Abby often since the kiss at Samantha's wedding, and she was annoyed with herself that she hadn't noticed how charming and funny and hot Abby was during all those times they had crossed paths at the Perfect Match mixers. But since the auction, when Abby put herself out there and put her money on the line, Sasha had been thinking about her almost constantly. So she decided to let Abby lead and see where it went. But she was determined to make sure it went somewhere. This felt a little too serendipitous to only put in the half effort. Abby was a beautiful, mysterious creature, and Sasha was more than eager to learn more about her.

She pulled up to the coffeehouse and smiled. Abby said this place was one of those new dual-purpose locations—coffeehouse and café during the day, intimate dining experience with locally harvested food at night. She had driven by probably a hundred times in the last few months and never noticed it. It was adorable. The outdoor patio was enclosed with wrought-iron railings adorned with white fairy lights. Planters with colorful, cascading flowers were placed evenly along the inside of the fence creating an urban garden feel under the soft cream-colored canopy that covered the seating space. Abby knew the owner, and they would have the place to themselves, or nearly so, during the restaurant's soft open. It had sounded so quaint and romantic, and so far, she was not disappointed.

She parked at a meter and took a moment to appreciate the quiet Cambridge street. The café was close to the center, but just off the beaten path enough to be a hidden jewel. She leaned against her car and checked her phone. She was early. But then again, she was always early. That was kind of her thing. If you were on time, you were late—that was something both her parents agreed on. For her father, time was money. When he was a construction foreman, getting to the job site first was a badge of honor—he perused the work from the night before and mapped out his plan for the day. Her mother was no different. They were a family that liked to be prepared. That didn't mean Sasha wasn't spontaneous. It just meant she liked to have a backup plan, to have all her bases covered. And arriving early afforded her that luxury.

She looked around for any sign of Abby before she decided this was her chance. She grabbed the flowers from the front seat of her car and headed toward the restaurant. When the front door of the café wouldn't open, she knocked on the glass. A young waitress met her with a smile.

"Hi. Are you Sasha or Abby?"

"Sasha. Is Abby here yet?"

"No, ma'am." The waitress opened the door to the café a little bit wider, inviting Sasha inside. "I'm Courtney, and I'll be working with you tonight."

"Hey, Court. Nice to meet you. Let's go ahead and drop that *ma'am* thing, stat."

"Yes, ma—" The waitress stopped herself with a laugh. "Sorry, force of habit."

Sasha took the moment to appreciate the amount of work it took to transform the indoor space from a café to a restaurant. Although all the tables and chairs had been relocated to the dinner setup, there were still tablecloths that needed to be laid out, napkins unfolded in piles by the bar, and about fifty votive candles waiting to be lit.

"Are you on your own with this stuff?" She motioned to the room around them.

"I am for a little bit longer—we weren't expecting you or Miss, uh, Abby, to arrive for another twenty minutes or so. I should have backup soon."

"Hey, can you do me a favor? Do you have any room to put these flowers in the refrigerator so they don't wilt while we're at dinner? I'd like them to be kind of a surprise."

"I'm sure we can find room." She took them and paused. "That's really sweet."

Sasha got the impression Courtney was checking her out. Normally, this kind of thing would segue into flirting, but she had every intention of making tonight a success with Abby, so she sidestepped the seemingly open door. "Thanks. Uh, while you do that, I'll light these zillion candles. Teamwork makes the dream work, ya know?"

Courtney seemed to consider this for a moment. "Sure. Thanks. The lighter is by the bar. Just don't hurt yourself."

"I'm pretty good with fire, trust me." Sasha didn't wait for a reply before she headed for the waiting candles. A quick glance in the mirror behind the bar showed Courtney watching Sasha's retreating frame—yup, she was definitely checking her out. Sasha smiled to herself as she appraised the candles. She took Courtney's attention as a win in the *I chose the right outfit* column.

She made quick work of her project and by the time Courtney had returned, she had lit all but five candles.

"Whoa. You're fast." Courtney grabbed the stack of cloth napkins and held them up. "Care to try your hand at folding?"

Sasha glanced up at the clock above the bar. She still had a few minutes before Abby arrived. "Sure. Lay it on me, sister."

"Okay, so you fold the napkin into an upside-down triangle, tuck this fold in like this, and then mirror it with the other side before you flip it over and fold down the top. Like so." Courtney was quick, so quick that Sasha thought she might have missed a step.

"I think you lost me." Sasha tried to follow the instructions Courtney outlined, but somehow her napkin didn't look anything like Courtney's.

A noise by the bar drew her attention. An older bartender looked their way and waved to Courtney.

"It's okay, I've got these." Courtney looked past her toward the door. "My backup just arrived and I think that's probably your friend Abby."

Sasha turned in her seat to find Abby watching her through the glass. "Yup. Gotta go. I guess, I'll see you…Where? Outside?"

"Yeah. I'll open the door and get you ladies seated." Courtney told the bartender to let the chef downstairs know his guests were here before she headed for the door. She stopped just short to ask, "This is a date, right?"

Sasha nodded. "It is."

Courtney frowned. "I figured. Anyway, if this doesn't work out, I'd be happy to have dinner with you sometime."

Well that was bold. Sasha wasn't sure what to say. Abby was about five inches away on the other side of the glass. It wasn't that she wasn't used to having a few girls in rotation at once, but this was a departure even for her. "Uh, I'll keep that in mind. Thanks."

"Sure thing." Courtney opened the door and greeted Abby. "Hi. You must be Abby. Micah said he'll be right up. Please let me show you and Sasha to your seats."

Abby appraised her with a look of suspicion. "Okay."

"Hey." Sasha stepped forward, trying to redirect Abby's attention to her. "How are you? I'm glad we're doing this."

"Hi." Abby still seemed a little distracted. "I'm good. Do you... know her?"

"Courtney?" It took Sasha a moment to recognize the look on Abby's face was jealousy. Shit. "No. Well, I know her name. I got here a little early and waited inside for you. That's all. Sorry, I'm sure that probably seemed a little strange."

Abby didn't say anything at first, so Sasha reached for her hand, eager to soothe her concerns. Abby looked down at their hands before looking back up at Sasha.

"Let's try this again." Sasha pulled Abby closer by their clasped hands, leaning in to kiss Abby on the cheek. She stayed close and spoke softly so that only Abby could hear. "I'm happy to be here with you. You look great. Thank you for bidding on me—I've really been looking forward to this." Abby squeezed her hand and she pulled back to see a small smile on Abby's face. Jackpot.

"Here you go, ladies." Courtney pulled out both of their chairs. Their table was along the edge of the patio space, a little removed from the others. Courtney had finished setting the table, and the linens were perfectly placed and menus awaited them. She filled their water glasses. "I'll be right back to take your order." Courtney disappeared and Sasha could not have been happier.

Sasha waited for Abby to sit before helping her adjust her chair. She settled in across from her and let herself appreciate Abby's outfit. She was dressed in a silk blouse and a short, flattering skirt with what Sasha would call a significant heel. It had occurred to her when she kissed Abby on the cheek that they were nearly the same height. At five foot eight, Sasha was used to being one of the tallest women in the room. She wondered how tall Abby was without her shoes on.

"Sorry." Abby cleared her throat and sipped her glass of water. "I don't know, I guess I thought you—"

"Were shacking up with the waitress?" Sasha didn't think being coy was her best choice here. She decided to go with her gut and her gut was telling her that Abby thought something more was going on.

Abby looked embarrassed. "Will you hate me if I say yes?"

"No." Sasha considered all the times in her life that she'd let her eye wander while on a date with another woman. This was probably some cosmic payback for her past bad behavior.

Abby cocked her head. "Why do I get the impression that this kind of thing happens a lot?"

"Me being accused of flirting with other women? Or being considered guilty before I'm given the benefit of the doubt?" Once the words left her mouth, she realized that was a little harsh.

Abby raised an eyebrow. "I suppose both."

"It happens more than I'd like. If that's what you're asking." Sasha shrugged.

"Why do you think that is?" Abby leaned back in her chair, her expression unreadable.

"I suppose it's because I'm friendly. I'm not afraid to strike up a conversation with anyone, female or otherwise. I'd say there have been more than a few instances in my past when I've been labeled a—"

"Womanizer?" Abby's gaze was focused on her face. She appeared to be watching Sasha's reaction.

Sasha was careful to mask her resentment of the word. Yes. She had been accused of that many, many times. And not wrongly so. But that was something she had sought to change. She wanted more than one-night stands and intense make-out sessions with strangers whose names she never made the attempt to learn. Samantha had told her that the change had to start with her. Today seemed like as good a time as any. "Yes."

Abby blinked. Sasha's honesty seemed to catch her off guard.

"Look." Sasha crossed her legs, her tight dress riding up as she leaned forward. "I'm not perfect. I've had my fair share of dates and hookups, and I'm not ashamed of that. But I'm also not into the whole judge-a-book-by-its-cover bullshit either. There's more to me than amazing cheekbones and legs for days. I promise you. And if you're willing to give me a chance, I'm sure you'll find out that I'm right. Because let's be honest, you paid for me to be here and I couldn't be more grateful. And honored. And pretty turned on that you took on that handsy lawyer chick for me. So I'm okay with you being a little suspicious as long as you give me a chance to prove you wrong. Okay?"

"Amazing cheekbones and legs for days, huh?"

"That's what you got out of all that?"

"Oh yeah. I have a pretty good narcissism radar." Abby's expression was playful.

She was teasing her. Sasha relaxed a little and decided to test the waters. "I mean, it's kinda true."

Abby's eyes followed Sasha's hand as she motioned to the large amount of leg exposed while she was sitting forward in her seat. "I'll give you that."

"Good." Sasha reached out and took Abby's hand again. "So we're agreed? Because I want to talk more about my amazing cheekbones."

Abby laughed and Sasha squeezed her hand briefly before releasing it. Courtney dropped off one of the votives Sasha had lit before and let them know Micah would be right up.

"So, who's this Micah character?" Sasha didn't bother looking at the menu. Abby was appetizing enough. She was reading the menu in front of her and twirling a strand of her blond hair around her finger. It was adorable.

"He's a bean guru I met a while ago. His café is notorious for having amazing aromas and unique blends. He mentioned a few months ago that he was thinking of converting his Cambridge location into a restaurant in the evenings but wanted to test it out a little before the grand opening." Abby looked up and caught Sasha watching her. She stopped twirling and looked a little shy. More adorable.

Abby cleared her throat. "Anyway. I figured this was a good place for us to get to know each other and help Micah finalize a menu. Are you a good eater?"

"The best." The innuendo wasn't lost on Sasha, and she wondered if it was intentional.

"Excellent." Abby winked. Definitely intentional. This date was going to be awesome.

CHAPTER ELEVEN

Abby's sides hurt from laughing. They had made it through dinner and were on to dessert, and she was pleasantly surprised to find out that Sasha was as funny as she was attractive. Sasha was in the middle of regaling her with a story about a false alarm at the firehouse, and she was convinced if she didn't stop laughing this very moment, she might hyperventilate. The thought would have alarmed her more if she didn't think Sasha would give her mouth-to-mouth afterward.

"So, here's the thing, right? We're firefighters. We literally do this for a living. But some asshole pulls the fire alarm at the station as a prank and every fireman and his mother are falling out of their bunker gear to get out of the building. I've never seen so many grown men shriek and run outside in their boxers and boots before in my life." Sasha was shaking her head as she recalled the incident from last month. "I swear to you, it was like *Candid Camera* was stationed outside. The best part though? It wasn't even a prank. The probie tried to microwave a cookie to make it warm and gooey for a midnight snack and it burst into flames in the microwave. That Burger kid is a complete moron."

Abby was wiping tears from her eyes and trying desperately not to smudge her mascara even though she bet it was a lost cause. "Wait, back up. You need to use layman's terms. What is a *bunker gear*? And why is a burger being probed?"

Sasha nearly spit out her sip of water. "Bunker gear is what we call our firefighting gear. It's the jacket and pants with suspenders and the boots we wear to a call."

"Yeah, see, I would just have called that your fire uniform."

"That works. I would have gotten the picture." Sasha smiled across at her and she had to remind herself to make conversation.

"And the person being probed?"

"Burger?" Sasha looked confused.

"Why are we talking about food again? You lost me." She could talk or not talk about food all day with Sasha. It was decided.

"Burger is the last name of the probie. In the firehouse, we often go by last name."

"Probie?"

"He's a probationary firefighter. He must pass the probationary stage before he can be considered for a permanent firefighter position. To see if he's got what it takes to be the real deal. It's kind of a nice way of calling him low man on the totem pole."

"Okay, I'm following."

"Good." Sasha leaned forward. "But I'm more than happy to give you a full tutorial, if you'd like."

Abby considered what that might mean and decided she hoped it meant hands-on training. "So, you love your job, right?"

"I do," Sasha replied.

"Why do you do catering on the side?" That was something that had been bothering Abby since the auction when she realized Sasha was a firefighter. Why the weekend waiter gig?

"Truthfully? It's for the money." Sasha frowned and Abby regretted asking. She hated talking about money. "My shifts are twenty-four hours at a time. I'll occasionally do a forty-eight-hour gig for overtime or to cover for someone, but it's usually a twenty-four-hour block. It works out that we tend to have quite a few days off between shifts to ensure we're well rested. Most of us have a secondary job. My parents really need the help making ends meet, so I do what I can." Sasha shrugged. "And my lieutenant owns the catering company, so scheduling is no problem."

Abby nodded. Sasha was a family person. She was also more complex than Abby had originally thought. It intrigued her.

"What about you? I know you're both beautiful *and* an accountant—we already reviewed that. But where do you... account?" Sasha paused. "I realize that's not a word but it's out there and I can't take it back. So work with me."

Abby laughed. "I work for a nonprofit. I help them manage their books. I find great joy in helping such a worthy cause maneuver the complex tax system. It's a good use of my love of numbers—at least I'm giving back."

"Basically, you're a money genius," Sasha said.

"I wouldn't say that." This money talk was making Abby itch. "I like order and organization and I don't mind filling out spreadsheets of itemized deductions. Maybe it's a control thing." She shrugged.

Sasha raised an eyebrow at this statement. "Do you have a thing for control?"

"Don't we all at some point in our lives?"

"Mm, maybe." Sasha cocked her head to the side and seemed to consider this. "I assumed you were a money genius because of the auction. That was an impressive amount of dough you shelled out for this date. A date I would have done for free a dozen times over."

"Really?" That was sweet.

"Really, really." Sasha sounded confident in that statement. It made Abby feel important, like she was valued. That was a strange feeling to have on a first date—she decided she would unpack that feeling later. "I guess I'm just impressed is all."

"Don't be," Abby said. "I work with numbers and money all day long. I'm the write-off queen. And it was a charitable donation." Abby was careful to downplay the bidding war. She didn't dare tell Sasha that the money she made at the nonprofit—a nonprofit her family ran—barely covered her living expenses. She especially didn't mention that her family's money ensured that she would never have to work a day in her lifetime if she didn't want to. Her lifetime and the lifetimes of her children and four or five generations of grandchildren at that. No need to mention that. Nope. Not at all.

Sasha was smiling.

"What?"

"Nothing. It's just, you're really refreshing." Sasha looked relieved. "I wasn't so sure about this whole matchmaking thing. To be honest, a lot of the women Samantha introduced me to were self-important and spoiled. I just don't understand people who don't have to work for a living. There is no way they can really understand and empathize with us regular folk if they live on another planet entirely, you know?" Sasha shrugged and Abby wanted to be invisible. "I was about to bail on the whole thing until I was introduced to Shelly. She was the first person I felt like I had a decent connection with who wasn't driven by greed or money lust. I guess that was the turning point for me—it was the first time I felt like there might be something legit to Samantha's process. In the end, I think Shelly found her perfect match in Claire, and I'm glad for her, really, but it was eye-opening for me, to say the least."

Abby nodded, unsure of what to say. Sasha was being so candid and honest with her, and Abby felt herself being envious of that quality. And a little afraid of it. Sasha gave so freely. They were just getting to know each other, yet she didn't seem inhibited at all.

Eager to change the direction of the conversation, she asked the question she had been dying to know all night. Sasha would be considered a catch by anyone's standards. She was tall, gorgeous, sexy as hell, smart, funny, and had an amazingly selfless job. All of that combined with the fact that she was apparently also an open book raised the question, why was she single? There had to be something wrong with her, right?

"All right, so tell me the truth, what brought you to Perfect Match?"

Sasha looked embarrassed. "I was hoping you wouldn't ask."

"And yet I did. Spill."

"A bet."

This was unexpected. "A what? You started working with Samantha on a bet? I need details."

Sasha told her the story and sighed. "The truth is, I was curious. The bet was a way for me to justify trying to get in the door, because I was a little too worried I'd be turned away."

Abby couldn't imagine why Sasha would be turned away from anything, ever.

"And you? What brought you to Samantha and Andrew?"

She supposed she set herself up for this one.

Sasha continued, "I work crazy hours and a lot of people think firefighters are dumb brutes. Which, to be fair, is kinda true some of the time. Exhibit A, the flaming cookie incident." Sasha rolled her eyes. "But you're smart and put together and sarcastic and beautiful—who wouldn't want to date you?"

The answer was simple. Most women she had met *did* want to date her. The trouble was the vast majority wanted to date her money and her family connections, not Abby herself. She had started working with Samantha in hopes of finding a perfect match with someone on an organic and intimate level. She wanted to remove the complications her family's wealth added to every layer of her life. She had joined the matchmaking service to find someone who was her perfect match in every way, outside of the financial side of things—that was the truth.

"Uh." Sasha's interest was genuine. Abby couldn't remember another time that someone had paid such close attention to the things she said. It was a little intoxicating. "I seem to find myself dating the same type of people over and over. But clearly, I've not found the right person, so it seemed like a wise idea to let a professional handle it. What did I have to lose?" Most of that was true. Sort of. Except for the part where she didn't mention hiring Samantha to make sure she wasn't matched with a gold digger.

"We're quite the pair, aren't we?" Sasha lightened the mood again and Abby was grateful. "Okay—regardless of how we got here, we're here. I made two hundred dollars on a bet and got out of kitchen duty for two whole shifts. And after a little bit of a journey, I met you. So it's all good."

"Oh yeah? And do you think I'm your perfect match?" Abby wasn't serious, but Sasha looked like she was.

"Maybe. Maybe not. Either way, I'm willing to find out."

Abby was charmed. "So it was a win-win then."

"Oh yeah. I'm totally winning."

Abby wondered if in fact she was the one winning tonight. Sasha's skin glowed in the soft light of the patio. Her dark hair framed her face perfectly; she wore a lighter shade on her lips tonight, almost subduing their fullness. But Sasha's eyes had her attention—her full, dark eyelashes showcased their deep brown color in a way Abby hadn't noticed before. The flicker of the votive candle reflected gold flecks in her irises. It was hypnotizing—she felt like she could stare at them all night and not get bored.

"Can I tell you something?" Sasha's voice was low.

"I wish you would." Abby was glad they were separated from the other diners Micah had invited for his tasting menu. The night was warm enough that they could sit comfortably outdoors for the entire evening, without any of the surrounding tables near enough to hear their conversation. She was grateful for that now especially. Because if Sasha lowered her voice to the sexy, honey-dripping level again, she wanted it to be for her ears only.

"I like you. I like you and I regret having met you before that night at the wedding and not taking the opportunity to get to know you better." Sasha reached across the table and traced her fingers along Abby's hand, making slow, sensual circles on the inside of her wrist. It was incredibly intimate and bold. Sasha's boldness drew her in deeper every time. In the short time they had known each other, there had been more than one occasion when Abby'd had her guard up to Sasha's charms and flirtations. But Sasha's sincerity and boldness broke down her walls and made Abby want to know more about her. This statement was one of many like that tonight. It was honest and vulnerable and bold. And Abby loved it.

"I'm glad we did this." She meant that. She turned her hand over and Sasha rested her fingers in Abby's palm, tapping and massaging lightly. Abby wondered what other parts of her Sasha could massage like that.

Courtney appeared with the check and Abby took it before Sasha had a chance to protest. When Sasha reached for her purse, Abby stopped her, intertwined the fingers of their joined hands, and squeezed. "You get the next one."

Sasha smiled and nodded, but said nothing.

When Courtney returned with her credit card and her copy of the check, she handed something wrapped in linen to Sasha with a wink. Abby raised an eyebrow in Sasha's direction and was met with a confident gaze.

"Thank you for dinner. And for being the highest bidder." Sasha unwrapped the linen and handed Abby one of the most intricate and beautiful bouquets of flowers she had ever seen. It was bursting with color: roses, Gerbera daisies, tulips—her knowledge of flower names was exhausted by the sheer variety of the bouquet. It was unlike anything she had ever seen and yet the many different flower types were so cohesively matched by their astonishing vibrancy, an organized chaos of color and the nicest arrangement she had ever been given. "I wasn't sure what your favorite flower might be, so I got a little creative and decided a rainbow would be safe."

"Sasha, they're beautiful." And heavy—there was probably thirty or more flowers in this arrangement. If she got another one of these anytime soon, she'd have to start weight training again.

Sasha helped her out of her chair and embraced her. "Are you trying to tell me that no one has ever given you a rainbow on your first date?"

Abby was aware that Sasha was holding her close and making no attempt to put space between them. "I am, in fact, saying just that."

"Good." Sasha pressed a gentle kiss to her lips and whispered, "Can I walk you to your car?"

Abby hummed against her lips in agreement and appreciation for what was easily her favorite part of Sasha—her boldness.

They walked hand in hand to the end of the street, Sasha graciously carrying the world's heaviest bouquet as Abby pressed the automatic starter on her key ring to warm the car up. Sometime between the end of dinner and the beginning of dessert, the temperature had dropped. The light cardigan she'd slipped on during dessert was doing little to keep her warm. She shivered and Sasha noticed.

Sasha placed the bouquet on top of the car and pulled Abby to her chest, rubbing her hands up and down Abby's arms and back to warm her. The affection appeared to come easily from Sasha, like an extension of herself. And it felt totally normal, which would have alarmed Abby if it didn't also feel so damn good. She purred involuntarily and Sasha let out a low chuckle just under her ear. She shivered again but for an entirely different reason this time.

"We spent all night talking about everything and nothing and at no point did we talk about what happens next." Sasha's lips were on her neck and Abby wasn't sure if that was a rhetorical question or not.

Sasha's lips were closer to her ear now, working their way up her neck as she asked, "When can I see you again? That is, assuming you had fun and want to do this again."

"Well this isn't exactly torture." Abby closed her eyes and breathed in Sasha's intoxicating scent.

"So sometime next week?" Sasha worked along her jaw and paused before kissing her lips, leaving her waiting. Abby hated waiting almost as much as she hated being late and talking about money.

"Sounds great." Abby leaned forward and kissed her, savoring the taste of Sasha on her lips. Sasha was just the right amount of playful and sensual—she kissed deeply and then flitted away before coming back and taking control of Abby's tongue. It was a skilled dance that Abby wanted to try again and again.

Abby realized she was pressed against her car when she felt it idle and turn off. They must have been kissing long enough to outlast the automatic starter timing window, but it felt like no time had passed at all.

Sasha laughed and Abby felt a little weak in the knees—and turned on. A *lot* turned on. It was a complicated feeling.

"I guess you'll have to restart your car." Sasha cupped Abby's face and kissed her slowly once more. "Unless you feel like you've warmed up a bit…"

Abby followed Sasha's mouth as she leaned back to separate them. She stole another kiss before nodding. "Yup. Definitely warmed up."

"Good." Sasha ran her thumb along Abby's lower lip and Abby contemplated inviting Sasha back to her place to see what the rest of Sasha's fingers felt like on her skin. Thankfully Sasha saved her from her horny self by politely ending the night. "I had a great time. I'll give you a call next week so we can get together again, but it's my treat round two. Fair?"

"I'm looking forward to it." She was. This night had been more fun than she had anticipated. And hot. Because evidently on top of being sexy as hell in her bunker gear, Sasha was also funny, charming, and a fantastic kisser. Abby didn't want to admit it, but if Sasha kissed her like that at the end of their next date, she'd probably let Sasha make all the decisions ever.

She watched Sasha walk away and made no effort to look anywhere other than at her impeccable ass. God, she had to get laid.

Chapter Twelve

Sasha tapped her fingers on the desk in her parents' den and thought about Abby for the umpteenth time today. They had spoken a few times on the phone and texted since their date last week, but they hadn't set up a formal second date. Sasha was beginning to wonder if Abby was stringing her along which baffled her because she had seemed really into the date. She was clearly really into the kissing if those delicious noises she was making up against her car were any indication. And yet, they still didn't have anything on the books. Sasha wasn't used to being in this position—she was usually the one who didn't call back or skirted a second date. She decided this was a humbling experience and not one that she enjoyed very much.

Before she could give it any further thought, she picked up the phone and dialed Abby.

"Davenport Charitable Foundation. Abby Rossmore speaking."

"That's a very official way to answer the phone, Abby." Sasha leaned back and put her feet up on the desk. Her mother was out grocery shopping and her father was napping—otherwise she wouldn't dare put her shoes on anything in this house. Rules were rules.

"Sasha. Hi." Sasha decided it sounded like Abby was smiling when she said that. She tested the waters a little.

"Hi, yourself. How's work?" Abby had given Sasha her work number after a few dropped calls last week. Abby had told her that even though she worked in a busy area downtown, the building she worked in was mostly cement, an architectural eyesore that had next to zero cell phone reception.

"Oh, you know, work-like." Abby's tone was playful, so Sasha decided to go for it.

"Listen, I know it's sort of short notice but I'm giving a little presentation at the Ashfield Elementary School by your office later and was hoping you could stop by. Maybe we could grab a quick lunch after if you have the time—there's a really cute restaurant right around the corner." Sasha knew this was a gamble but when Casey called in sick and asked her to fill in for him this morning, Abby was the first person she had thought of. Maybe this would be the jumpstart she needed to see Abby again.

There was a pause before Abby answered. Sasha's heart sank. She knew it was a long shot, but she had been hopeful.

"What time?"

Sasha fist pumped in celebration and nearly fell out of the chair in the process. "I'll be there around eleven fifteen, and the presentation is about thirty minutes long. It'll be fun."

"Sure. Sounds great. Okay, I have to go and move some things around on my end, but I'll be there."

Sasha felt like it was Christmas morning. "Awesome. Cool. Okay, I'll make sure they have a visitor pass for you at the main office. Just bring your ID so you can get in."

"Will do. See you later, Sash." Abby ended the call and Sasha's father cleared his throat behind her.

"You know, you'd be a hell of a lot less likely to fall your ass out of that chair if you didn't have your feet on your mother's antique desk."

Sasha cringed and lowered her feet to the floor, giving her father a pleading expression. "I won't tell if you don't."

"What's in it for me? The only entertainment I get around here is watching your mother chew you out." Her father laughed and coughed. He took in a steadying breath of his oxygen and stretched out on the couch.

"I happen to have on good authority that Mom is hiding a stash of your favorite cookies above the fridge by the Tupperware. I might be inclined to help a few fall into your mouth if we can come to an agreement."

"Always by the Tupperware...she's so sneaky." Her father shook his head and gave her a sly smile. "Deal. But I want the deets on the phone call, too."

"No way, that was not part of the negotiation." Sasha waved her finger at her father. "No freebies."

"Let me remind you that I was innocently napping here when you decided to make a phone call within earshot. It's not my fault that you didn't consider you might be interrupting my slumber. I'm a dying man, Sash. I need my beauty rest."

Ouch. That hurt. Her father never shied away from the reality of his situation. His bluntness was usually accompanied by his trademark humor and sarcasm, but it was still a bluntness that pained her and her mother. She wondered if this was how he coped with his decline; he tackled this head-on just like every obstacle he had ever encountered. It was moments like this Sasha was reminded of why he was her hero.

"Okay. Fine. But only because I don't trust you to keep quiet with cookies alone." She smiled more for herself than for him, hoping to pull strength from it.

"You're probably right about that." Her father pulled the blanket up higher on his chest. "Go on..."

Sasha spun the chair around so she was facing him entirely and she lounged backward, placing her hands behind her head with a yawn. "Casey called out this morning and asked if I could cover his fire prevention chat at the school. I may or may not have agreed when I recognized that the address was close to Abby's work."

"You sly dog, you. That sounds a little stalker-like, but continue."

Sasha shrugged. "I like doing those talks. It was just good fortune that she works nearby."

Her father nodded. "And good fortune that she agreed to go. I assume that's what the arm flailing was, right? She's gonna show up?"

"That wasn't arm flailing, Dad. That was the very confident fist pump of a complete stud."

"Sure thing, Sash." He was humoring her, and she was glad. "You like this girl, huh?"

"Why do you say that?" She did. But she wanted to know what made him think that.

"Well aside from the arm flailing—"

"Victorious fist pumping," she corrected.

"Yeah, whatever. Aside from that, you sounded nervous and all giggly. And you twirled your finger through your hair like a total girl."

"I am a girl," Sasha pointed out. "And I so totally did not."

"You did." Her father shifted against the armrest of the couch and adjusted his pillows to prop himself up. "You like her and you twirled your hair like a giddy little schoolgirl when she said she'd meet you for lunch."

Sasha frowned. "Was it that obvious?"

"Probably only to me and anyone with eyes and ears."

"Oh, good. So, no then."

"Right. Not obvious at all." He winked at her. "Now about those cookies?"

She stood up with a stretch and headed toward the kitchen. "On it."

"Don't forget the milk," her father called out from the living room and she smiled. Her firefighting gig afforded her a lot more time to spend with him during the week and gave her mother the much needed break to work part-time or get errands done or have an afternoon to herself. Truthfully, she really loved these moments with him. She had almost passed on the chance to fill in for Casey today because it was her afternoon with her father. But it would only be a couple of hours, and like her father so keenly pointed out, she was kinda really into the idea of seeing Abby again. Kinda. Really.

"Sasha. Did yah get lost out there?" Her father interrupted her daydream with his thick Boston accent. "Don't make me have to hobble my broken ass in there for nothing. You better be bleeding or dead or I'm not getting up. My shows are about to start."

"Sorry, Dad. Be right there." She grabbed the cookies and ignored the Post-it left on the box by her mother, warning her to only give her father a few at a time. She added an extra one to his plate for good measure.

❖

"Do you guys know what this is?" Sasha held up something that looked like an alien mask and the kids all oohed and aahed. It was adorable. They were so captivated by her.

"This is an SCBA. That stands for self-contained breathing apparatus. Do you know what we use this for?"

"To breathe in a fire?" a little blond girl from the front row called out.

"Exactly. And do you know why we use this instead of an oxygen tank?"

The children looked around at each other. From her vantage point in the back of the room, Abby could see two little girls in the back of the classroom wiggle in their seats. They had been talking excitedly to each other when Sasha first pulled out all of her gear.

"C'mon. Take a guess," Sasha encouraged the class. "Do any of you have grandmas or grandpas that use oxygen at home?"

A few hands went up.

"Have you seen this little symbol on a sign they have on their front door or somewhere in the house?" Sasha held up the image of a little flame in a diamond shape.

One of the little wiggly girls in the back nodded and stood up. "That's the fire symbol. Momma says no firecrackers at Grammy's house because it's dangerous."

"Right." Sasha smiled and pointed to the sign again. "This symbol means something is flammable. Oxygen is flammable in a fire—so we use this SCBA which has compressed air instead of pure oxygen to breathe safely while in a fire."

"Like the people in the water? In *Finding Dory*?" A little boy pointed to his shirt with a cartoon fish on it.

"Sort of. That's a scuba tank"—she spelled it out for them—"and the extra letter means *underwater*. But it's the same idea, just a different mask." Sasha held the mask up a little higher to show the class. "Okay, who wants to see what it looks like on? It makes me sound a little funny, wanna hear?"

The class cheered and Sasha proceeded to don the mask and her helmet. Abby noticed that Sasha had started the talk in some sort of uniform dark blue cargo pants and a polo shirt, but had slowly put on her bunker gear as the presentation went on. She would ask about that later.

"Okay, guys, you can come up and check out the gear and ask me anything you want." Sasha sounded a little muffled and far away. Another one of the firefighters off to the side waved the kids forward and knelt to show them a flashing badge thing.

"She's great with kids." A voice to her left drew her attention from Sasha, who was kneeling and letting one of the wiggly girls touch her jacket.

"Yeah, she is." Abby looked at the man next to her. His uniform shirt read *Burger* over the right chest, and she laughed.

"What?" He looked down at his shirt. "It's a funny name, I know. I'm Aaron."

She shook his extended hand and nodded. "I've heard about you, Aaron."

He puffed out his chest, apparently taking her comment as an invitation to flirt. "Oh yeah? Well it's all true. I'm pretty amazing." He paused, seeming to reconsider his statement. "Well, it's all true if it's good. You know, all the stories of me being brave and heroic. Wait, who told you about me?"

"I did." Sasha rested her helmet on her hip, her arm draped over it and her jacket unbuttoned, exposing her suspenders. Abby remember the last time she had seen Sasha in those suspenders and was sad to see she was wearing a shirt.

"Oh. In that case, everything she said was a total and complete lie." Aaron was blushing. "She embellishes."

Abby gave him a sympathetic look. "So the cookie story wasn't actually true, huh? Because I really enjoyed that one."

"Seriously, Sash?" Aaron pouted at Sasha and ran a hand through his hair. "You're like the big sister I never had. And never wanted, by the way."

Sasha gave him a solemn nod. "And you're like the annoying little brother I never had and am grateful for that fact every day." She handed him her helmet and stepped out of her gear before passing it off to him. "Put that in the truck for me, would you? I have a meeting with Abby."

"Fine. Whatever." Aaron took her gear and stuck his tongue out at her before turning to go.

"Hi, Abby." Sasha adjusted her ponytail and looked perfect, even in her blue ensemble. It fit her well—snug in all the right places—while still looking professional and practical for what she imagined firefighters did when they weren't all geared up, whatever that was. More questions for Sasha, she mused.

"Hi." Abby had been surprised by Sasha's phone call, but glad, too. She enjoyed the times she and Sasha spent together. Granted, both times there was kissing. But this might be a nice departure—a midday lunch and get-to-know each other opportunity was exactly the kind of thing Samantha would encourage. Less physicality, more vulnerability. It was a mantra she had introduced to Abby after discussing a dating disaster. Abby liked women. She liked kissing, she liked sex, and she liked all the stuff in between. But her problem had always been opening up to other people, and Samantha had made a point to remind her of that often. Maybe it was time she listened.

"I'm glad you made it. Tell me the truth, was I lame?" Sasha reached out and touched her arm. "I can take it, lay it on me."

Abby wanted to do more than lay it on Sasha. The way she interacted with those kids was adorable—it showed Abby a completely different side to Sasha than the charming lady-killer side she had seen before. It was all kinds of hot, which was exactly the

kind of thought process she was supposed to avoid. *Bad, Abby, bad.*
"No, actually, you were really great with them."

Sasha beamed. "Did you have a favorite part?"

"The stop, drop, and roll. That was easily the best part. Very serious business that shimmy demonstration you did on the floor."

"I take my job as an educator and public servant very seriously," Sasha deadpanned.

"Clearly." Abby looked down at the hand Sasha still had resting gently on her forearm.

"I hope you don't mind. You just look really...touchable." Sasha met her gaze when she looked up, but made no attempt to move her hand. There was that boldness that Abby was so fond of.

"That's a compliment I haven't gotten in a while." She turned her palm upward and took Sasha's hand. "Still have time for lunch?"

"It just so happens to be my day off, so you're in luck," Sasha teased her before asking, "But you were at work, not me. Do you have time?"

"For you? Yeah, I can probably swing it." Abby didn't bother telling Sasha she was the head of her department and could take as much or as little time for lunch as she wanted. She preferred to let the mystery linger.

"'Scuse me, Miss Sasha." A small voice behind Sasha interrupted them. Abby went to release Sasha's hand, but Sasha held it tight.

"That's me. What's your name?" Sasha bent at the waist to bring herself to eye level with one of the wiggly girls Abby recognized from the back of the classroom.

"Leah." The little girl danced in place, her excitement infectious.

"Well, hi, Leah. What's up?"

"Um. I want to be a lady fireman, too. I think you're great." Her wiggly friend appeared at her side and nodded enthusiastically. Leah pointed to her classmate with her thumb. "So does Chrissy. She's my best friend."

"Aw. Thanks, ladies. I bet you'll be the best lady firemen ever. Make sure you come find me after you finish the academy. I'll tell you some of my favorite firefighting stories and show you all the cool equipment that I couldn't bring today." Sasha paused and released Abby's hand to reach into the cargo pocket of her uniform pants. She pulled out two embroidered patches and handed them to the girls. "You know, if you want to swing by the station with your parents one day when I'm on shift, I can give you a special tour. This is my firehouse, Engine 28. This patch says you're an honorary firefighter friend. Stop by anytime, okay?"

The girls squealed and each grabbed one of Sasha's legs in a hug. She laughed and patted their heads, telling them to keep their patches safe, and she gave each girl a pinkie squeeze before they ran off to show their friends the new swag. Sasha stood back up and took Abby's hand as though it were a normal occurrence. "Ready?"

It did feel completely normal. All of this did. "Let's do it."

❖

The restaurant was cute. It was small with only a few tables but it boasted an enormous three-page menu. Most importantly though, Abby was impressed that the food was delicious.

"So, this is your station uniform?" Abby motioned toward Sasha's polo shirt getup.

"Right. We wear this around the firehouse and only put on the bunker gear for calls." She pulled on the collar of her shirt and gave Abby a flirty smile. "It's not the sexiest of work attire, but it gets the job done."

"I don't know about that." The words fell out of her mouth before she could stop them. She seemed to struggle with a filter around Sasha. Sasha licked her lips in response, real slow like. Tease. She had to get control of this conversation if she had any hopes of following Samantha's advice, though trying to block her physical attraction to Sasha seemed impossible. Seeing her interact with those kids like a pro did nothing to squelch her libido. Sasha was a complete package and a half.

She tried again. "I noticed that you started the presentation dressed in your station uniform but slowly put the gear on. Why not just come in that way?" How was it that they were talking about Sasha in some stage of undress again? Even when trying, she couldn't keep her mind out of the gutter.

"Oh. I do that for a few reasons. First and foremost, I don't want to scare the kids. It's really terrifying when we storm into a room in heavy boots and gear with a mask on. It's important that they not be afraid of us and know we're here to help. Lots of times children will hide during a fire rescue—the more comfortable they are with us, the easier it is to help get them to safety." That made sense. Sasha added, "Aside from that, the gear is heavy. Like fifty pounds plus, depending on what I'm wearing. It's a lot easier to stop, drop, and roll in cargo pants than the whole fire shebang."

"I still can't believe how great you were with those kids." Abby reached for a warm dinner roll and Sasha pushed the whipped butter in her direction. "Also, this bread is amazing."

"I know, right?" Sasha pointed toward the roll with her fork. "I was talking about the bread, not the kids thing."

"I figured." Abby savored the warm carby deliciousness. This bread was unreal.

Sasha ran her thumb along her bottom lip and gestured for Abby to do the same. "You have a little…There's some rogue butter you might want to attend to."

Abby narrowed her eyes at Sasha. "Do you find it distracting?"

"Not really. I find it kind of adorable." Sasha grabbed the last roll out of the basket and broke it into pieces, juggling them in the air. "This is really freaking hot."

"Said the lady fireman." Abby wiped her mouth with a napkin.

"Damn skippy." Sasha nodded and popped a piece of bread into her mouth, chewing with her mouth open likely to limit the pain of the delicious flaming bread morsel. Abby had done the same thing moments earlier—sacrifices had to be made in the name of hot carbs. Sasha sipped her water and said, "Lady fireman, ha-ha. I love kids. Those presentations are some of my favorite things."

"Well, the kids were clearly captivated by you. You're great with them." Abby had been most impressed with how at ease Sasha had seemed during the whole thing. She answered all the questions, no matter how silly or misguided, and she always made sure to get down to their level whenever she had one-on-one time with any child. It hadn't occurred to Abby that the vantage point might impact the message. But the children responded better to Sasha than a few of her other firefighter colleagues who also spoke, and that seemed to be one of the main reasons. She wondered if Sasha had had much exposure to children in the past. "Do you come from a big family?"

"Not at all. I'm an only child. My mother doesn't have any real family to speak of and my father isn't close to any of his. We're a small unit, the three of us. I think that's why I like kids so much—I want a big family, lots of people gathered around a table for the holidays. The beautiful chaos of many smiling faces in the same place." Sasha shrugged. "I didn't mind being an only child for most of my life, but as I get older, I wonder what it would be like to have someone to share the burden of aging parents with. Like what a built-in friend must be like. That's something I think about from time to time."

Abby knew exactly what Sasha meant. "I'm an only child, too. I completely get what you're saying."

Sasha looked surprised. "Wow. I guess I figured you were the oldest or, like, the mature and stable middle child."

"When is the middle child ever mature or stable?"

"This is a valid point. I, as previously determined, have no experience in this department. My parents stopped at perfection. I know nothing less." Sasha's laugh was full and hearty. Abby joined in easily. She loved Sasha's sense of humor and self-deprecation. It was easy to be around her. She had contemplated setting up a date with Sasha a few times over the last week. But every time she reached for the phone, she chickened out. Sasha's comments about people of wealth being detached from society had felt like a stone in her gut. And yet she still wanted to know more about her. She wanted to find out what made Sasha tick.

"Are you and your parents close?"

"We are. Maybe too close." Sasha rolled her eyes. "My dad likes to keep abreast of my love life, and my mother just wants me to settle down and find a nice girl before she's dead and gone."

"They sound great."

"They are. I'm lucky, I know that." Sasha's eyes were so expressive. Abby searched them for the flecks of gold she had seen the other night. They were gorgeous. "What about you?"

Abby let herself get lost in those eyes as she answered. "My father passed away a few years ago from leukemia. My mother and I are very close." She found herself getting very relaxed, almost too relaxed. It occurred to her that the more they shared with each other the more invested she was starting to feel. She broke eye contact. She needed to catch her breath, slow down. She needed space from this feeling she had toward Sasha.

"I'm sorry to hear about your father." Sasha's voice was empathetic but not in a pitying way. She looked up to find Sasha staring off into the distance, her attention on the people passing by. Sasha didn't turn back when she asked, "What's your mother like?"

Abby felt a pang of remorse. Sasha had already met her mother—she just didn't know it. Abby warred with herself. Why had she denied their relationship again? If things continued to progress with Sasha, the truth would come out eventually. It seemed foolish now to have set up those walls for no reason. Bad habits rearing their ugly head. It occurred to her that this was exactly what Samantha had warned her about—she made it nearly impossible for people to get close to her. She was the reason these things didn't work out. She sighed. "My mother is great—funny, smart, nurturing, sarcastic… all the best things a mom is, I guess." And yet she denied her. This conversation had her feeling like an awful daughter.

Sasha nodded, her gaze still directed out the window. Abby took the opportunity to appreciate the profile before her, the contour of Sasha's cheeks and lovely pout of her full lips. Her hair was pulled up into a high ponytail, its long dark layers falling past Sasha's shoulders. It looked so soft. Abby wanted to touch it.

Sasha's eyes were on hers again but the light from before had dimmed in them a bit. Abby wanted to ask why, but Sasha spoke first.

"I'm glad you came today." Her voice was soft. Her face looked contemplative. And beautiful. She was beautiful. But there was a sadness there that Abby hadn't seen before.

"I am, too. It was really fun and enlightening."

"Yeah?" Sasha's smile returned.

"Yes. I learned a lot about fire safety today and I feel much better about leaving appliances plugged in during an electrical storm."

Sasha took a mock bow, her usual playfulness reemerging. "Then my work here is done."

CHAPTER THIRTEEN

Sasha stopped by the firehouse to pick up some last-minute things from her locker before her big date with Abby tonight. She had been over the moon when Abby agreed to watch her presentation, and the lunch afterward had been fun and light. Mostly light. Until Abby brought up her father and Sasha was reminded of her own father's failing health. As much as she enjoyed Abby's company, a wave of guilt about leaving her father on their scheduled afternoon together had taken over. She didn't want him to be alone, ever.

It had been a foolish concern, of course. When she got back to her parents' house he was watching *Family Feud* and yelling answers at the television screen and beating all the contestants because he was positively unstoppable at that game. There was no competition—he was a *Family Feud* phenom. As soon as the first commercial break rolled through, he started grilling her about the lunch date. As much as she pretended to be annoyed by her father's interest in her love life, she loved it. Especially when they were talking about Abby. It gave her a chance to be reflective in a way she wouldn't have before. As she recalled their conversations and exchanges, she realized just how much attention she had paid to Abby. Just how much she liked her.

When Abby had entered the classroom, her heartbeat increased. There wasn't enough time to chat before the presentation, but just knowing she was there gave Sasha butterflies. She was nervous. Nervous that she would make a mistake or come across as ill prepared. She'd done literally dozens of these presentations in the past few months, but with Abby there, it felt like this was her first time ever. She wanted to impress her. This was a new feeling. Sasha wasn't used to feeling like she had to prove herself to anyone.

The more time she spent with Abby though, the more she liked her. And although they had agreed that Sasha would be in charge of their second date, she didn't consider the fire safety school event and the lunch to count. They were a date lite, at best. Before she parted ways with Abby at the restaurant, she'd convinced her to go out with her again, her treat, to try something special. Abby had been almost shy when Sasha suggested it.

And then there was kissing again. Like, all the kissing. She was incredibly attracted to Abby—it was almost carnal. And she felt like that same intensity was thrumming between them. There was something about the way she caught Abby watching her, the way her eyes landed on Sasha's lips when they talked. The physical spark had been there since that night at the wedding, and Sasha was more than eager to see what kind of blaze they could start together. It had been on her mind when she had planned tonight's date; she was going to see if that spark would ignite.

She parked outside the station and headed to her locker. She grabbed the spare key and work gloves she kept there for the nights she went to the glass studio. It wasn't common knowledge that she did this for a hobby; she wasn't ashamed of it, but it felt like something private that she wanted to keep to herself. Until tonight. Tonight, she wanted to share it with Abby. It felt right.

She said hello to the other shift working tonight and was walking past the chief's office when she noticed him struggling with a bow tie.

"Need a little help?" She'd helped dress her father a million times—she was a bow tying professional.

The chief sighed, looking defeated. "Yes, please."

"Sure thing, Chief." Sasha set aside the things she was holding and stepped up to help. She untied the knot and evened out the fabric to ensure both sides were an equal length before she began looping the pieces into place.

"You're a lifesaver." Luke looked at the final product in the mirror on the back of his office door and breathed a sigh of relief. "I was afraid I'd have to run out and buy a clip-on."

Sasha laughed. "No worries, Chief. If you want, I can show you how to do it sometime, in case you're ever in a pickle. A very formal pickle, but a pickle nonetheless."

"Thanks." His appreciation seemed genuine.

"So, fancy tux, snazzy bow tie. You doing something special tonight?" Sasha stepped back to take in his full form—he looked great. Very dapper. In fact, this was the nicest and most well-dressed she had ever seen him. It occurred to her that he was also clean shaven save for his newly shaped goatee. "I don't think I've ever seen you without a full face of five o'clock shadow."

His attempt to give her a look of warning was completely undermined by his blush. "That's enough of that, McCray."

"Right." She tried to hide her amusement. "You were just about to tell me about your fancy dinner plans."

"I probably wasn't." There was the gruff chief she knew and loved. "But since you asked, I'm going out with that woman from the fundraising auction. We're attending opening night at the symphony. There's a cocktail party beforehand that she wants to go to, something about an award being given out. It's a big deal, or so I'm told."

Sasha thought back to the auction and a wave of realization washed over her. "Edie!"

He looked alarmed. "Yes?"

"Why didn't I make the connection earlier?" Sasha put a palm to her forehead. "You're going out with Edie. I met her once before—she's awesome. And a total fox. Good for you, Chief."

He blushed again and grumbled something under his breath. He slipped on a slightly oversized trench coat and ushered her out of his office. "What are you doing here tonight? You're not on shift."

"I am also going on a date with my auction bidder tonight." She held up the things she retrieved from her locker. "I had to pick up supplies."

He pointed to the work gloves she was holding. "You aren't planning on tossing her in a ditch and hiding the body, right? Because now I'm officially going to be an accomplice since you told me. And I really don't want to be late to meet Edie."

He was teasing her. She liked this new chief. "No one is being buried in ditch, not by me anyway. Have a great time tonight—Edie seems like a wonderful person."

"She is." Sasha swore he had hearts in his eyes. It was the cutest thing ever.

❖

Sasha flicked on the lights of the back room and started organizing supplies. She was grateful the studio was empty tonight. With the owner on vacation for the rest of the month, the usual nightly classes had been canceled. This was her favorite time to be here, in the quiet, alone. It was one of the only times she had a chance to really think and find herself.

"Okay, Sash. The furnace is all heated up and the vent fans are on. I'm going to head out. You'll turn everything off and lock up, right?" Jose asked as he shrugged on his coat.

She held up the studio key she'd retrieved from her locker and nodded. "I'll make sure everything is tight as a drum and cool as a cuke before I leave. Promise."

"Sounds good. Have fun. Call me if you need anything." Jose gave her a wave and headed out through the small glass door by the office.

Sasha checked the clock on the wall and headed toward the large garage door in the front of the building—Abby should be there any minute. She opened the door and the cool night air crept in. She savored the feeling. It would be hot in here in a matter of minutes.

"Hey." Abby was right on time. And she was dressed to kill—she had clearly taken some liberties with Sasha's clothing recommendations for tonight. Sasha had told her to wear something lightweight but close fitting and to come prepared to remove layers if she got too warm. Abby's skintight tank top and short, flowing miniskirt left almost nothing to the imagination. Sasha felt her temperature rising already.

"Hey, you look great." She greeted Abby with a hug, both to welcome her and selfishly to feel Abby pressed against her. Ain't no shame in her game.

Abby hugged her back and held up an oversized water bottle. "I come fully prepared."

"That's good. You're going to want to stay hydrated—it's going to get hot in there."

"That's what you keep threatening me." Abby reached out and took her hand first this time, and Sasha warmed to the contact.

"I'm excited to try this with you. I think you'll like it. Have you ever done this before?" Sasha guided her through the studio toward the kilns at the back. She stopped to watch Abby take in the surroundings: shelves of colorful glass art lined the small gift-shop designated section of the studio. There were vases, mugs, drinking glasses, figurines, fruit bowls, ornaments, pumpkins, and dishes of all shapes and sizes that were ready for purchase. This studio relied on the sale of their goods to help fund classes for local area kids in the evenings. Sasha loved how they gave back to the community.

"Glassblowing? No, never." She released Sasha's hand to glide her finger along the smooth curve of a waved fruit bowl. "These are gorgeous. The colors are fantastic. This is all handmade?"

Sasha nodded. Her reaction had been the same the first time she had ventured into this studio five years ago. A lot had changed in that time, she mused.

"Are we the only ones here?" Abby sounded shocked.

"We are." Sasha led her to the station she had set up at the most rear furnace.

"Is that safe? I mean, shouldn't there be a professional here?" Although she verbalized concern, Sasha noted that Abby was following her freely. She wondered if Abby was a follow-the-rules kind of good girl. She hadn't gotten that impression up to this point, but maybe she'd missed something.

"I'm a firefighter. I work with fire all day long. Who is better suited to captain this date than me?" Sasha nudged her and smiled broadly. "Truth is, I come here a lot. And I'm good friends with the glass artists and owners. They let me have the shop to myself tonight to teach you some glassblowing techniques. Normally there are night classes, but the owner is out of town so it's their slow period. Long story short—I called in a favor. But I promise it will be safe and fun."

"And hot. Don't forget the hot part." Abby fanned herself as they stepped closer to the furnace. "That is no joke. You weren't kidding when you said dress for high heat."

Sasha laughed and offered a hair tie to Abby. "You may want this for later."

"How hot is that thing?" Abby pulled her long blond hair up into a messy ponytail and Sasha admired the soft, pale skin of Abby's neck.

"To get the molten glass consistency it can go up to twenty-four hundred degrees Fahrenheit, but this is around twenty-one hundred since there's only two of us and we have small stuff to do."

"Did you say twenty-one *hundred*?"

That was most people's response.

"Indeed, I did. I told you, it's hot stuff." Sasha took a sip of the water bottle she had sitting on the table by her station. "What do you think—are you ready?"

Abby looked at her with big eyes. "Ready as I'm ever going to be, I guess."

"Okay. First things first. We have to go over a few ground rules. Just some basic stuff to keep us both safe and the building intact. Sound good?"

Abby's brow furrowed in focus. "Do I have to take notes?"

"Only mental ones."

Abby pointed to her temple and nodded. "Mentally note taking as we speak."

Sasha chuckled. "This is the furnace that we get the molten glass from. We pick it up with a blowpipe, and this"—she pointed to a taller furnace with a circular opening in the front—"this is the glory hole we put it in to—"

"I'm going to stop you right there because there is no way that is actually called a glory hole and absolutely no way you expect me to stick my blowpipe in that glory hole to make glass art." Abby crossed her arms in skepticism causing her breasts to swell slightly above the confines of her tight tank top.

"I promise you it is, and yes, I want you to stick your blowpipe in the glory hole a few times tonight." The innuendos surrounding this conversation were not lost on Sasha, nor on Abby, if the look on her face was indicative of anything.

"I don't believe you." Abby had a small smile on her face, but she continued to keep her arms crossed. The visual combination was titillating.

"Check Google. Look up glassblowing. I'm going to put on some music because once the vents go on and it's pretty noisy in here, the music helps to drown out the industrial fan sound." Sasha stepped toward the back of the studio and used her smartphone to access her sound cloud and pipe music in through the studio speakers.

Abby shook her head as she put her phone back in her purse when Sasha returned to the workstation. "I can't believe it."

"Told you." Sasha stepped closer to Abby and leaned in as the vent fans surged louder. "Tell me, Abby. Are you ready for me to put my blowpipe in your glory hole?"

Abby's shudder in response told her everything she needed to know and more.

CHAPTER FOURTEEN

Sasha had gravely undersold how hot this date was going to be. Like melt on the sun hot. They were literally standing in front of a furnace twirling a scalding-hot metal pole in something called a glory hole. What was she thinking?

Sasha took the pole from her hands and spun it quickly along the bench set up to their right. She motioned for Abby to head to the end of the pole and encouraged her to blow as hard as she could into the tiny opening. This was really happening.

"C'mon, Abby. Show me what you can do." Sasha appeared to be enjoying every second of this. "Squat down, put your lips on the end of the pole, and blow like you're trying to inflate a balloon."

"I can't believe I'm doing this." Abby wasn't really complaining. She swept a loose hair behind her ear and wiped her forehead. Her makeup had probably melted off her face by now, yet she wasn't that concerned. This was far and beyond the most interesting and unique date she had ever been on. She was excited to learn something new. Doing it with Sasha was an added bonus.

Abby blew into the pole and Sasha helped her continue to spin it along the support bars that came off the bench. Just when she thought she was going to pass out from breathlessness, Sasha finally told her to stop and motioned for Abby to follow her over to the flat metal table to the left. Abby took the opportunity to trail behind Sasha and take her in. Sasha was wearing a fitted black tank top that complemented the dark hair she kept off her neck in a ponytail. But what Abby was most appreciative of was the cut of the tank top;

Sasha's strong, muscular shoulders flexed and rolled as she spun the bar while she walked. Abby had been surprised at how heavy the bar was, but Sasha maneuvered it like it was weightless. Abby's stomach tightened as she let herself imagine all the ways Sasha could show Abby just how strong she really was.

"Jesus. That is harder than it looks." Abby huffed and puffed next to Sasha for more than one reason, as Sasha continued to spin the pole slowly, keeping the hot orange glowing ball of glass on the end of the pole in a round shape.

"It is." Sasha nodded toward the table. There were eight flat metal blow-like things with different shades of colored powder in each. "Pick your first color. We're going to use three altogether, so consider that when you choose."

Abby was drawn to the purples and blues on the table. She pointed to them and added a lime green to break them up. Sasha refused to tell her what they were making, so she was blindly choosing her colors—she hoped they would work. "How about those three?"

"Ooh, that's gonna look great." Sasha pressed the hot orange glass along the metal table and formed a cylinder. She reached for Abby's hand and gave her the rod. "Okay, let's put some color on this."

Sasha helped her coat each side of the cylinder with the purple powder before guiding her to the glory hole then back to the furnace to coat the cylinder with fresh glass. They repeated this three times until all of the colors Abby picked were folded into the glowing cylinder.

"I know it looks all orange but I promise you the colors are there." Sasha put a hand on Abby's low back. She had been particularly affectionate today. Abby wondered if it was to communicate with her over the loudness of the vent. Sasha had been right—the music helped to cancel out some of the droning noise.

Sasha leaned close, her hand settling on Abby's hip while Abby spun the pole to keep the shape at the end. Sasha nudged Abby's foot with her own, guiding her legs apart just a bit as she leaned into Abby's ear. "Let's open this up a bit, shall we?"

Abby wasn't sure what Sasha's intention was, but she was definitely open for her. Open and ready. She turned toward Sasha, their faces close. "What are we opening, Sash?"

Sasha's eyes were dark, her pupils full, and her lips parted slightly. "Let's start with the glass and then we'll see what else we can loosen up along the way." She made no attempt to put any space between them. Instead, she placed her hands above and below Abby's on the pole and helped her spin a little faster. She looked over her shoulder, and her collarbone shifted as she raised the pole. Abby didn't miss the slight glistening of sweat along Sasha's neck. She resisted the urge to lean in and lick along it. They were so close. It wouldn't take much effort.

Sasha maneuvered Abby and the pole back toward the workbench, staying very close, her body brushing against Abby's, distracting her in all the best ways. She let Sasha lead, eager to have the opportunity to watch Sasha's physical prowess.

What happened next was sort of a blur. There was more spinning and blowing, the two of them working together while Sasha used wet newspapers and tongs of some sort to shape and pull the cylinder into a longer tube. Sasha had Abby stand above it and blow downward as she spun the pole even faster causing the glass to thin and fan out. She used the wet wooden tools on the bench to press and pull on the hot orange glass until it started to take the shape of a—

"Bowl. You're making a bowl?" Abby had helped the entire time and yet she still didn't believe this had come out of that little glowing ball.

"*You* are making a bowl. I'm just helping." Sasha dipped the tongs in cold water and motioned for Abby to don the gloves on the workbench. "Put those on and form a cup with your hands. I'm going to disconnect the glass from the rod and we're going to finish the shaping process."

Abby slipped on the gloves and watched as Sasha separated the glass from the rod with a series of taps on the metal and a pinching motion with some giant tweezers. The bowl dropped from the rod into Abby's hands so quickly that she almost dropped it. Sasha's hand steadied the underside of her glove to keep the glass from hitting the ground.

"That was close." Abby exhaled and blew a loose hair off her forehead.

"I got you, babe." Sasha winked. "Lean back a little—this is going to be very, very warm." She pulled out a small blowtorch and heated the bottom of the bowl, smoothing the surface with a wet wooden spoon.

She was right. The heat from the torch felt smothering when combined with the blazing furnace and the sight of Sasha's sexy arm muscles pulsating. Abby thought she might combust.

Sasha grabbed another set of gloves and took the bowl from Abby's hands, placing it into a large closet-looking thing and sealing it tight. She was back at Abby's side in a flash, her hands on Abby's hips, a look of concern on her face. "Are you okay?"

"I'm fine." That was a lie. She wasn't fine. Quite the contrary, she felt a little light-headed. She swayed on the spot and Sasha's hands were all over her.

"Let's get you cooled off." Sasha half walked, half carried her over to a cushioned bench on the other side of the room, as far away from the furnaces as possible. Abby had a glass of cold water in her hand before she even realized what was happening. When had she gotten so thirsty? "Drink that, and lean back a little."

She greedily gulped the water, finishing it quickly. Sasha replaced the empty glass with a new ice-cold one as she settled next to Abby. She brushed hair off Abby's forehead, her fingers pausing at Abby's neck before she stroked the skin.

Abby closed her eyes, savoring the coolness of the water on her tongue and the gentle pressure of Sasha's touch on her skin.

"Your pulse is a little fast." Sasha's fingers continued their dance along her neck. Abby blinked her eyes open to find Sasha watching her closely.

"I feel fine." She did. Well, now she did. "I think I just got a little overheated."

Sasha didn't say anything at first. She just continued watching her, pressing her wrist to Abby's forehead briefly before she rubbed her thumb along Abby's cheek. "And now? Do you still feel hot?"

That was a complicated question: Sasha's attention and clear concern were making her hot, but the turned-on kinda hot not walking-on-the-sun kinda hot like a few minutes ago. Sasha's lips were parted slightly. She looked thirsty. "I'm fine. Really." She offered the remainder of the cold water to Sasha. "You should have some, too."

Sasha hesitated before she accepted it, finishing the glass with ease. She had a little droplet of water under her bottom lip. Abby reached for it to wipe it away when she had a better idea.

"You've got a little water under your lip." Abby leaned forward, bringing her face closer to Sasha's.

"Yeah?" Sasha's eyes were on Abby's lips when she spoke. "Do you find it distracting?"

Abby smiled at the reference to their exchange from the other day. "I do, actually."

Sasha was so close to her now, her head slightly angled to the side, her lips close enough to…"Maybe you should do something about that, then."

That was all the invitation Abby needed to close the distance between them. She couldn't remember a time when she'd wanted to kiss someone as badly as this. Sasha met her passion immediately, her tongue tracing patterns along Abby's lips, teasing and licking until Abby couldn't stop the moan from tumbling out of her mouth. Before she knew it, Sasha was taking over. The kiss was escaping her—her head was spinning. She reached out and gripped Sasha's shoulders to steady herself.

Sasha pulled back, and that look of concern from earlier was back. "Are you okay? Is this too much?"

"Yes." Abby was trying to catch her breath. Since when did kissing make her so breathless? Oh, about since Samantha's wedding.

"Yes, this is too much? Or…?" Sasha was holding her close, but not close enough for Abby's liking.

"Yes, I'm okay. No, this is not too much." She pulled Sasha back to her and kissed her hard. Sasha's hand was in her hair, her thumb teasing at Abby's jaw, imploring her to open her mouth wider.

She complied and was rewarded with Sasha's tongue on her own, her other hand gripping Abby's ribs, and she wanted to be rid of her shirt now. She wanted to feel Sasha's hand on the naked skin of her torso. She pulled up her shirt while Sasha continued to massage her tongue. It was a struggle to maintain enough focus to do both, but luckily Sasha caught on, and before she knew it, she was out of her shirt and Sasha was sucking on her neck. She felt herself getting wetter by the second. Sasha was so sexy it was overwhelming. "More. Sasha, I need more."

Sasha leaned into her, guiding her back onto the cushions of the bench, and Abby felt her insides tighten. She had thought about this often, the moment when Sasha would top her, how badly she had wanted to feel Sasha over her, around her, in her. She was climbing too quickly. She needed to slow down but her body moved against Sasha's at an almost frantic pace.

Sasha's hand moved to her thigh. She stroked the skin above her knee and dipped inward before sliding back out. She was teasing her. "As much fun as I've had on this date, I'd be lying if I said I didn't think about taking this skirt off you the minute you walked in." Her hand moved up higher on Abby's thigh, disappearing under the hem of the skirt to tickle the soft, supple skin there.

Abby moaned again, grabbing at Sasha's tank top and pulling her on top of her, trapping Sasha's hand between her thighs. "Tell me more about that, Sash. Did you like my outfit tonight?"

Sasha purred in response, her lips by Abby's ear as her fingers continued to tease and dance along Abby's thigh, moving higher and higher, her skirt flipped up against the sweat-slick skin of her waist. "Why do you think I had you squat and bend over so much tonight? I'm not about to let legs like those and an ass like that"—Sasha squeezed Abby's ass and pulled her tight against her—"go to waste."

"Fuck." Abby sucked her bottom lip into her mouth when Sasha discarded her tank top and lowered her body on top of her, Sasha's strong shoulder flexing as she held her chest up enough to reconnect their lips, silencing Abby's panting with her mouth. Sasha's skin was scorching against her own, their sweat mixing in the most deliciously sticky way.

Abby spread her legs, accommodating Sasha's hips to rest between her own. Sasha massaged up her side, palming at the lace of her bra while her mouth continued to do terrible things to Abby's jaw and pulse point. And suddenly Abby was there again, right at that line where if she didn't slow, she would come hard and fast, and this was the hardest decision she had ever made in her life. To fuck or not to fuck?

Sasha's polite teasing came to an end when her fingers brushed across the flimsy front of Abby's thong. Abby surged upward, crying out as her clit twitched under Sasha's exploratory touch. "*Sasha.*"

"More?" Sasha's breath was short and fast across her lips. "Are you ready for more, Abby?" Her fingers pressed inward and Abby couldn't remember another time when she had gotten so wet, so fast.

"Yes, Sasha, please." She wasn't above begging. Her body was buzzing with all kinds of sensations and she needed relief, now. "Fuck me."

"You are so fucking hot." Sasha slipped under her panties and stroked her wetness and Abby thought she saw Jesus.

"Oh, oh, my…yes. Sasha. *Yes.*" Sasha's fingers entered her and Abby clenched around them as they slid in and out of her with a practiced ease that Abby was so very, very grateful for. "Don't stop. *Harder.*"

Sasha's full weight was on her now as she gave Abby everything she asked for and more. Her thumb circled Abby's clit as she stroked and curled her fingers inside her until Abby couldn't hold out any longer—her orgasm erupted after a well-timed thrust by Sasha and she cried out as her body ignited with a rush of heat and tremors.

Sasha kissed along her jaw while she gasped for breath and Abby was grateful for the tenderness that followed the dominance. If this was just a glimpse of what Sasha was capable of, Abby was more than interested in doing more one-on-one research.

"You make the sexiest noises." Sasha kissed her ear and rolled her hips, the buckle on her belt sending a shock wave through Abby's clit.

She hissed at the sensation—too much, too soon—and yet she wanted to feel it again. Sasha's fingers traced along Abby's belly button before sliding up to cup her still-clothed breast. Her nipple strained against the fabric and Sasha rubbed it between her thumb and forefinger. Sasha didn't let up and soon a smaller orgasm followed the first. Abby saw stars and decided that if this was the end, then this was the best death she could ever have wished for.

"Mm, that was…" Abby had no words. Especially since Sasha didn't seem quite done with her.

"Hot?" Sasha found her lips and abandoned her teasing in favor of cupping Abby's face. She was equal parts appreciative and sad that Sasha's hand had moved.

"That does seem to be the theme tonight." Abby exhaled as her muscles relaxed. Sasha's body against her felt like a warm blanket. She wanted to be wrapped up in her immediately. She rolled to her side to make room for Sasha in front of her. Sasha settled into the space and Abby kissed her slowly, savoring the taste of Sasha's mouth.

Sasha wrapped her arms around her and held her while she recovered. She pressed a kiss to her head and breathed, "Thank you for coming tonight."

Abby laughed. "Which time?"

"Mm." Sasha tapped her chin in thought. "All the times."

Abby snuggled closer to her. The sweat on her skin made her feel cold even though the furnaces raged not far from them. Sasha rubbed up and down her arms to keep her warm and she felt safe. She tucked her head into Sasha's neck. "This was really, I don't know, perfect."

Sasha hummed in agreement, her fingers tracing delicate circles on Abby's shoulder and the back of her neck.

"How did you get into this?" She closed her eyes and focused on Sasha's touch—it was heavenly.

"Lesbianism? Or glassblowing?"

Abby swatted at Sasha's chest and Sasha caught her hand, kissing her palm. This woman was unreal—flirty one minute, tender the next. She was enthralling.

"I first dabbled in lesbianism in high school." Sasha's lips stayed on her skin, kissing along the inside of her palm. "The glassblowing happened a few years ago when we had a call here for a small fire. I got to know the owner and took a few classes. It really drew me in and helped me overcome some of my fears."

Abby wanted to know more about the high school lesbianism but something Sasha said drew her attention. "Fears?" She turned her hand to caress Sasha's face. Sasha's lips found her wrist.

"Yeah. When I got into firefighting, I had a fear of fire. I know that sounds crazy, but it's pretty common. One of the reasons I pursued this work was to overcome that fear. I wanted to know more about it, take the power away from my ignorance, you know? Anyway, there was a small fire in the back and I was introduced to this amazing art form. It really helped ground me to see the beauty from the chaos of the fire. It's all about how you harness it." She shrugged, sucking on Abby's wrist for a moment before continuing. "I found myself back here more and more often, trying to learn how to make different things. The fragility and immensity of the inferno personified. I find this really peaceful."

"Wow." Abby wasn't sure what to say. That was really...deep.

She smiled against Abby's wrist before she nibbled the skin a little. "I meant the glassblowing, but I find this really peaceful, too."

"It's definitely something, I'll give you that." Abby pulled Sasha's leg over her hip, bringing their centers closer. "Peaceful isn't the word that comes to mind at first."

Sasha's eyes closed and her lips formed a small *o*. As much as Abby enjoyed receiving, she was more than willing to return the favor. If the way Sasha's breathing increased was any indication, Sasha was just as turned-on as Abby had been. How turned-on she still was.

She pulled at Sasha's belt buckle, her lips brushing against Sasha's as she repeated Sasha's phrase from earlier, "Let's open this up a bit, shall we?"

Sasha moaned and Abby decided that was her new favorite sound.

CHAPTER FIFTEEN

Sasha drummed her fingers on the steering wheel as she sat outside the fire station and let her mind wander back to last week's date. Everything had gone off without a hitch. Like, it couldn't have gone better. And yet, it got better, twice before the night was over, and still it felt like a dream.

But it wasn't a dream. She and Abby had spoken daily since the glassblowing date and they had plans to get together tonight after this ridiculous training session was over. She hated these things—they took up whole shifts and were boring and redundant. She'd much rather be fighting fires or hanging out with Abby.

The thought made her smile. She really liked Abby, enough so that she found herself thinking of her often. She had noticed a change in their interaction after that night; she'd been worried that maybe Abby was keeping her at arm's length, but she had felt a real connection to her during that date. Especially toward the end when she *physically* connected with her on so many amazing levels. Abby was playful and funny, but she was smart and sarcastic and really, really sexy. Like super sexy. So far, Abby'd had no problem matching Sasha's physicality or endurance in the bedroom department, which made Sasha want to see all the sides Abby had to show her.

She reached for her phone and shot off a quick text. *Hey. Thinking of you. I'm looking forward to later.*

Text bubbles popped up on the screen indicating Abby was writing back but they stopped and Sasha frowned. That was the absolute worst thing about texting—knowing a response was being drafted only to have it never sent.

Her phone rang.

"You're pouting about the text bubble thing again, aren't you?" Abby teased her.

"How do you know me that well already?" Sasha leaned back in her seat, resting her head on the headrest. She regretted ever telling Abby about that pet peeve.

"I can just imagine the frustrated forehead crease. That must have been agony."

"Kick a gal while she's down, why dontcha." Sasha was glad Abby called, and she decided to tell her that. "I'm glad you called."

"I'm driving—it was safer." Abby paused. "Plus, I wanted to keep you on your text bubble loving toes."

Abby's sarcasm was one of Sasha's favorite things about her.

"So, when does your shift start?"

Sasha could hear traffic sounds in the background when Abby spoke. "In about ten minutes." She glanced at the clock on her dash to confirm. Yup. Time hadn't stood still yet; she still had to do this class. "I would rather be doing just about anything right now."

"Just about anything, huh?" Abby's voice had that lilt in it that Sasha was growing to love. It was that little bit of subtle provocation that she somehow managed to sneak into all their conversations of late. Sasha lived for it.

"Or anyone," she replied.

Abby hummed. "Anyone? That's a pretty broad net to cast."

"Well, I should be more specific." Sasha cleared her throat. "I'd much rather be doing *you* than this. Or anything, really." She wondered if that was an overshare, but it was true. Spending time with Abby, talking to Abby, thinking about spending time with Abby: all those things were pastimes that were becoming top priority in her day-to-day. It worried her a little bit, but at the same time, it was refreshing.

"That's better." Abby sounded pleased.

Good. They hadn't discussed exclusivity or anything, but when their banter entered this level, Sasha figured it was clear that her interests were with Abby and Abby only. Perhaps they ought to discuss that, she thought.

"Speaking of which"—Sasha figured this was a good segue—"did you have anything in mind for tonight?"

"Oh. I have the day from hell. A midmorning meeting after my breakfast meeting, then a lunch meeting, then an afternoon meeting... basically I'm meeting everyone in the world ever today and all I want is for it to be tonight so I can get reacquainted with you."

"But not *meet* me," Sasha pointed out.

"Oh no, we've already met. I'm the attractive, charming blonde with a sharp wit and endless capacity of sarcasm. And you're the dashing lady fireman with perfect shoulders, a great sense of humor, and a mouth that makes me think bad things all day long." Abby's voice was so low Sasha had to strain to hear it.

"So maybe tonight we Netflix and chill? You know, unwind, de-stress, maximize that reacquainting thing?" Sasha was already thinking of movies she could put on and not watch with Abby.

"Yes. All the yes to that. Sign me up. That sounds perfect. God, I could really use some...reacquainting. With you. Tonight."

Sasha laughed. "My place or yours?"

"There's a TV in my bedroom," Abby offered.

"Your place it is."

"Great—call me when you're out and we'll finalize the details. I have to head in. Good luck today."

"Will do. Thanks." Sasha paused before disconnecting to add, "I'm really looking forward to seeing you. You know, outside of the reacquainting part."

"Me, too." Abby's confident reply gave Sasha all the motivation she needed to get out of her car and get this day over with. Great things awaited her tonight.

❖

Sasha had been staring off into the distance for the better part of an hour. It wasn't that she found the mandatory training boring, per se, it's just that she found it incredibly...boring.

"Turn to page ninety-four and pair up with a buddy." The nasally instructor licked his finger when he turned the page. That never ceased to gross Sasha out. How many people licked their fingers and touched that book in a day? In a week? She could think of just about a million things she'd rather lick, Abby being at the very top of that list.

"Hey, partner. You ready?" Burger plopped down next to her and she cursed. Served her right for daydreaming.

"Uh, yeah. Sure." She checked the clock on the wall again, willing the minute hand to move faster so she could meet with Samantha over her lunch break. Samantha was coming by the station to drop off the check from the fundraiser and Sasha wanted to take the opportunity to debrief about the glassblowing date with Abby last week that ended up, well, mind-blowing.

"You got somewhere better to be?" Burger scratched his forehead as he read the booklet in front of him. It was common knowledge that he had barely passed the written part of the firefighter exam. These semi-annual reviews were for people like Burgertime, not people like Sasha.

She sighed. "Don't we all?"

He snorted. "They're paying us to be here. I say we should enjoy it."

"You were a lot less annoying when you weren't all rainbows and sunshine trying to get back on Casey's good side." She rolled her eyes and picked up her pencil, doodling in the margin of page ninety-four.

"Do you think he's noticed?" He looked so hopeful she almost didn't want to insult him. Almost.

"How could he have missed it? You shined the back bumper of the rig with a toothbrush and it wasn't even his." Sasha slow-clapped for effect. "That's some serious ass kissing, Burger."

"Thanks." The poor kid didn't even know to be offended. Her sarcasm was wasted on him, yet again. "So do you think I should ask him about a shift or two with the catering company again? Enough time has passed, right?"

Sasha did a quick mental calculation of the approximate repair bill from Aaron's coat check fur debacle at Samantha's wedding. "It's not about time, Burger. It's about money. You cost Casey a lot of money because you're a lovable—but bumbling—oaf."

"Aw, you think I'm lovable?" He looked touched. Sasha tried not to gag.

"What I'm saying, you big lug, is that you're worth more on a barter system than an ass-kissing one."

"I'm not following."

Sasha was afraid if she didn't break it down for him, his eyes would remain permanently crossed from this amount of concentration.

"Offer to work off the repair bill. Find out how much it was and work those hours for Casey unpaid. Erase the debt with your time. That's where I would start if I was you." Sasha shrugged.

"Really? You think that would work?" He had a look of confusion and consideration on his face. It was impossible to tell which was winning out.

"I think it's worth a try." Sasha's doodle had become an entire mountain range populated by tiny stick figure skiers. "Casey's not an unfair guy. It's better to ask and be denied than to continue to drive the rest of us at the station insane. Because it's only a matter of time before someone leaves you at the top of a building with a hundred pounds of uncoiled hose and a pat on the back."

Aaron gave her a look. "How tall is this building?"

"Real tall. No elevators, only stairs, on the hottest day of the year in full gear, while someone pumps Michael Bolton music at full blast through the stairwell."

"Michael Bolton? Like the nerd from *Office Space*? He sings? I thought he was a rapper…"

And the dead space between his ears won again.

"All right—now that you've had a chance to go over the scenario with your partner, each pair will be randomly called to demonstrate the fire safety technique to the class. Let's break for lunch. See you all back here in an hour." The instructor saved her from having to YouTube Bolton's greatest hits to prove her point.

"Oh, shit, Sasha. We'd better review the case over lunch." He looked genuinely worried. It was almost cute.

She picked up the manual and skimmed it aloud. "Old lady at home trips over cat, breaks hip, soup burns on stove. Easy-peasy. This is a teachable moment for you, Burger. You lead and I'll be your wingman this time around."

"Really? I can call the case?" He rubbed his hands together in excitement.

"Sure." Sasha would say just about anything to get out of here faster—she was supposed to meet Samantha five minutes ago.

"Great, you wanna grab a—"

"I've got plans, Burger. See you in a bit." She was out the door before he had a chance to reply.

She found Samantha in the common area talking to the chief on the couch, her designer suit and heels looking out of place against the worn, cracked leather of the sofa. Sasha would bet that Samantha's purse cost more than her monthly rent.

"Sorry to keep you waiting." Sasha meant that. She was an early bird whenever she could be.

"No worries, Sash." Samantha kissed her on the cheek when she stood. "Luke was just telling me all about his gala last week."

The chief was smiling until he noticed Sasha staring. She couldn't help it—this was a new side to him she had never seen before. He cleared his throat and looked away. "McCray."

"Chief." She liked seeing him squirm—it made him so *human*. She doubted he'd reprimand her with Samantha around, so she decided to test her luck. "Oh, that's the night I helped you with your bow tie. How'd it go, stud?"

"McCray." His tone held warning.

"Too far? I took it too far, didn't I?" Samantha laughed and Sasha decided it was worth the death stare from the chief. "Just kidding, Chief. You looked dapper and handsome and I hope it was fun."

He stared at her for a minute, his face an expressionless stone until he turned back to Samantha. Then he was all smiles and sunshine. Figured. "I can't thank you enough, Samantha. That auction raised a record amount of money for the firehouse. It's going to make such a huge impact on the station and the neighborhood."

"I'm glad to have helped." Samantha gave him a hug. "Keep me posted on how things go with Edie."

"I will." He was beaming, and he had this googly-eyed, faraway look. Sasha tried to stifle her laugh, but self-control wasn't a strong suit of hers. He growled in her direction. "Don't you have a training course today, McCray?"

"Yes, sir." She plastered on the most serious face she could muster. "We're on break, sir."

He grunted. "Well, then. I'll leave you ladies to it."

This time Sasha was at least able to keep it together until he was out of the room. Then the giggles took over and Samantha swatted her on the arm.

"Leave him alone. He's happy. It's cute." Samantha grabbed her purse and pulled out her phone.

"I know, I know." Sasha wiped tears from her eyes as she tried to catch her breath.

"Anyway, troublemaker, tell me about Abby. Did you two go on a date after the auction?" Samantha's eyes shined as she leaned against the arm of the couch.

Sasha remembered the café in Cambridge. But mostly she remembered the kissing afterward. "Yeah, a couple of times since then, too."

Samantha raised an eyebrow at this information. "Really? How many times?"

"Twice." Sasha paused. "Once was a lunch date thingy, but I'm still counting it."

"A date is a date." Samantha nodded in agreement. "And? How'd it go?"

"The lunch date?"

"Yeah, let's start there." Samantha waved her hand, indicating Sasha should get to the details.

"Right, so I had a fire safety lesson at an elementary school by Abby's work, so she came to observe and then we grabbed lunch afterward. It was nice."

"Oh, wow. She saw you interacting with little kids while all firefighter-y? Nice work, Sash." Samantha patted her on the shoulder. "That explains date number two."

Sasha feigned offense. "Are you saying I couldn't have snagged a second date night without adorable children learning how to prevent forest fires?"

Samantha gave her a knowing smile. "I'm saying that Abby isn't just like every other girl—she takes a little more finesse to figure out. Clearly, you're on the right path. Tell me about date number two."

Sasha was glad Samantha seemed to think she was on to something with Abby. "We had a private glassblowing session last week at a studio I frequent from time to time."

"That sounds—"

"Hot," Sasha interjected. "It was. Five alarm hot. For sure."

Samantha's perfect teeth were on display when she smiled this time. "That's excellent news." She seemed to consider something for a moment before adding, "You and Abby are a great physical match—that won't be an issue for you. Can I make a suggestion?"

"I'm all ears." Sasha wanted to hear this. When the notorious Miss Match offered to give you dating advice, you listened.

"Don't lose sight of what brought you to my office originally. You have had lots of great—let's call them *moments*—with plenty of women, but you told me you wanted something more than that. Something that mirrored your parents' relationship. You wanted a life partner. Don't let yourself forget the importance of that. Abby may very well be that person, but you may have to do the work outside of the bedroom, too."

Sasha let this statement sink in. Samantha had a way about her that kept these sorts of conversations from feeling preachy. It didn't offend Sasha that Samantha reminded her of their first few meetings—if anything, it made her feel very secure in her choices. Samantha seemed to have her best interests in mind, even when Sasha lost track along the way. "Thank you, I appreciate that insight."

"I'm here to help. Let me know if I can do anything else for you, but I'm glad it's working out." Samantha gave her a hug. "Keep me posted—I want all the juicy details. All of them."

"Will do." Sasha watched Samantha leave and thought back to where she'd been fifteen months ago, taking a dare with the hopes of maybe finding a perfect match in the process. She wondered if she and Abby would burn too bright and fizzle out before what they had became something more. She hoped—for once—that this fire would continue to burn for a very long time.

Her phone rang—her mother. She checked the time and decided she could squeeze in a quick call before she had to team back up with Burger for the second half of their day.

"Hey, Ma. What's up?"

CHAPTER SIXTEEN

Abby's hand hurt from all the signatures she'd signed today. It seemed like every meeting required her to sign off on or approve some ungodly amount of spending—her brain felt like mush. She should have known when she looked at the calendar that today would be her quarterly review day for the foundation. But truthfully, her mind had been elsewhere for the past week.

Talking to Sasha this morning before work had done nothing to help organize her thoughts. If anything, she was more distracted than usual. Her phone vibrated on the table, and she reached for it just as Evelyn walked in with a new stack of forms for her to sign. The phone would have to wait.

"All right, Ms. Rossmore, here are the last of the grant approvals for this year. Color coded and organized, just like you like them." Evelyn had been with her family's foundation for the past fifteen years. She made sure everything was organized, on time, and brand representative of the Davenport name.

"You're too good to me, Evelyn." She took the stack and separated them. Evelyn had outlined each document with flags for Abby's signature, so she could skim the content. These forms were nothing new—only the recipients of the grants and the amounts changed over time. The process was long and arduous, but Abby's involvement was—thankfully—minimal. The board decided whose applications were accepted, and all she needed to do was make sure the money was there to allocate. And sign off on them, of course.

Abby flipped through the stack and made sure her initials were on all the necessary lines before she handed them back to Evelyn with a sigh. "It's a pleasure doing business with you, Evelyn."

"I'll make sure copies make it into this quarter's files. They will be up on the cloud tonight." Evelyn filed them into a neat folder and stowed them into her leather attaché case.

"That little briefcase makes you look like a secret agent, Evelyn, darling." Abby's mother entered the room with a broad grin. "My two favorite ladies. How are you today?"

Evelyn gave Abby a confused glance. "Very well, Mrs. Davenport."

"Edie. It's Edie. It's been Edie since you started here, Secret Agent Evelyn." She put her hand on Evelyn's shoulder and asked, "How long has it been now?"

"Fifteen years," Abby replied from her seat at the conference room table.

"Ah, my math genius strikes again." Edie settled into the seat across from her. "How'd it go today? Everything in order? Grant day is my favorite day of the quarter."

As much as her mother loved the expensive and beautiful things that she surrounded herself with, Abby had to admit she gave away as much as she spent. Her mother's selflessness was what had driven her to get into the nonprofit accounting business to begin with. It was nice to be able to share the wealth, so to speak. If she was being honest, grant day was one of her favorite days as well.

"A great new crop of applicants this quarter, Mrs., er, Edie." Evelyn pushed the glasses up her nose and read the summary sheet that she attached to every batch of quarterly forms. She had been a bookkeeper in a past life and that was an invaluable asset to Abby, particularly for days like these. Evelyn never missed a single form, staple, or tittle. You could set your watch by her.

"That's great news. So I assume all the community outreach we've done of late is working, then?" She directed her question to no one in particular.

"I'd assume so. The board attached a brief note stating as much, but I missed the meeting last week so I'd have to check the minutes for details." Abby handed the pen to Evelyn and she excused herself, leaving Abby and her mother alone in the high-rise conference room.

"Oh? You never miss a board meeting. Everything okay?" Her mother inspected her manicure as she spoke. Abby hoped she would be too preoccupied to notice her shifting uncomfortably in her seat.

"Uh. No. I mean, yes. Everything is fine, I just had a..." Abby wasn't quite sure she was ready to open this Pandora's box with her mother. The truth was she'd missed the board meeting because Sasha had invited her to the school safety thing. She couldn't remember ever having skipped a board meeting before. There seemed to be a lot of those—firsts—these days.

Her mother's attention was directed at her now. "A what?"

Abby looked everywhere but her mother's face. "A date."

Edie leaned forward. "A date. With whom? Wait." She clapped her hands excitedly. "It's that dashing Sasha woman, isn't it?"

Abby sighed. There was no use avoiding the inevitable. She found Edie's blue eyes looking at her expectantly and she replied, "Yes."

Her mother squealed with excitement. "Oh, goody. Tell me all about it. How has it been going? When can I meet her?"

"Whoa, Mom. Pump the brakes." Abby's hands were up in alarm. "Let's not smother the woman with your expectations of a daughter-in-law and babies."

Edie gave her a look. "Don't be so obtuse, Abigail. I can have grandbabies without a daughter-in-law." She winked and cackled that carefree laugh that Abby loved so very much.

"This is true. And yet, unlikely." Abby stretched in her seat and reached for her phone, long forgotten on the tabletop. "We have a date toni—shit." The words were barely out of her lips before the frown had settled there. Sasha had texted her. Something had come up and she had to reschedule.

"What?"

"Well, we had plans. But those don't appear to be happening now." The disappointment was real. Dammit.

"Oh, honey. I'm sorry." She knew her mother was being sincere, and that was comforting. Sort of.

"Me, too." She had been telling herself all day that Sasha would be the light at the end of the tunnel of this very long week. This very long month. Sasha had been on her mind a lot since their glassblowing date—she'd be lying if she said she wasn't itching to be under her again.

"Come over for dinner tonight. We're having duck."

"Who's *we*?" Her mother didn't often speak in plural. The last thing she wanted to do after being stood up for a sexy date with her lady fireman was spend the night with her mother and her bridge partners gossiping about the country club biddies.

"Luke is coming by. I'd like to formally introduce you. You'll like him."

Scratch that. Having dinner with her mother and her new boyfriend was a thousand times worse than the Brookline Bridge Babes. "I don't know, Mom."

"Abby, come on. You said yourself that your plans have changed. There's no reason to mope at home when you can socialize with your favorite mother and her new friend, Luke."

"You're my *only* mother, Mother," Abby pointed out and already knew she wasn't getting out of this.

"All the more reason to humor me and have dinner with us. I'll make sure to limit the number of baby photos of you that I show him to five. I think five is completely fair." She nodded to herself as though it were already agreed upon.

"No baby photos or no deal."

"One." She looked determined.

"Zero, or I'm eating cold lo mein at home with a Lifetime movie on."

"Oh Lord. That's just depressing, Abby." Her mother looked scandalized. "Fine. No baby photos. Just promise me you won't show up in sweatpants nursing a half-eaten box of bonbons."

"No promises."

❖

Luke was completely and totally charming. And it was clear her mother genuinely liked him. She wasn't laughing at his jokes or humoring him in any way with her patented fake laugh—she was one hundred percent interested in what he had to say.

Abby had to admit that she was, too. He was handsome and very much old-school in his chivalrous ways. He was a great conversationalist and regaled them with stories of his experience as a firefighter and a chief. Everything was going well until he started talking about his current firehouse—Engine 28.

"Twenty-eight?" Abby rarely spoke with her mouth full, but her surprise negated her charm school training.

Luke nodded. "Yes, for about five years now."

Edie gave her a curious look. "Isn't that where Sasha works?"

It was Luke's turn to look surprised. "You know Sasha?"

Abby tried not to choke when she swallowed. Why hadn't she made the correlation before that they worked at the same station? She thought back to the night of the auction—there were many different houses represented between firemen, EMTs, and the like. They were from all over the New England area. What were the chances that Sasha and Luke were from the same house? Evidently, pretty good.

"Abby and Sasha are dating." Edie's timing couldn't be worse.

"Dating?" Luke looked between them before he asked, "Wait. I thought you looked familiar. Didn't you bid on Sasha at the auction?"

Abby felt like she was being backed into a corner. She said nothing.

Luke directed his question to Edie. "Why didn't you tell me that Abby was your daughter that night? I never would have made the connection otherwise."

Edie shrugged. "I guess it didn't seem pertinent. Plus, Abby didn't want Sasha to know we were related."

"Why?" Luke asked. Abby had to remind herself why, because this was getting unnecessarily messy.

"Because my mother, as you may have noticed, is a Davenport. And I'd like very much to find a partner in life outside of the shadow of my name." Abby wondered if she sounded like she was trying to convince herself of that. Because the more she got to know Sasha and the closer they got, the more she questioned her initial motives. Why so many walls?

Luke put down his fork and wiped his mouth, seemingly in contemplation. After a moment he asked, "Sasha has no idea that Edie is your mother, does she?"

"No." That same guilt from before came rushing back up.

Edie huffed and rolled her eyes. "She's bound to find out eventually. I mean, Abby, you're dating the woman."

"I wouldn't say that…" They hadn't discussed what was happening between them. Just that it was happening and happening faster than Abby had expected. "We're not—, well, I'm not sure what we're doing."

Luke's brow furrowed. "Sasha's a great kid. She's hardworking and she's extremely dedicated to her family. It hasn't been easy for her with her parents and their needs. Don't get me wrong, I give Sasha a hard time from time to time, but it's because she's so great—I think of her like a daughter." He frowned. "She deserves better than to be lied to. You should tell her the truth—it wouldn't change anything. If she likes you, then she likes you for you."

Ouch. That hurt. The last person Abby thought she'd be getting a lecture from was her mother's new boyfriend, yet it felt like a necessary slap in the face all the same. Luke's affection for Sasha was clear and so was his statement. She deserved better.

"I'll tell her. I will." Abby felt properly chastised. His comments about Sasha and her devotion to her family seemed specific. She wanted to ask what he meant by that.

Luke nodded. "How's she doing anyway? I know she called out for the rest of her shifts this week because her father's in the hospital again." His face was somber when he turned to Edie. "It sounded serious. That kid's had a tough go of it with her father."

"Oh, dear." Edie's hand was on her heart and Abby felt like she'd been kicked in the stomach. "Why didn't you mention that earlier, Abby? We should send flowers…"

"I didn't know." Abby hated the shame associated with that statement. She had no idea about Sasha's family or her father's illness. Why hadn't Sasha mentioned it before? Is that why their date had to be canceled? Abby felt awful for being disappointed that their plans fell through. What if Sasha was going through a major personal crisis and Abby was just worried about getting laid the whole time? "I'm an idiot."

Luke and her mother gave her confused looks.

She stood from the table and folded her napkin as she excused herself. "Listen, dinner's been great. Thanks for having me. Luke, you seem like a great guy, I can see why my mother is crazy about you. I have to head out, but thanks again."

Edie began to protest but Abby stopped her. "Mom, I love you. I'll call you tomorrow."

She grabbed her jacket and slipped out the front door into the night, more confused and lost than she had ever been.

CHAPTER SEVENTEEN

The beeps of the monitors and whooshing sound of the ventilator had begun to sound like some haunting symphonic lullaby. Sasha looked at the clock on the other side of the hospital room and sighed. There had been no change in forty-eight hours.

She leaned back in her chair and balanced her heels on the end of her father's hospital bed. She was going to be alone for a bit—her mother had gone home to check on the house and do some laundry. Sasha was sure she was also cooking her father's favorite meals for when he woke up. If he woke up. Sasha felt nauseous just thinking about the possibility of him not waking up. It was unbelievable how quickly things had changed. Just two days ago she was in a training session, teasing Burger and chatting with Samantha at the firehouse when her mother called to tell her that her father had to be rushed to the emergency room—he was coughing up blood and looked pale. She'd rushed out of the station and met them at the hospital. Aside from a trip or two home to shower, she'd been there ever since.

Her pocket vibrated; it was a text from Abby. She smiled, grateful for the distraction.

How are you?

Sasha drafted a whole text and deleted it, deciding to text only *Okay* instead. But she wasn't okay. She was scared.

Uh-oh. Deleted text bubbles. This is serious. I'm coming over. Where are you?

Sasha laughed. Abby had reached out to her the night Sasha had to cancel their plans. She filled her in on what was happening, sort of. She didn't know anything at the time, but she knew she had to be here for her parents. Abby had been checking in regularly since then. It was nice to not feel like she was doing this alone.

At the hospital, hanging with Dad

There was a pause before Abby wrote back.

What can I bring? Clothes? Food? All the rum? ;)

Sasha appreciated the winky face and the offer of copious amounts of alcohol. Her stomach grumbled in response.

I'm starving. Donations of food are being accepted.

Abby's reply was immediate.

On it. What hospital are you at? What room?

Sasha texted her back the location and room number and let out a heavy sigh. She felt exhausted, like even breathing was difficult. She looked back at her father and wondered if he felt the same way. The tubes coming out of his nose and mouth looked uncomfortable, but they were keeping him alive all the same. She wondered if he would want this, to be kept alive by machines. They had avoided end-of-life planning for the longest time, but now that seemed like a foolish oversight.

She closed her eyes and tried to calm the panic that was bubbling up inside her.

"Sasha?" She felt a hand on her forearm. She blinked her eyes open. It was darker out. She must have fallen asleep in the chair. Abby was kneeling in front of her, her expression tender. "Hey there."

Sasha stretched and rolled her shoulders. Her neck was killing her from sleeping upright in this chair. "Hi." Her voice was gravelly with sleep.

"You know that chair is a recliner, right? I'm pretty sure it pulls out into a full bed." Abby gave her a small smile and patted her arm.

Sasha yawned. "I wasn't planning on sleeping. But you make a good point."

Abby nodded toward her father. "How's he doing?"

Sasha looked to her right and assessed the situation. Someone must have come in and adjusted her father's pillow while she slept. The volume of the monitors seemed to be lower as well. "No change. He's being sedated until they can get a handle on the infection. The machines are helping him breathe. It's just a waiting game now. He's got to let his body do the work to get better."

She felt like she was having an out of body experience. Her strong, construction foreman father looked so frail and small in that bed. His muscular frame had dwindled over the years of the disease's progression. His skin was so pale it was almost clear. Sasha felt her lip tremble but didn't have the energy to resist the emotions.

Abby stood and embraced her. That was the final straw for Sasha—all the tears she had kept at bay in front of her mother spilled out in that moment. How could this be happening? How was it that just days ago she and her father were joking about *Family Feud* and today he was in a coma? What was she going to do without him?

"Sh, sh," Abby soothed in her ear. "It's going to be okay."

Sasha wanted badly to believe her. She just nodded and let herself be held. There was nothing she could do and that's what hurt the most.

Abby caressed her hair and rubbed her back. Sasha slowed her breathing and tried to compose herself. She couldn't remember a time when she had felt this tired before, and considering the number of overnights she did on the job, that was a feat. "Thanks."

Abby pulled back and gave her a sad smile. "Sure thing. I'm here, okay?"

"Okay." Sasha took the opportunity to take Abby in. She was a natural beauty—that was something Sasha had never missed about her. She wore minimal makeup, and it suited her. Her blond hair was half up in a delicate, twisting braid that kept the hair off her forehead and out of her eyes. Those eyes looked at her closely now, the green vibrant today against the color of Abby's shirt. Sasha made no attempt to conceal her admiration. Seeing Abby felt like a breath of fresh air. "You're beautiful."

Abby blushed as she brushed a stray hair behind Sasha's ear. "So are you."

Sasha smiled the first genuine smile she had in days. She reached for Abby's hand. "I'm glad you're here."

"Me, too." Abby rubbed her thumb along Sasha's cheek before she stood back up, her fingers loosely entwined with Sasha's. "Hungry?"

She was hungry for a multitude of things at the moment. She tried to relay that information to Abby, holding Abby's gaze as she spoke. "Yes."

Abby paused and nodded almost infinitesimally. She leaned forward and kissed Sasha gently, holding her lips against Sasha's, her breath skating across Sasha's lips, helping to ground her. It was exactly what Sasha needed in that moment but didn't know how to ask for.

Sasha kissed her back and smiled against her lips. "Much better."

Abby giggled and pulled back. "Now, how about some food?"

"Yes, please." Sasha released Abby's hand so she could reach into the bags she'd carried in, but she missed her touch immediately. She was surprised how relieved she felt with Abby here. She warmed her.

❖

"Wait. Tell me again. He did what?" Abby stole a fry off Sasha's plate and waited for her to continue. They sat at the little table in the corner of Sasha's father's room where Sasha was telling her all about the time her father rescued their cat from the tree in their neighbor's yard.

"I shit you not. He's in his boxers just after dawn on a stepladder that was far too short for the tree in question. And the whole time I'm crying and screaming because Mr. Wadsworth is climbing higher and higher, wailing the whole time." Sasha dipped her fry in to the ketchup dish between them and shook her head. "The long story short is that my father ended up in the tree with the cat, and my mother had to call the fire department to get them both down. That was my first experience with firefighters. Needless to say, it was a memorable one."

"And you loved it ever since?" Abby was glad to see the smile back on Sasha's face again. She had observed her for a few minutes when she'd arrived before she woke her. Sasha looked like she needed the rest—dark bags were under her eyes even as she snoozed. Seeing Duncan on the machines and monitors reminded Abby of her father in his final days. She remembered the exhaustion and the feeling of endless sorrow that followed his passing. There was no way around it—losing your parent sucked every day no matter how much time had passed. She hoped Duncan's outcome would be different from her father's, if only for Sasha's sake alone. Abby had seen the devotion in her face when Sasha had tried to fill her in on what happened. She saw Sasha break then, too. It was devastating.

"Ha. Not quite." Sasha offered Abby a sip of her fountain soda and Abby took it while Sasha spoke. "Remember at the glassblowing, how I mentioned I was afraid of fire?"

"I remember a lot about the glassblowing. Sometimes I let myself be reminded in the shower and before bed." Abby shrugged, pulling on the straw with her lips before handing it back to Sasha.

Sasha's eyes flashed and she shook her head while taking a sip. "You're a naughty little thing, aren't you?"

Abby fluttered her eyelashes as innocently as she could. "I have no idea what you're talking about. But yes, I remember. Please, continue."

Sasha reached across the table and stroked Abby's fingers as she spoke. "I was afraid of fire for a long time because a few summers after the Adventures of Mr. Wadsworth and the Tree, we had a pretty significant house fire and lost just about everything."

"Oh, Sasha. I'm so sorry." Abby was glad to be close enough to take Sasha's hand.

Sasha looked over at her father and sighed. "My father ran back into the house to save the family photos and make sure the cat got out. And he did. That damn cat had nary a singed fur on his tail and all of my baby photos survived the fire. But my father was badly injured—he had burns along his chest and arms. But the real damage was in his lungs. He had such bad smoke inhalation damage that his lungs and throat scarred over. He had surgery after surgery to release the scar tissue and try to repair the damage from the fire, but he eventually developed this respiratory disease."

She wiped a tear from her eye with her free hand. "My father was a strong, strapping man. He was a general contractor and foreman for a large construction company and he was invincible. But over the years since the fire, slowly he started getting sicker and weaker. He got hit with bouts of pneumonia and bronchitis more and more often. He had to be hospitalized for long periods at a time, on steroids and antibiotics around the clock. At first he needed oxygen at night to help him sleep, but soon it was oxygen with activity, and then oxygen all the time. Everything changed for my family after that one night.

"So yeah, for a long time I was afraid of fire. That's why I got into firefighting—because the firefighters saved my father's life, but also because my father always told me to tackle my fears head-on. To take the power away from them." She looked back at Abby, the sadness from before settling heavily on her face. "But none of it seems worth the life of that stupid cat or a couple hundred pageant photos of me as a little kid, does it?"

"I bet he doesn't see it that way." Abby took a shot in the dark with that one, but if Duncan was as devoted to Sasha as she clearly was to him, then she had no doubt in her mind that he would have moved heaven and earth for her. "I bet he thinks you've taken a brave and selfless job to help others, and I bet he treasures those photos. I'm sure you do too now, as well."

"You're probably right." Sasha sighed and finished off another french fry. "You know? That damned cat lived to be twenty-one years old."

"Now you're lying." Abby teased and was glad to see a small smile on Sasha's face again.

"I swear to you—he lived to be twenty-one and never missed a meal in his life. It's a friggin' miracle he got up into the tree to begin with because even as a little guy he weighed eighteen pounds at least."

"I don't believe you."

Sasha chuckled. "Well, thanks to Dad, I've got pictures to prove it."

"I'd like to see them sometime." Abby meant that.

Sasha nodded. "I'd like to show them to you."

They sat quietly for a few moments before something occurred to Abby. "Did you say *pageant* photos?"

Sasha winced. "Ooh, you caught that, huh?"

"Oh, yeah. Details, please."

The door to Duncan's room opened and an older woman entered. She was weary but still beautiful, and her resemblance to Sasha was clear in the woman's strong cheekbones and sculpted brow line. This must be her mother.

"Hey, Ma." Sasha went to her, hugging her for a minute and carrying her bags over to where Abby was seated.

"Hello." The older woman gave her a curious smile. "I don't think we've met."

Abby took her hand and shook it. "Abby Rossmore. It's nice to meet you."

"Sorry, where are my manners? Ma, this is Abby. Abby this is my mother, Valeria." Sasha winked at Abby and pulled up a chair for her mother.

"I've heard good things about you, Abby." Sasha's mother gave her a tired but friendly smile.

"Sasha was just about to tell me about her apparent past in the pageant circuit." Abby hoped with Valeria here, she'd get the full scoop.

"Was she now?" Valeria looked amused. "Sasha was quite the showboat. She had trophies and awards in every category at every age. She could twirl a baton like no one else. But it was her Irish step dancing that drew the most attention."

"Shut up. You can Irish step dance?" Abby's mouth was practically on the floor. She didn't bother to close it.

Sasha looked shy. "I used to be able to. Much to the chagrin of my Russian ballerina mother. Irish step dancing was...What did you call it, Ma? The devil's jig?"

Valeria laughed. "I only called it that to piss off your grandmother. She was obsessed with your father and his Irish heritage. We nearly came to blows over her enrolling you in that jig class. Joke was on me though—you loved the little flowing skirts."

"I need to see these pictures." Abby could almost picture Sasha as a little girl, dark hair in pigtails, flouncy bouncy skirt, and tap shoes. "You must have been adorable."

"Hey." Sasha looked scandalized. "I'll have you know I am *still* adorable."

After watching Sasha's interaction with her mother, Abby decided she was right.

Valeria looked over at Duncan with fresh tears in her eyes. "How is he?"

Sasha exhaled. "No change. Vitals are good, urine output is appropriate. I'm getting the feeling that this is the uninterrupted nap he kept complaining that he needed."

Valeria smiled at her daughter. "You have his humor, but thank God you have my good looks."

Sasha blew her mother a kiss. "What's in the bags, Ma?"

"All your father's favorites. Including those cookies from above the fridge that I see you have been helping him to." She narrowed her eyes at Sasha and Sasha shrugged.

"I surely have no idea what you're talking about."

"Surely." Valeria rolled her eyes. "I brought a few changes of clothes and that awful album your father likes."

"The one with the drunk guy singing 'Danny Boy'?" Sasha rifled through the bag's contents and pulled out a battered CD case. "Jackpot."

Valeria shuddered. "You and your father have the same taste in music—awful."

Sasha turned to Abby. "My mother is much more dignified in every aspect of life. Right down to her love of Tchaikovsky."

Abby appreciated their banter. It reminded her of the relationship she had with her own mother. Which was why she had come here in the first place—to tell Sasha about her mother. Well, that and offer moral support. Both of which would have been a lot easier if Sasha's father hadn't been admitted to the hospital that Abby's great-grandfather built and her family's foundation ran. Of all the hospitals in Boston, why did he have to end up at Davenport Memorial? Probably because it was the best. Dammit.

Valeria looked at the remnants of their dinner. "Are you still hungry?"

Abby patted her stomach. "Oh, no. I'll bust, but thank you."

Sasha's eyebrow raised. "What do you have to offer, woman?"

"Your grandmother's Irish whiskey cake." Valeria placed the tinfoil-wrapped dish on the table.

"Devil's jig cake for the win." Sasha high-fived her mother and turned to Abby. "You have to try some of this. It's out of this world."

Abby believed that it probably was.

Chapter Eighteen

They keyed into Sasha's family home and she gave Abby a quick tour.

"This is the kitchen, over there is the den. My parents' bedroom is on the first floor by the enclosed sunporch. My childhood bedroom, a guest room, and the office are upstairs." Sasha went to the sink and closed the window, making sure to lock it.

Her mother had sat with them for a while at the hospital but sent Sasha home, saying she would do the overnight with her father tonight. Sasha had protested, but her mother had been adamant, saying it was her husband and she would spend the night with him. Sasha had been pretty sore about it until her mother remembered that she had left most of the windows open on the first floor. There was a storm threatening and she wanted Sasha to swing by the house and lock everything up tight. At least then Sasha felt like she was being useful.

"Do you live here still?" Abby leaned against the entryway in the kitchen, as her father had so many times before to catch his breath. She tried to push those memories away.

"No. I haven't lived here since I got out of the fire academy. I have a place about fifteen minutes away, but I spend a few nights a month here, off and on, if my mother needs a night off or picks up a shift to make extra money. My father really can't be alone."

Abby nodded. "Why move out at all?"

Sasha finished closing the downstairs windows and stood in the den. "For a multitude of reasons. First and foremost because I'd never get laid in my childhood bed with my parents downstairs. Ever." She winked and Abby laughed. She could listen to Abby laugh all day—it was quickly becoming one of her favorite sounds.

"Secondly, my firefighting gear has a tendency to off-gas even after it's been washed at the station. The smells irritate my father's asthma and makes his breathing more difficult. But at my apartment I leave my gear and clothes in the hallway outside the back door, so the smell doesn't fill my entire apartment. It's hard enough getting the smell of smoke out of my hair—it never leaves my clothes."

"What does off-gas mean?" Abby was never shy about asking Sasha things about her job, and she appreciated her interest.

Sasha settled on the couch and motioned for Abby to join her—her fatigue was winning out, and she needed to sit. "It's the gas given off as a byproduct to a chemical process. Which in layman's terms means it's stinky and can be toxic. Most of us shower after shift and keep a change of clothes in our lockers, but occasionally I'll pop home in my blue uniform that you saw at the school, and that can be a little funky at the end of a twenty-four-hour shift."

"I see." Abby sank onto the couch near her, but not touching her. Sasha rectified this by reaching out and pulling Abby closer. Abby settled into her side and rested her head on Sasha's shoulder. Sasha could feel the heat of Abby's body against her own. It soothed her. She felt sleepy.

"You didn't have to come back to my parents' house to help me close the windows, you know. I probably could have managed on my own." Sasha pressed a kiss to Abby's head. She breathed in the scent of her shampoo and felt the stress of the day start to melt away.

"Oh, it was completely selfish. I have an agenda here." Abby looked up at her.

They were so close, Sasha knew if she leaned a little closer, their lips would touch. She moved in a bit, stopping short of her goal. "Oh? And what agenda is that?"

"To see your pageant photos, of course. Duh." Abby pecked her lips and laughed as Sasha tickled her sides.

"I knew it was too good to be true." She continued to tickle Abby as she squirmed next to her.

"What is?" Abby swatted her hands away, gasping to catch her breath. "What's too good to be true?"

"You." Sasha hadn't meant to reveal that, but she'd thought it since their dinner at the café in Cambridge. Abby was perfect. She backpedaled. "You, joining me to be helpful, I mean."

Abby's face was unreadable for a moment. Sasha got a little anxious, worried that she'd shared too much of herself. And yet, tonight Abby had met both of her parents, well, sort of. The overshare part seemed to be behind them. Sasha couldn't remember the last woman she'd introduced to her parents. And no one had seen her be as vulnerable as she had been at her father's bedside. Abby was different. And she liked that about her. She didn't mind sharing things with her.

"Oh, I have full confidence that if I hadn't breached the threshold under the pretense of being helpful, you never would have shown me those photos. I'm on a mission here. Nothing will stop me." Abby laughed manically and Sasha rolled her eyes.

"They're in the fireproof cabinet over there, by the front door. Close to the exit in case of a fire emergency." Sasha waved toward the black box by the stairwell and Abby scampered over to it. She gave Abby the code, and within minutes Abby had the books spread out on the coffee table in front of them, asking questions and exclaiming over Sasha's outfits. It would have been embarrassing if Sasha hadn't been so damned cute. She patted herself on the shoulder when one little nude tub photo from her first birthday made its way into Abby's hands.

"You. Were. *So.* Cute." Abby's eyes shined.

"Correction. I *am* so cute. Just because I'm older doesn't mean I'm any less cute." Sasha pointed between her face and the little smiling face on the picture. She mimicked the smile as best she could. "See?"

Abby leaned back in mock examination. "Well, I'd argue that your teeth are significantly better now."

"Now that I have teeth."

"Yes. Teeth are nice. You have nice teeth," Abby noted.

"You're easy to please." Sasha nudged her with her elbow.

"Are you calling me easy?" Abby scoffed.

"I wouldn't dare. But you did sleep with me on our third date." Sasha tickled Abby's side again, leaning closer to her in the process.

"I don't recall much sleeping." Abby wiggled under Sasha's touch, but she stayed close.

Sasha let her eyes drop to the pink gloss on Abby's lips. She thought about that night, that date. She thought about the heat between them and the spark that ignited. She wanted to feel that again. "I feel comfortable saying that was the best date of my adult life. Hands down. No questions asked."

"Your adult life, huh? Is this the time you tell me about the high school lesbianism you hinted at before?" Abby was making no attempt at eye contact. Her gaze seemed to trace the outline of Sasha's hand, which had ceased tickling and instead rested on her thigh.

Sasha moved her hand up on Abby's thigh and was rewarded when Abby stifled a moan. She leaned close to reply, "I dabbled a bit here and there. After school, at weekend parties, under the bleachers. But like I said, I never got any action in my childhood bedroom. If I'm being honest, I got most of my hands-on training in college."

Abby licked her lips and looked up at Sasha, her pupils large and dark as she asked, "And were you a good student in college?"

"The best." Sasha doubted they were talking about her academics.

"I'll be the judge of that." Abby's hands gripped at Sasha's shirt, tugging her off the couch. "Why don't you show me that bedroom you keep talking about? Maybe we can, oh, I don't know, turn your luck around up there?"

Sasha didn't have a chance to think, let alone agree, before Abby's lips were on her own. Abby was pressed against her, pulling at her shirt, sucking on her lips. That passion from their date flared and Sasha had no desire to extinguish it.

They stumbled up the stairs, Sasha climbing up backward so as not to break away from Abby's mouth. By the time they fell through the door into her room, Abby had Sasha's shirt off, the fabric bunched in her fist while she palmed at Sasha's breast with her other hand. Sasha's arms were around Abby, holding her close when the backs of her knees hit the bed. They tumbled onto it and Abby was on her in a flash.

Sasha shifted up the bed, scooting toward the headboard, when she came in contact with something large and hard. She paused and Abby stopped kissing her.

"What? Everything okay?" Abby was adorably flustered, her lips kiss-bruised, and her hair coming loose from the delicate braid of earlier.

"Yeah. Yes." Sasha looked at the offending object and laughed. "Hold on a second."

It was a box with all of her athletic trophies from her high school days. Her mother had warned her that she was clearing out the sun porch to make room for her father's growing medical equipment collection. Evidently her mother had been in here recently. When she unceremoniously shoved the box off the bed, the contents clanged and jingled as it hit the floor.

Sasha grabbed Abby by the collar of her shirt and pulled her back down to her lips.

"So I take it that whatever that is, it isn't important." Abby teased kisses around Sasha's mouth, kissing her briefly before traveling to Sasha's neck and sucking the skin there.

"Not even close to being as important as this." Sasha's hand was under Abby's shirt, scratching at her abdomen. Abby's stomach was firm but soft. Her abdomen flexed and lengthened as she climbed up Sasha's body. Sasha reveled in the feel of Abby's body under her hands.

Abby's hands worked to undo Sasha's belt while she continued to lavish attention on the soft, sensitive skin of Sasha's neck. Sasha shuddered when Abby's tongue hit a particularly erogenous spot. "I could suck on this skin all day. You're delicious."

Sasha was soaked. She couldn't remember another time she had been so turned on so quickly. She pulled Abby's shirt over her head and threw it off to the side. Abby was a vision in an off-white lace bra. Her breasts strained against the flimsy lace cups and Sasha's mouth watered at the outline of perky nipples just inches from her lips. Sasha was panting now. "You're driving me crazy."

Abby released Sasha's belt and unbuttoned her jeans, pulling them off Sasha before climbing back on top of her, straddling her as she claimed her mouth again. Abby's hands cupped Sasha's still-clothed breasts, tweaking her nipples in frustration. "Take this off, Sash." She snapped Sasha's bra strap and licked her lips.

She leaned forward and licked the swell of Abby's left breast, while she unhooked her own bra, sliding it off her arms and dropping it off the bed. Once her breasts were free, Abby's hands were on them, massaging and teasing the skin, making it almost impossible for Sasha to keep tending to the soft skin above Abby's nipple. She tugged down on the offending cup and freed Abby's left nipple, sucking it into her mouth hungrily. Abby moaned and her hand was in Sasha's hair, holding her lips in place. Sasha maneuvered the rest of the bra out of the way and savored the weight of Abby's other breast in her hand, her nipple in her mouth. Abby abandoned Sasha's breasts in favor of massaging Sasha's scalp, which would have disappointed Sasha had Abby not then begun to grind her hips down on Sasha's abdomen.

"You are so fucking hot, baby." Sasha worked her mouth across Abby's chest to her other nipple as she dragged her fingers down Abby's abdomen, punctuating her statement with a gentle scratch to the taut skin below her hand. Abby hissed and threw her head back as Sasha unbuttoned her pants and pulled at her panties. "I want to see you naked, Abs. Can you get naked for me?"

Abby moaned again as Sasha gripped her sides and pulled her down to her mouth. She worked her tongue against Abby's, matching her grind roll for roll. She kissed her hard and fast until she couldn't catch her breath, and then Abby was off her, slipping out of her pants and helping Sasha pull down the covers of her childhood bed.

"I've never been so happy to fuck in a twin bed." Abby's lips were on the skin under her ear, her body pressed flush against Sasha's. The sensation of their naked flesh rubbing breast to breast, thigh to thigh, was making Sasha's clit throb.

"Yeah? Why's that, babe?" Sasha's hand trailed down Abby's naked back to her thong, toying with the waistband before grabbing the exposed flesh of her ass hard and pulling Abby's core against hers in a practiced roll.

"Fuck," Abby cried out before she sucked Sasha's earlobe between her lips.

"You were saying?" Sasha could feel the heat of Abby's center against her own. She wanted to feel how wet she was, too. She'd bet anything that Abby was dripping like she was. She released her ass and slid inward, the tips of her fingers brushing against the swollen lips of Abby's sex from behind. The barely there material of Abby's thong was long since soaked through and moved easily aside to grant Sasha the access she so desperately sought. Sasha vibrated with excitement at the thought of entering Abby. She wanted so badly to be inside her. "What was that about fucking in a twin?"

Abby groaned as Sasha swirled her fingers in her wetness. Abby bit down on Sasha's earlobe when she entered her with two confident fingers and pumped her hips down in response, pulling Sasha in deeper. She panted in Sasha's ear as they began to work on a rhythm, Sasha thrusting in with Abby pumping down and back against her open hand. "This bed. It's the perfect size." Abby's breath was short and fast. "No matter where I am on it, I'm on you, too. Twin for the win."

Sasha connected their lips as she slipped a third finger in Abby on the next thrust. Abby moaned in pleasure and Sasha wondered if she could come from the sounds Abby was making alone. It seemed more than likely when Abby grabbed at her breasts to anchor herself. Her fingers tweaked and pulled at Sasha's nipples in time with her thrusts, and Sasha felt herself start to shake and twitch, her body winding up as Abby started to reach her peak.

"Oh, fuck. Sasha, don't stop," Abby pleaded and Sasha kissed her harder, trying to show her that she had no intention of stopping anytime soon. Not when Abby was so wet in her hand she was practically slipping out of her. Not when Abby's thighs gripped Sasha's hips so tightly it almost hurt. No. She had no intention of stopping until Abby couldn't come anymore.

"You are so tight, Abby." Sasha strained to curl her fingers inside Abby to prolong the pleasure for them both. Abby's muscles pulsed and pulled her in deeper yet again.

Abby pulled back from Sasha's lips long enough to beg, her hands abandoning Sasha's chest in favor of gripping at her shoulders. "Sasha. Baby, please. Please."

Sasha nodded and leaned up again, curling her fingers and stroking backward as Abby rolled her hips against her hand. "Kiss me, Abby. Kiss me while you come."

Abby kissed her with such passion that Sasha lost her breath. Abby followed suit as her hips bucked and her muscles clenched around Sasha's fingers. Abby's orgasm rolled through her so fiercely that Sasha's clit twitched in response. They were so close, so tightly pressed together that every shudder Abby endured quaked back against Sasha, priming her for her own orgasm.

"Jesus. Fucking A, that was…unreal." Abby gasped and crumpled against her, her head on Sasha's chest as she caught her breath.

Sasha laughed, taking the opportunity to breathe in the smell of Abby's perfume mixed with their combined sweat. It was intoxicating.

Abby shifted and when her thigh rubbed against Sasha's swollen sex, she shuddered. Abby looked up at her and shifted again, smiling when Sasha's reaction was the same, only amplified this time. Abby kept eye contact with Sasha as she lowered her lips to the skin between Sasha's bare breasts. "Remember before when I told you I could suck on your skin all day? That I thought you were delicious?"

Abby moved lower and Sasha had a hard time forming words. "Yes."

Abby hummed, her tongue dragging slow zigzags down Sasha's abdomen, stopping to suck on one of the defined abs Sasha worked so hard to maintain. She had never been so glad she put in those extra hours at the gym between calls at the station as she was in this moment.

When Abby's nose brushed against Sasha's navel, she curled up reflexively. This was too much and not enough all at the same time. She clawed at her own thigh for something to do with her hands as Abby licked across the band of her panties, pulling them down with her mouth.

"I think the only way to really prove that statement is"—Abby kissed the inside of her thigh as her hands worked the soaked panties off her hips, exposing Sasha's naked, quivering sex to the cold room air—"to taste you."

Sasha couldn't stop the whine that tumbled from her lips in response to Abby's slow torture. She felt like her heart was going to beat right out of her chest when Abby's mouth began to tease at her opening. Sasha nearly fainted when Abby sucked on her swollen lips, spreading them with her tongue to flick across her clit.

Sasha's hips bucked up in response and Abby's hand pressed her back to the bed, her lips and tongue everywhere at once. Sasha closed her eyes and let her head drop back as Abby's mouth brought her to a new level of ecstasy she'd never experienced before. She gripped Abby's hair, more to ground herself than for anything else, but when Abby's fingers entered her, Sasha's resolve faded. She cried out as she came hard and fast in Abby's mouth, the climax coming on so quickly it surprised her.

Abby stayed between her legs, sucking and licking until it became too much for Sasha to bear. The intensity of the tremors felt like one long-drawn-out orgasm sending little shock waves while it ramped up and slowed down, only to repeat again.

"I think I'm dead." Sasha spoke to test her theory that she had died and gone to heaven. This was heaven, right? An endless orgasm from an amazingly attractive woman who showed no signs of stopping. At all. Ever.

Abby sucked on her clit in response and Sasha was sure then that her life had ended. If this was the eternity she was destined for, then so be it.

"I sure hope not," Abby purred against her and another wave shook through her. "I'm hoping to do that again, immediately."

Sasha cursed. "Which part?"

Abby pressed a kiss to the inside of her thigh and Sasha felt her settle on her chest, her body spread over Sasha's in a warm blanket of sex-sticky flesh. It was exquisite. "All the parts."

Sasha opened her eyes and looked down. Abby was propped up on her elbows, her chin resting on Sasha's sternum between her breasts. Abby dragged her thumb and forefinger under her lips, wiping her mouth, and Sasha had a revelation. "You are the sexiest thing I have ever seen in my entire life. And that's saying something since I'm talking to you from the grave. Literal grave. Dead."

Abby laughed and Sasha pulled her up to kiss her lips, savoring the warmth and taste of Abby's mouth. She didn't want this moment to end.

"You look so good for dead, though." Abby slid to her side and Sasha turned to face her. "It's kind of a sin how good you look."

"Marry me." Sasha was half kidding. Half.

Abby laughed and cuddled close to her, reaching for the blankets to cover them. "I don't even know if you snore yet. How can you expect me to make that kind of commitment without important information like that?"

Sasha pulled Abby to her chest and wrapped her limbs around her as sleep threatened to interrupt their evening. Abby's arms slid around her waist in response and she felt safe and warm and cared for in a way that she hadn't in a very long time. From her vantage point, she could see the picture on the nightstand of her with her parents, and she was reminded of why Abby was here tonight to begin with. The euphoria of the evening started to fade. Sasha didn't want to be alone. "Stay with me tonight."

Abby looked up at her, her expression soft, the teasing from before gone now. "To see if you snore?"

"What better way to find out?" Sasha hoped the need in her voice was concealed.

Abby's eyes traced her face before she replied. It felt like minutes had passed. "There is nowhere else I'd rather be."

Sasha kissed her, long and slow, trying to relay how much that meant to her. She didn't have the words for it yet, but something about tonight and Abby and everything that transpired felt very different from anything she had experienced before. As Abby's breath skated across her collarbone and her eyes got heavy, she decided she'd worry about all of that later. Abby was naked in her arms and sleep was calling. Everything else could wait.

CHAPTER NINETEEN

Abby stood by the coffee machine and made a mental note to upgrade it, immediately. She cocked her head to the side as the sludge parading around as coffee dripped from the opening into the cheap paper cup, and she was disgusted that this had somehow evaded the normally scrupulous standards of the customer service department of the hospital. Her family's hospital.

She sighed.

"Yeah. If I were you, I'd take the five-minute walk to the café at the north end of the building. This stuff looks toxic." Sasha leaned against the wall next to the antiquated machine.

"I wonder if it's ever been cleaned. I'm not talking about in this century either—I mean just since its original manufacturing." Abby dumped the brown tar into the small trash can nearby. "I'm offended that people actually drink it."

"Luckily for you, I know my way around this place and can give you a few pointers about the best place to get a scone, a latte, or, on Thursdays, who to talk to about getting chicken fingers off the secret cafeteria menu." Sasha's smile didn't reach her eyes. She looked tired. Abby should feel guilty about that fatigue, but she didn't. She had thoroughly enjoyed herself with Sasha last night and she had a feeling if she inquired, Sasha would agree. Last night had been...memorable.

"You're so useful. I'll keep you." Abby extended her hand in Sasha's direction and Sasha took it. She had woken up blissfully in Sasha's arms at Sasha's parents' house this morning but had to go to the office to finish some work she'd been putting off. Before she left, she promised to swing by the hospital later to check in. It had been a long day and she was in desperate need of caffeine. This coffee machine issue was a definite wrench in the plans.

"I can live with that." Sasha kissed her on the cheek and yawned. "I have to make a quick phone call. The signal here sucks—I'm going to pop outside to call the station and check on the updated schedule. I'll swing by the café on the way back. What can I get you?"

"A latte. Caramel, light foam." Abby squeezed Sasha's hand before letting go.

"If I get heavy foam, can I watch you lick it off?" Sasha's smile was mischievous.

"Just watch?" Abby couldn't help herself. Last night was fresh in her mind and her body. She was still a little sore from their second round of play in the early morning. It was a delightful reminder of what had transpired. She regretted nothing.

Sasha let out a low whistle. "You make a valid point. I'd much rather be involved in the process than just observe."

There was that boldness that Abby adored. "You make sure there's light foam on my latte and we can see what type of *involvement* we can work out for later."

"Consider it done." Sasha placed a lingering kiss on Abby's lips before she left and Abby stood there for a moment, appreciating the tingling sensations that Sasha sent all throughout her body with something as simple as a kiss and a promise for more.

"She likes you." Valeria appeared at her side as Sasha walked away.

"I like her, too." The words left her mouth before she could stop them. She did like Sasha. But maybe admitting that out loud for the first time—to Sasha's mother no less—wasn't the wisest idea. She blamed Sasha's blistering kiss for knocking her off her game.

Valeria nodded. "What's not to like? She's a gift." Spoken like a true mother and sounding so much like Sasha. "But that's not what I mean."

"It's not?" Abby was confused and more than a little worried Valeria overheard some of their exchange before Sasha left—that would be embarrassing.

"No." Valeria shook her head and sighed. She walked toward the solarium outside Duncan's room and sat heavily on a bench, patting the space next to her for Abby to join her.

"Duncan has always been Sasha's hero. She was a daddy's girl from birth. Everything he ever did she tried to mimic, to emulate him in some way. After the fire, that reverence doubled. She was dead set on finding a career in which she could help people and make a positive impact in people's lives like her father had in hers. It was a cruel irony that she found that passion in firefighting." Valeria looked at the door to Duncan's room as she spoke, almost like if she spoke too loudly, he might hear. "I'm terrified she will meet the same fate as her father, being brave and foolish and doing something rash that takes her from me far too soon. She doesn't need to fight fires to be someone's hero—she's got all the qualities to be that now. She already *is*. She has kept our family together. She's our savior, her father's champion—none of that has ever been in question."

Her brow creased and the stress of her life settled on her beautiful features. Abby could read in Valeria's face how Duncan's decision had forever changed this family. She looked at Abby in that moment. "Sasha is bullheaded like me. Fearless like her father. But soft and gentle like herself. She's sweet and kind and would give you the shirt off her back if she thought it would make your day better." She paused, appraising Abby briefly before she continued. "She likes you. But I see the way she looks at you. It's more than that. You're special to her."

An alarm sounded in Duncan's room and a nurse ran in. Valeria's whole body tensed and Abby reached for her hand out of instinct. The noise ceased and the nurse exited the room, informing them not to worry, that one of the wires had come loose. But Abby did worry. And clearly, Valeria worried as well.

Valeria squeezed her hand and patted it as she exhaled, the crisis seemingly averted for the moment. Her dark eyes, so like Sasha's and yet so different as well, looked at Abby almost pleadingly. "She will need help now. Her hero is failing. Everything she has ever known will be extinguished before she's ready for it. Before any of us are…"

Her wording was not lost on Abby. She shifted closer and took Valeria's hand in her own, cradling it. "She's special to me, too. I won't let her down."

Abby was having an out of body experience. It was like her mouth had a mind of its own. She was hearing these words and living them for the first time, at the same time.

"What's wrong? Did something happen?" Sasha stood over them carrying a tray of coffees with a look of concern on her face.

Abby was too caught up in her own thoughts to figure out what Sasha was talking about. Thankfully, Valeria seemed to have her shit together. She squeezed Abby's hand before she released it. "It's nothing, love. We were just talking." Abby didn't miss the warning glance Valeria gave her as Sasha paced by the door of her father's room. She figured there was no need to tell Sasha about the alarm shock that she just missed.

"Jesus, Ma. I'm glad you and Abby get along and all but if you're gonna be all cuddled up like that holding hands, I'm going to think the worst." Sasha looked a little pale.

"What? That she realizes I'm a much more attractive, mature version of you? Really, Sasha. I thought I raised a more confident woman than to be jealous of your own mother." Valeria stood and accepted the coffee Sasha handed her. She kissed Sasha's cheek. "She only has eyes for you, dear. Don't worry."

"Ma. I wasn't worried about…That's not what I—" Sasha sputtered. It was cute.

"Sh. I know. I'm joking. Your father's fine. I'm going to sit with him now." Valeria patted her on the shoulder and headed toward the door, pausing to add, "She's got very soft hands though, Sash."

The wadded-up napkin narrowly missed her as she walked through the door.

Abby popped the lid off her latte and inspected the foam level. Sasha was watching her with great interest. She dipped her finger in, gathering some foam, and proceeded to lick it off, making sure Sasha had a clear view. She recapped the latte and leaned in to Sasha's ear to whisper, "Maybe you can do more than just watch, later."

Sasha laughed and kissed her. She handed Abby a bag containing an assortment of pastries and said, "I got you something special."

Her conversation with Valeria was fresh in her mind as she broke the chocolate croissant in two, handing a piece to Sasha, their fingers brushing briefly. This was something special indeed.

❖

Sasha sighed and closed her eyes as Abby's mouth descended upon her breast, her tongue working Sasha's nipple in that tantalizing way that made Sasha shiver and quake all over. It was something that Abby had picked up on over the last nights that she and Sasha had gotten close. Truthfully, Sasha hadn't even been aware she had such a sensitive trigger spot but—evidently—she did.

"Your skin is so soft." Abby's lips broke contact with her skin just long enough to tease her. "This is my favorite part of the morning."

Sasha threaded her fingers through Abby's hair, tousling the blond mass on her chest and holding her close. Her chest rose and fell with increased frequency as Abby's fingers skimmed the inside of her thigh, pressing in and skating away, only to return and repeat the torture. Her sex buzzed with anticipation and want. Abby had a way of winding her up and leaving her there to drown in her arousal. It was agony.

"More than coffee?" Sasha tried to relieve some of the building pressure by spreading her legs a little, inviting Abby to touch her instead of only tease her.

Abby sucked hard on her nipple and she saw stars. "Mm-hmm. More than coffee."

Sasha's shifted again, trying to bring her center closer to Abby's hand, which was tauntingly evasive at the moment. "Abby."

"Sasha." Abby moved to her other breast, licking along the skin while she massaged the skin of the breast she had just abandoned, the nipple sore and erect from Abby's mouth play. It all felt amazing and Sasha's body twitched with pleasure, but her focus was on the fingers that now danced around her lips, gathering wetness and spreading them slightly before retreating. Sasha felt like she might explode.

"Abby." She tried again, her voice shaky at best.

"Tell me." Abby spread her lips and dipped in just enough to send a wave of pleasure through Sasha's abdomen. "Tell me, Sash."

"Fuck." Sasha palmed her own breast to keep from touching herself—this was the most fantastic torture she had ever experienced.

Abby released her nipple to kiss along her sternum, settling just under Sasha's chin, licking the skin along her neck. She pressed her body down on Sasha's, trapping Sasha's hand at her breast while her right hand continued its teasing ministrations. She husked in Sasha's ear, "Tell me. Tell me and make the teasing stop."

Sasha bit her lip to quiet the moan that was bubbling up in the back of her throat. This was her favorite sex with Abby—the long, teasing, sensual kind where Abby wanted her to beg for release. It was exactly the kind of thing that Sasha dreamed about when they were apart—ceding control to Abby to give her what had turned out to be the best sex of her life. But she had to say it. She had to ask to come.

"Fuck me, Abby. Please. Fuck me." Sasha had reached her breaking point. If Abby didn't help her, she'd come from the teasing alone, something that had happened more than once over the course of their new relationship. She couldn't remember another time in her sexual life that just the foreplay and promise of sex could bring her to the finish line. And yet, it had. A few times. "Make me come."

"Good girl." Abby rewarded her with slick, coated fingers inside her, moving slow and steady until Sasha bucked her hips, taking Abby in deeper. Abby bit down on her earlobe and breathed encouragement in her ear with every deepened thrust. "You're so tight, Sash. So wet. Does that feel good? Tell me more, Sasha. Tell me what feels the best."

Sasha couldn't form words. She wasn't even sure she was breathing. She felt light-headed, all her blood rushing everywhere but her brain. Abby's thumb brushed over her clit and the room spun. "There. Please, Abby, there. Don't stop. I need—"

"What? What do you need?" Abby's mouth was on hers, her tongue coaxing Sasha's to speak, to ask, to beg. She pressed on Sasha's clit and Sasha cried out. "Is this what you need?"

"*Yes.*" Sasha was right at the brink. She tried desperately to slow the crescendo, wanting Abby to bring her over the edge, but she was so close, it would be a matter of only seconds now if she—

Abby kissed her hard and pressed her thumb to Sasha's clit as she thrust in and out slowly, bringing Sasha across the precipice and drawing out Sasha's tremors, prolonging her ecstasy.

Sasha curled into Abby, her muscles twitching and her body on fire. Her sweat-covered skin pressed against Abby's as Abby continued her unhurried thrusts, bringing her down gently until the sensation was too much for Sasha to handle.

She grabbed Abby's wrist for respite, trying to catch her breath. Abby turned her hand and guided Sasha's hand between her own legs, coating Sasha's fingers with her own wetness.

"That. That's the best part of my morning. How wet you get for me. How turned on you are. That never gets old." Abby slid to Sasha's side and licked the tips of Sasha's fingers before intertwining their fingers.

Sasha's body hummed. She tattooed the image of Abby cleaning her fingers to memory and vowed to revisit it often. "You're something else, you know that? I—I can't even. You're perfect." She leaned forward and kissed her, overwhelmed by everything that was Abby Rossmore.

"I'm not. But thank you." Abby's eyes were so green in this light, the low light of the morning, when the sun peeked over the trees and spilled into her childhood bedroom. It seemed silly that they continued to return here, and yet, it felt right.

Abby snuggled up to her side and yawned as she rested her head on Sasha's collarbone. Sasha felt such peace in that moment. Having Abby here by her side was making her feel all sorts of things. She felt such a deep connection with Abby. One that she hadn't expected would be possible. One that she might have missed out on had she not run into Abby at Samantha's wedding. How many times had they almost made a connection during those mixers? How close had she come to not realizing that Abby was everything she had been looking for and more? "You know, we could do this sometime in an adult-sized bed."

Abby's laugh vibrated across her chest. Her eyes were closed, her lips bright pink and plump from their wake-up today. They looked delicious. "I feel like I'd never be able to find you in a regular-sized bed. You'd be so far away."

"I'd never go too far. I like being this close to you." She did. In more ways than one. She'd realized she was starting to fall for Abby the night she showed up at the hospital, when her father was first admitted. Something about Abby walking into that room gave her such hope, such lightness. Like, no matter what happened, she could get through it. She never would have thought that such tragedy would have brought her such clarity. Abby wasn't just some fling or physical crutch she was using to get through a difficult time. Abby was the calm at the end of a rough day of machine beeps and her father's failing health. Abby was the rainbow at the end of the storm, and yet, even in the thick of this family crisis, Sasha felt safe and cared for.

"I love that." Abby opened her eyes and Sasha let herself get lost in them for a minute.

Sasha loved that, too. She loved that Abby wasn't uncomfortable with her desire for closeness. She felt so grounded when she could reach out and touch Abby, even just on the hand at the hospital when the doctors made rounds and spoke about her father like he was some nameless face, all clinical and detached. She knew she could just touch Abby's hand and not be alone in this for once. It was everything to her. "Listen, why don't we do something together this week. You know, outside of the hospital and the *reacquainting* we've been doing. Let's go out. Together. I'd like to take you out."

Abby gave her that lazy, satiated smile that she loved so much, the one that followed their lovemaking. The one that greeted her every night and every morning they spent together. "More glassblowing?"

"Ha-ha. No, something more, I don't know, intimate." Sasha realized she had to pick up their bowl at some point. She had all but forgotten about it when her father went into the hospital.

"I thought that was a pretty intimate date." Abby licked her lips. "I mean, you got pretty intimately acquainted with my pussy that night. There are few things more intimate than that, if you ask me."

Sasha moaned. Abby had the filthiest mouth and mind ever. She had always prided herself on being a sexual being, but Abby brought it to a whole other level entirely. "This is true."

"I only speak in truths." Abby kissed her, sucking on her lips for a moment. "And unfortunately, the truth is I have to go to work today, but there aren't any clothes for me here, so I have to do the walk of shame into my building and change beforehand."

"That truth sucks." Sasha pouted. She had the next two days off from the firehouse and she wanted to spend every moment with Abby. "It's too bad you're just a lowly bachelorette candidate like me and not some wildly wealthy socialite like the ones Samantha tried to pair us with, because then you'd have no responsibilities in the world and could just stay in bed with me all day."

Abby's brow furrowed and she blinked. She almost looked... offended.

Sasha backpedaled. "I'm not complaining. I'm thrilled you're normal and approachable and down-to-earth—"

"And fuckable," Abby deadpanned.

"Right, that, too." Sasha exhaled. "I'm not doing this very eloquently, but I'm just so grateful that you didn't get scooped up by some entitled, privileged lady who lunches."

"Good thing." Abby's smile didn't reach her eyes. She pecked Sasha on the lips and slipped out from under the sheets, dressing quickly. "I'll swing by the hospital after work. Will you be there around dinnertime?"

Sasha stretched, grateful she had time to nap before relieving her mother later. "I should be. Just text me."

Abby finished buttoning her shirt and dug her purse out from under the discarded comforter on the floor. She blew Sasha a kiss as she headed out of Sasha's bedroom. "I'll lock up when I leave. Have a good day."

And just like that, Abby was gone. Sasha lay there for a moment, replaying the morning. Had she offended Abby? She felt like Abby left a little abruptly. But then again, Abby did say she had to go home and change before work. She looked over at the clock. It was almost eight in the morning. Abby would probably have to hustle to get a start on the day. She closed her eyes and felt sleep tugging at her. She decided she was overthinking it. She just needed a little rest and she could worry or not worry about it later. Things with Abby were going so well. Why let her insecurity ruin everything?

CHAPTER TWENTY

Abby woke up in Sasha's childhood bed, wrapped up in Sasha's arms, for the seventh time in the past two weeks. Someone had once told Abby that two weeks was the amount of time it took for a habit or routine to form.

They had fallen into a sort of after-work routine, where Abby would join Sasha and her mother at the hospital before she retired for the night. If Sasha didn't have a station shift the following morning, they went back to her parents' house. They'd catch up with each other about their days, they would kiss and have a passionate exchange that lasted hours into the evening or spilled into the early morning, and then Sasha would snuggle up to Abby—at which time she'd forget all about the life that existed outside that bedroom door. They had joked about going to their respective apartments once or twice, but there was something so safe and inviting about Sasha's childhood home. It seemed like Sasha felt better being in such close proximity to the hospital in case something happened, but also that it was familiar to her.

Abby had seen her stare off into the distance or get lost looking at family photos. She knew this was a difficult time for her, so it had been completely fine with her that they continue this little tradition. It was working, so why stop? But it was more than that. Selfishly Abby didn't want to disrupt the way things were going. Being with Sasha made her feel so...complete. So whole. The sex was divine, but there was so much more to Sasha than just that. She was sensitive but cocky at the same time. Their conversations were easy and engaging, and they never struggled to find something to talk or laugh about. And getting to know Sasha's mother was an unexpected bonus. Valeria was sweet and playful—Abby could see where Sasha got her humor and sarcasm. She loved the opportunity to get to know Valeria almost as much as she loved her nights with Sasha. Almost.

This relationship was the whole package. The more time she spent with Sasha, the more invested she felt. She wanted to be there for Sasha, to be with her. But she knew that she could only avoid the elephant in the room for so long. Abby still hadn't come clean to Sasha, and if she'd had Sasha up to her penthouse downtown, the jig would have been up. Her home, although modest compared to her mother's palatial estate, was not the home of a nonprofit accountant. It was the home of an heiress, with a multimillion dollar view of the city, and it came with all the perks that such a luxurious lifestyle could afford. The doorman and concierge made sure she never entered the building without a smile or someone offering to carry her bags. The valet made sure her car was maintained and temperature controlled whenever she called for it. In fact, she couldn't remember the last time she'd had to have her car serviced or had to fill her own gas tank. This was the kind of lifestyle she had grown accustomed to, the kind of thing she had taken for granted. And now, suddenly, it felt shameful.

So she made no attempt to disrupt their routine. Because it benefited her. Because she loved the safety of it. Because it allowed her to avoid the part of her life that she was desperately trying to keep hidden for fear of it driving Sasha away. And she had wholly done this to herself. If she had been honest from the start, would Sasha still want to be with her?

If this morning's postcoital conversation was any indication, the answer was no. Sasha was so emotional, so communicative with Abby. She was never dishonest, ever. That's what was killing Abby. Sasha had been entirely open and vulnerable this whole time and Abby couldn't meet her at that level. She was hiding so much, and for what? For fear of losing something she didn't think she'd ever find with someone. Ever.

And Sasha's statements this morning all but proved that fear to be true. Sasha had a clear contempt for those who fortune favored, for those who were given advantages that were completely unattainable to hardworking blue-collar people like Sasha and her parents. She had overheard the whispered conversations between Valeria and Sasha at the hospital when the days turned to weeks and Valeria worried about the bills. And yet every time, Sasha soothed her. She picked up extra shifts and worked catering jobs when her mother could sit by her father's bedside, only taking time off work to take Valeria's place, sitting vigil, hoping and praying for his infection to pass and to get a glimmer of her father back.

Abby had seen it all. And the knot in her stomach tightened even more, a vise that kept her frozen in fear. She had withheld the truth for far too long and now she had everything to lose. Sasha would hate her. And she had every right to. After all, Abby was everything that Sasha loathed in this world. She was financially care free.

Two weeks. They'd had two amazingly emotional and eye-opening weeks in which Abby had never felt more connected to another human being. Time to come clean.

❖

"Hey, Abby." Dianna Rabin sauntered up to her in the hospital corridor, her smile genuine.

"Dianna. Hi." She kissed her on the cheek and gave her a one-armed hug.

"What are you doing here? The board meeting isn't until next week." Dianna was on the hospital board as well, or more accurately, her family had a seat. Dianna was merely the current placeholder for the Rabin family. Their donated wing housed the colorectal unit and was one of the newest additions to the main campus.

"I could ask the same of you." Abby didn't feel like talking to Dianna about Sasha or her father. It wasn't that she didn't trust Dianna or anything. It was just that, well, it was none of her damn business.

Dianna laughed. "Never change, Abby. You're as charming as ever." Dianna was flirting. Abby had forgotten that her interactions with Dianna in the past had been mostly sarcastic and saturated with sexual tension. She was inadvertently falling into bad habits. Except this time, she was just trying to be evasive. Not mysterious. *Abort, abort mission.*

"Oh, um, no. Not like that." She cleared her throat. "I'm visiting a friend."

"Oh? Anyone I know?" Dianna leaned against the wall and crossed her ankles. Abby didn't miss the way Dianna checked her out. She was so predatory that way. It made Abby miss Sasha.

"I don't think so. No." Abby was itching to end this conversation. Sasha would be here any moment and she didn't really feel like introducing them, considering last time they'd met, Sasha was half naked and writhing around onstage. Part of Abby was still a little possessive over Sasha. Dianna had, after all, gotten a little handsy in the bidding war at the dating auction.

"Hey, Abs." Right on cue, Sasha walked up. Because of course she did. "What's cooking, good lookin'?" Sasha slid her arm around Abby's waist and it took all her power not to pull away.

"Bachelorette number twenty-seven. No shit." Dianna stood to her full height and gave Sasha a wave, but not before she surveyed the arm Sasha had around Abby's waist. A look of understanding crossed her face. "Fancy meeting you here."

Sasha looked between them, clearly confused. "Uh, hey."

"We haven't been formally introduced." Dianna extended her hand to Sasha. "I'm Dianna Rabin. Nice to meet you."

"Sasha McCray. Likewise." Sasha shook her hand and looked back at Abby. "You two know each other?"

"Yeah, we, uh…" Abby felt like a deer caught in headlights. This was bad. Very bad.

Dianna spoke first. "Our families go way back."

Abby was grateful Dianna chose the more conservative response. That was technically true. It was also true that they used to have a lot of sex. But that didn't seem pertinent right now.

"Oh, that's nice." Sasha's expression was unreadable.

"Well, I won't keep you." Dianna looked back at Abby. "Oh, before I forget, I wanted to tell you that I tried out that new coffee machine you ordered. It's fantastic."

How was it that she hadn't noticed the gourmet coffee cup in Dianna's hand? Oh, probably because she was having a full-blown panic attack from running into her here in the first place. No big deal.

"Coffee machine?" Sasha asked.

Dianna pointed behind them to the space where the antiquated sludge machine had been two weeks prior. Abby had made a few phone calls and requested that all the self-serve machines be upgraded in the hospital. She hadn't given it much thought beyond that—in fact, she'd completely forgotten about it until now.

Dianna continued, "They're mighty fancy. It was surely a splurge for the board. But since you're queen of the write-offs, I'm sure it all worked out. The coffee is top notch—I think the patients and their families are going to be thrilled."

"Thanks," Abby replied dumbly. Sasha's hand twitched on her hip and she wondered how quickly she could get Dianna to leave.

"Anyway, it was nice meeting you, Sasha." Dianna turned to go and Abby thought she might have gotten away scot-free until Dianna turned back to add, "Do me a favor? Tell your mother to return my mom's phone calls. She's been bitching that Edie's missed three bridge games this month. Their team is in a tailspin. She swears the whole country club is talking about them." Dianna rolled her eyes and sighed. "Lord knows we don't need that kind of drama."

"Sure thing." She could feel Sasha's eyes boring a hole in the side of her head. Fuck.

Dianna waved good-bye and was gone before Abby could think of an escape plan to join her.

"Edie's your *mother*?" Sasha's arm was off her waist faster than she had a chance to comprehend what had just happened. "And what board is she talking about?"

"Sasha. I can explain." She couldn't look at her though. Abby hated herself.

When Sasha didn't say anything, Abby mustered her courage to look up at her and immediately regretted it. Sasha looked so betrayed Abby didn't think she'd ever get the image out of her head.

"What the fuck, Abby?" Sasha ran her hand through her dark hair and Abby felt nauseous.

"It's not—it's just that..." She didn't know what to say.

A look of understanding crossed Sasha's face and the betrayed expression shifted to one of anger. "Let me help you here. How many times have I met Edie, your mother, and you didn't think to mention that to me? Come to think of it, I recall you telling me that you were colleagues, colleagues through your nonprofit job, except she was more of the philanthropic type. Because she's a *Davenport*." Sasha turned and pointed to the sign over the elevator, her voice a sharp hiss. "As in Davenport Memorial Hospital. As in Davenport Charitable Services. As in you are a fucking Davenport and you didn't think to mention it to me?"

"Sasha, it's complicated—" Abby felt faint.

"Complicated? What's complicated is that you have been fucking me for weeks and you didn't think that warranted you being honest with me? Like I didn't deserve the simple courtesy of knowing that the woman we kept running into, who is dating my frigging boss by the way, is your mother?" Sasha shook with rage.

"Sasha—" Abby didn't get anything else out.

Sasha shook her head, her eyes welling with tears. "How am I supposed to even look at you right now? I *needed* you, I trusted you. I thought we had something special. I've spent the last few weeks falling in love with someone I know nothing about." Sasha wiped away a tear before something appeared to occur to her. "What else don't I know about you, Abby? What other secrets are you keeping? Were you even a member of Samantha's bachelorette Rolodex or is that a bunch of bullshit, too?"

Abby wasn't sure at what point during Sasha's speech she had started to cry, but she was full-on bawling now. "Sasha, please."

Sasha scoffed. "Forget it. I don't want to know anymore. Our entire relationship is built on a lie." She shook her head. "Just leave."

Abby was panicking. This had gone horribly wrong, but there had to be something she could do, something she could say. She reached for Sasha's hand but Sasha pulled it back like she'd been burned.

"How foolish of me to ask you to go, being as you own this hospital and all." The hurt on Sasha's face made Abby sob even harder. "Just leave my family alone. You've done enough damage already. Let me watch my father die in peace."

Sasha cursed under her breath and turned, walking right out of Abby's life.

CHAPTER TWENTY-ONE

Did you try calling her?" Her mother nudged her elbow with her designer bag and Abby contemplated launching it across the room.

"Of course I called her, Mom. I've called her about a hundred times. She doesn't want to talk to me." Abby was sick of talking about Sasha. She was sick of thinking about Sasha. And yet she couldn't seem to stop missing Sasha. None of that mattered though, not anymore.

Her mother looked pained. But to her credit, she didn't say anything. Which Abby would have preferred if instead of prying her mother wasn't giving her the most pathetic expression she had ever seen.

"What, Mom?"

Her mother seemed to hesitate. She sat down next to Abby and helped her put on her necklace. "She's mad." Her voice was soft and soothing. "She has every right to be—"

"This pep talk sucks, Mom." Abby knew her mother was right, but that didn't mean she wanted to hear it.

Her mother tried again. "Clearly you feel very strongly about her and she let you know that she felt very strongly about you."

Abby had replayed that fight over and over in her mind these past few weeks and the part that always stung the worst was when Sasha had told her she was falling in love with her. In *love*. Love was easily the most profound and important four-letter word Sasha had ever uttered in her presence, and what should have been a joyous feeling surrounding it was instead shame and devastation. Sasha had been falling in love with her and she'd ruined it. It kept her up at night. It kept her up at night because somewhere along the way, she'd felt the same way about Sasha and hadn't been brave enough to admit it. She hadn't been brave during any of this. At all.

"Mom. You're making me feel worse with every word. Please. Just let it go." Abby brushed her mother's hand away and flattened the necklace to her collarbone, using the reflection in the mirror in front of them to help her center it.

"You need to tell her you love her and that you were wrong, because this Abby"—her mother motioned up and down her frame—"this Abby is grouchy and sad and miserable to be around."

Abby had no more bark left. Her mother's words hit all the right spots and she was melting into a puddle of tears before she could stop herself.

Her mother rubbed her back and pulled her against her chest, soothing along her back and her neck. "Sh, sh. It's not too late, you can fix this. Pick up your bootstraps and apologize. Start fresh."

"It's too late," Abby cried into her mother's neck. "It's too late and I'm a terrible person and I deserve to be heartbroken."

Her mother's hand stopped its soothing circles and instead pushed Abby back so that they were facing each other, eye to eye. Her mother smoothed her thumb under Abby's eyes and she sighed. "You are not a terrible person. You made a decision that may not have been the best, but you did it out of a sense of self-preservation." She brushed a loose strand of hair behind Abby's ear before she continued. "Abby, all along you told me that you wanted the chance to get out from under the shadow of your name. I get it. I do. So tell her that. Give her a chance to understand where you were coming from."

"You're assuming I could even get her to listen. Even if I could, she'd never forgive me." Abby's shoulders slumped. That was the realization she had come to after a series of unanswered texts and sleepless nights. Why should Sasha even give her the time of day?

"You've got nothing to lose, Abigail." Her mother stood and pulled her into a hug. "Don't give up on love, Abby. It's all there is in life."

There was a knock at the door before it opened and Luke joined them. "Ready, ladies? The gala starts in twenty minutes."

"Luke, honey. Give us five minutes to fix our makeup and we'll be right down."

He nodded but not before giving Abby an understanding nod. "Take all the time you need."

Abby sighed as she looked in the mirror. "This is going to take more than five minutes."

"I'll help. Many hands make light work." Her mother nudged her and she laughed.

"You make it sound like this is going to be a lot of heavy lifting." Abby picked up a tissue and dabbed under her eyes.

"I'm just being a realist, darling." Her mother was teasing her, and she was grateful for a reprieve from the hurt, even for just a moment.

❖

Samantha Monteiro smiled and graciously thanked what seemed like the dozenth guest to offer her congratulations on her recent nuptials. This was one of the first public events since her wedding to Lucinda and the glow had not worn off. She loved celebrating her love.

"This newlywed thing is the best." She slid her hand into Lucinda's and leaned against her. "Why didn't I do this earlier?"

Lucinda scrunched her nose with a laugh. "I should have proposed sooner?"

Samantha considered this. "At the end of our first date would have been more than appropriate. I definitely would have said yes."

"Oh? Is that so?" Lucinda pulled her close by their clasped hands and brushed her nose along Samantha's ear. "Because if I recall, our first date ended with some really fantastic and mind-blowing kissing. The kind of kissing that made me want a million more dates with you."

Samantha turned her head to bring their lips together. She never got tired of kissing Lucinda. "Precisely my point. No one is saying remove the kissing part, but perhaps you could have proposed after—or even, if you wanted to be really romantic, during—the kissing. Then you would have guaranteed *all* the dates. Forever."

"If you'd said yes, you mean." Lucinda's blue eyes sparkled as she spoke.

"I already told you I would have said yes." Samantha wiggled her ring finger as proof. "That's clearly a given in this scenario."

"What if you were terrible in bed though? Wasn't it in both of our best interests to try that out a few times before we made it all death-do-us-part?" Lucinda teased.

Samantha scoffed. "As if that was ever in question."

Lucinda shrugged.

"Are you serious?" Samantha was offended.

"No." Lucinda kissed her again, smiling against her lips. "But you could have been a total pillow princess. The hot ones always are."

"Sweeping generalizations abound." Samantha nipped at Lucinda's bottom lip. "Luckily for you, I'm not."

"Far from it." Lucinda's expression was genuine. "You're everything I ever could've asked for and more. That's my favorite part about being a newlywed. The part where I'm actually married to you."

Samantha's heart doubled in size. "So not just all the hot, newlywed sex then?"

"That helps." Lucinda ran her hands along Samantha's sides, settling at her hips. "But we had pretty hot pre-newlywed sex, too. I think we do just fine in that department."

"Says you," Samantha purred. "I personally think we should have more of it."

Lucinda gave her a very serious nod. "You're right. Let's bail on this thing and get to work immediately. That dress looks much too constricting. Let's get it off."

Samantha slapped at Lucinda's hands and shook her head. "I've created a monster."

"A sex monster," Lucinda corrected her.

"As much as that sounds like the ideal way to spend this evening, and don't get me wrong, I really, really mean that, we have some work to do tonight."

Lucinda regarded her with suspicion. "Work? We're working tonight? I thought we were attending a friendly neighborhood museum gala—" She stopped herself. "Forget it. Forget I said anything at all. Clearly, you're the mastermind here. So, tell me, love, what kind of work are we doing tonight?"

Samantha loved that Lucinda could be playful and teasing one moment and sexy the next moment without any apparent change of gears. But what she loved most about Lucinda was the way she always supported her, in every crazy endeavor. Always. Tonight was no different.

"The most important work, Lucy. The work of love." She blinked flirtatiously and Lucinda chuckled.

"I figured. Who are we helping tonight?" Lucinda looked around the room, scanning the gala guests.

"Abby." Samantha had met with Edie twice in the last few weeks to see how things were progressing with Luke. She was pleasantly surprised to hear they were doing well and on the road to a more serious courting relationship. But during their meetings, Edie had mentioned that things were in flux between Abby and Sasha. This was devastating news. Samantha had really felt like they were a perfect pair, but had stepped out of the matchmaking process since the night of the auction. Abby had to do this work on her own if it was going to work out this time, and any involvement from Samantha would only slow down the spark that Samantha could see from a mile away. They were perfect for each other. She knew it. There was no way this flame was going to fizzle out. Not on her watch, anyway.

"Abby?" Lucinda's brow furrowed. "What's wrong with Abby? I thought she had a good thing going with Sasha. I'm lost."

"She does." Samantha corrected herself. "Well, she did. She still can. There's been a little setback. We're trying to right the train on the tracks, so to speak."

"All right, I'm game. How're we doing that?" Lucinda looked focused, motivated. Samantha fell in love with her a little more.

"By making sure Sasha knows exactly how Abby feels." Samantha glanced left and right before lowering her voice. "The hard part will be getting them in the same room at the same time."

Lucinda dipped her head to hear what she had to say. "Why's that?"

"I get the impression Sasha is avoiding her." Samantha was undeterred. "We may have to be a little sneaky about making it happen."

"I'm shocked. Really?" Lucinda deadpanned.

Samantha rolled her eyes. "It's already in motion. I had a contingency plan in place weeks ago. Now it's all about the execution and timing."

"I'll never understand the inner workings of your matchmaking brain, but I'll be the first to admit it never ceases to amaze me. You're kind of incredible."

"Good thing you married me, then. Even if I had to propose first." Samantha scanned the room until she found the person she'd been looking for. "It's go time."

She led Lucinda in the direction of her target and hoped she would be able to live up to Lucinda's praise. She hoped her intuition had been enough and that tonight she would help reignite a match, and not strike out in the process.

❖

Abby accepted a champagne flute from the passing waiter and watched her mother socialize in the corner. She was so good at this. And she glowed as she introduced Luke to all of her country club friends. He was handsome and dapper and good for her, but he also made her look good, which on a night like tonight mattered very much. The fact that they seemed to be a good match in real life outside of this pomp and circumstance was just the cherry on top.

Abby reached into her purse to check her cell phone for the time. There weren't any pockets in couture and a watch wouldn't work with this dress, so she was chained to her phone for timekeeping. She had twenty minutes before the work of the evening began. Work. Her mother was exceptional at this kind of stuff, but to Abby, this was work.

Her mother and the Davenport Charitable Foundation were being honored tonight at the Isabella Stewart Gardner Museum. As one of the sole board members who was also family, Abby had been asked to say a few words in addition to presenting the public service award to her mother. If not for that, she would have skipped this event entirely. The last thing she wanted to do was be social and pretend to be normal when she felt anything but.

She sipped her glass and assessed her audience. The crowd was full of the usual suspects—the shrimp cocktail hoarder from the dating auction, and a few of her mother's bridge friends, including Rachel Rabin, although her daughter Dianna seemed to be absent tonight, much to Abby's relief. It was a plethora of Boston's wealthiest art supporters, hobnobbing over passed hors d'oeuvres and getting an early peek at the newest art exhibition hosted by the Gardner.

A familiar laugh off to her left drew her attention. She hadn't expected to see Samantha here, and yet, there she was. A part of her wanted to run over and talk with her to ask for help or guidance in getting Sasha back. But another part was terrified of admitting that things with Sasha had fallen apart. She was torn. Before she could decide to be brave she noticed who Samantha was talking to—it was Aaron Burger and he was dressed like a waiter.

Her mouth got dry and her throat felt tight as she looked around the room. If Burger was here as a catering waiter, then that meant Sasha's lieutenant's catering company was probably in charge of the evening. Which meant there was a very good possibility that Sasha was here as well. Fuck. What would she say to her?

As if her panic were audible, Samantha looked over in her direction. Samantha pointed to her and Aaron nodded before he disappeared. Samantha walked toward her and Abby actually considered fleeing. Where would she go?

"You look like someone just kicked your puppy." Samantha kissed her cheek and handed Abby's empty glass to a passing waiter, a waiter she recognized as Jonah from Samantha's wedding. This was definitely the same catering company.

"I'm allergic to dogs." Abby sighed, understanding what she meant. "I've been meaning to talk to you."

"I assume you mean *return your calls*, right? Because I've left you a voicemail or two." Samantha's face was kind—she wasn't chastising her. Abby was grateful for that.

"Yeah. That. I'm the worst." Abby felt unsettled. Every time someone with dark hair walked by, she panicked and thought it was Sasha. It had been a few weeks since she had seen her, and the anticipation of possibly seeing her again felt like dying.

"She's not here." Samantha took her hand and soothed it.

"Oh." A wave of disappointment washed over her. She had the sudden urge to cry.

Samantha stepped in front of her, a small smile on her face. "Yet. She's not here, yet."

Abby's heart rate picked back up. "What do you mean *yet*?"

Samantha's smile broadened. "I mean *yet*. She's on her way. She'll be here shortly. She got a little delayed leaving the house—they're transitioning her father back home."

Luke had been secretly giving Abby updates about Sasha and her family over the past few weeks. She had respected Sasha's wishes and distanced herself, but Luke would sneak Sasha updates into conversation over the family dinners she'd had with him and her mother of late. It was a nice thing, the reinstated family dinners. She liked the feeling of a family unit. It was an opportunity for her and Luke to bond. He clearly respected and cared for Sasha and he acknowledged Abby's feelings for her as well. Sasha had brought them closer together.

"I'd heard that." Abby was glad to have another source confirming the news, but saddened also that she wasn't able to be there for Sasha during what was likely a difficult time in her life. It was a double-edged sword, the elation she felt about Duncan getting better paired with the deep-seated regret she had about missing a moment in Sasha's life. It was not lost on Abby how quickly she had fallen for her.

"Listen, we don't have much time, so let's get to it." Samantha put her hands on Abby's shoulders, grounding her. "Your mother filled me in on what happened. I'm all up to date. But that's not important. What's important is that you're going to win Sasha back tonight. And I'm going to help."

It sounded too good to be true. Abby didn't think she could stomach seeing Sasha again face to face, let alone be rejected. "Wait. My mother *what?*"

"Focus." Samantha shook her gently. "We're running out of time. You're going to go onstage in no time flat and we have some work to do ahead of time. But first I need you to answer two very important questions."

Abby felt like she was on a Tilt-A-Whirl. "Questions? What kind of questions?"

Samantha's hands slid down her shoulders and loosely clasped her hands. "Your mother tells me you love Sasha. Is that true?"

"Yes." Abby didn't have to think about that one. She'd thought about it long and hard every night she'd spent alone since their fight at the hospital. The more time she was apart from Sasha, the clearer it was: she'd been in love with Sasha since their glassblowing date, maybe even since the safety training at the school. Somehow, without her knowing it, Sasha had broken through her walls and become the one person she didn't want to live without.

"Great." Samantha looked elated. "Okay, how do you feel about grand gestures?"

If it helped her win Sasha back, she'd do just about anything. "How grand are we talking?"

"The grandest." Samantha looked so sure of herself, Abby couldn't help but feel encouraged.

CHAPTER TWENTY-TWO

Sasha pulled up to the designated parking area for the catering employees behind the museum and checked the time. Damn. She was *real* late. And not the late like on-time late that she already disliked—she was like an hour after the set-up time kinda late.

She hopped out of the car and pulled on the vest she had hanging in the back seat, using the car's side mirror to make sure the shirt was tucked and her hair looked good. She'd had time to do her makeup while she was waiting for her mother to get home from her shift at work, but they'd had to train a new home health aide, and it had taken longer than anticipated to orient her to all of Duncan's new and complex needs. Luckily, Casey had been super understanding and told Sasha to turn up when she could. But still, she didn't want him to think she was taking advantage of him. She needed this money and this job. She couldn't afford to miss out on an opportunity like this one. Especially not now.

As she headed through the back entrance of the museum to the pop-up kitchen Elise and Casey would be using for hors d'oeuvres, she let herself think about all of the changes that had happened lately. Her father's health had improved almost overnight. His white blood cell count decreased and his oxygen saturation improved as his infection began to recede. He was off the ventilator and using the nasal cannula for oxygen after a very short wean. Gradually, his color returned, and although he was still very weak and still very pale, he had some life in him that had been missing for weeks. She almost couldn't believe her good fortune; she'd all but resigned herself to losing him. But having him back home brought on a new batch of trouble and worries. He needed around-the-clock care to help him return to his prior level of functioning. He would still be dependent on oxygen and medication to help him breathe for the rest of his life, but at least he would be able to resume his *Family Feud* marathons and hassle her mother again. Her mother had increased her work hours to help cover costs on the now necessary aides that her father needed, and Sasha had maxed out her overtime at the firehouse. This catering job was the only thing keeping their heads above water. And at this rate, soon this wouldn't be enough.

"Sasha, good to see you. Everything okay at home?" Casey greeted her with a handshake and a slap on the arm. His concern was genuine. She was grateful for his friendship during this time.

"Yeah. No. It is now. New girl working tonight, long story. All set now, though. Thanks for asking." Sasha straightened out her vest. "I'm good to go. Where can I help?"

Casey nodded and she was grateful he didn't press her for any more information. She was keeping it together, but just barely. Talking about her father's improved health always had her just at the brink of tears these days. It was a terrible feeling to have your joy stamped out by the fear of inescapable debt.

"Shaun is managing the main bar in the back, and Jonah is running between the floor and the kitchen but he could use some help." Casey pulled out his clipboard and showed her a map of the event space. "There's an award presentation that happens after the cocktail hour finishes." He checked his watch. "Which will be any minute or so now. We're serving light apps and hors d'oeuvres afterward to be handed out in the new exhibit area that opens after the ceremony. We'll need lots of man power here and here, as this is where the most foot traffic will be."

Sasha nodded and followed along as he drew Xs on the paper, à la football drills. "Got it."

"Burger is back on shift tonight." Casey sighed and ran his hand through his hair. "We needed the extra hands and he's been begging to get back to work. So keep an eye out for him. There's a lot of expensive art on display tonight and the last thing I need is to be responsible for any damage again."

"Wow. Desperate times, desperate measures, huh, Lieutenant?" Sasha was teasing him. She was glad Burger was back in his good graces. He was a good kid, after all. "I'll make sure he limits his clumsiness to the kitchen."

"I heard that," Elise supplied over Casey's shoulder, her chef's whites already covered in a variety of colorful stains. She pointed a wooden spoon at Sasha. "You best keep him away from the dessert trays. It's taken me more than three days to get those three-dimensional sugar bridges perfect. One rogue swipe of his hand and all of those cheesecake toppers will be shattered."

She looked over at the dessert area and was floored—dozens of small dessert plates were in position, each featuring two bite-sized cheesecake morsels topped with fresh raspberries and a sort of red sugar glaze, connected by arching sugar bridges, so tissue thin they were almost clear. Sasha could see why Elise was concerned—they looked so fragile even she was afraid to walk near them.

"I would never dream of letting him ruin dessert." She crossed her heart and nodded, holding up three fingers. "Girl Scout's honor."

Elise exhaled, a look of relief on her face. "God, I'm glad you're here."

"Me, too," Casey added as he handed Sasha an empty tray. "Start with helping Jonah."

Sasha took the tray and headed for the door when Elise called out to her. "Hey!"

"Yeah?"

"Take this. You could use a little pop on those lips tonight." Elise tossed Sasha the red lipstick she'd used at Samantha's wedding.

Sasha caught it and tried not to frown. This was the lipstick she'd used to try to convince Abby to forgive her, to dance with her...It'd worked. That night started what had become one of the most important and profoundly emotional relationships she'd had in her adult life. It had started with an unintended insult but ended with a kiss. A kiss that led to many more and many nights of unbridled passion. Abby's presence in her life had been sorely missed these past few weeks, especially with the change in her father's health. It had saddened Sasha to feel so alone again, after having had Abby by her side during the worst of her father's health crisis. She'd missed her touch, her kiss, but mostly she'd missed the feeling of closeness. She'd felt empty since Abby had been gone. But Samantha's wedding was a long time ago, long before she'd found out that Abby had been intentionally keeping things from her. She looked at the tube in her hand and shook her head, walking back to Elise to hand it back to her. "I don't know about this tonight, Elise."

Elise shoved it back in her hand and closed her fingers around it. "Trust me. Wear it. You look great in red, Sash. Look good, feel good—remember?"

Sasha sighed. "I'll think about it."

"Put it on, or you're washing dishes with me all night." Elise crossed her arms, blocking Sasha's way to the exit.

"You should probably do as she tells you, McCray," Casey added from behind his clipboard. "She's the real boss around here. What she says goes."

Sasha decided not to argue. "Fine. Thank you."

Once the lipstick had been applied and inspected by Elise, Sasha was shuttled out of the kitchen just as the crowd began to take their seats. The emcee took the stage and began introducing the night's award recipient. She headed to Shaun at the main bar to see where she was most needed.

"Hey, Sash." Shaun smiled at her broadly as he lined up rows and rows of wineglasses. "Glad you made it."

"Me, too." Sasha was happy for the distraction. She pointed to the glass army he was assembling. "Wine on the agenda tonight?"

"Lots of it." Shaun nodded and pointed to the schedule Casey had left behind the bar. "Passed champagne with the cocktail hour, open bar with mixed drinks and beer at the three bars in the room, passed house wine during the museum tour portion of the evening."

Sasha nodded. She was so impressed with Casey and Elise. Since Samantha's wedding, they'd been booked for no less than three major events. By the presence of the press assembled at the back right of the room, tonight's event was no different. This was a job Casey had been very excited about, a job Samantha had first mentioned that time she came by the station to talk to Sasha about the auction. Ugh. The auction. Her heart sank. Everything seemed to remind her of Abby these days.

"Say," she asked Shaun, "what's tonight about anyway? I've been so busy with my old man, I didn't have a chance to ask Casey what we're here for." The audience behind Sasha applauded, but she'd missed all of what the emcee had said. It didn't concern her, not really anyway, but she was curious just the same. There was a flash to her right from the photographer's camera. This seemed like kind of a big deal.

Shaun topped off a row of white wine glasses before uncorking a red. "We're here to serve food and merriment." He winked at her. "But I've been told someone's getting a big humanitarian award or something before the museum debuts their new exhibit."

"No kidding? Wow."

Burger appeared at Sasha's side. He looked a little nervous. "Hey, Sasha."

"Burger." She reached out and fixed the button on his vest that had come undone. "Don't tell me you broke something already. I just got here."

"Broke something?" Burger pouted when he realized she was teasing him. "I didn't break anything—"

"Yet." Shaun chuckled behind them as he lined up more glasses.

Burger rolled his eyes. "One time, it was one time."

Sasha patted his arm. "Glad you're back, bud."

Burger smiled. "I took your advice and offered to work for free. Casey thought it was a great idea. Hopefully, after tonight I'll have almost paid off my debt. Thanks for the suggestion, Sash."

"Anytime, probie."

His smile faltered as he looked past her. She pivoted to see what he was looking at, but he grabbed her shoulder, turning her toward him again.

"Okay, that's enough bonding, Burger. Hands off the merchandise." Sasha tried to shrug off his grip but he tightened it.

"No can do, Sash. I need you to, uh, stick around here for a moment." That nervousness from before was back.

"What're you talking about?" Sasha tried to shake him off again, this time nearly succeeding.

He lunged forward and wrapped her up in a bear hug, easily using his height and strength to lift her feet off the floor, pinning her against him.

"Burger. What the hell?" Sasha squirmed and kicked at his shins.

"Ouch. McCray! Quit it." Burger hissed in her ear, his voice a harsh whisper. "Listen, listen. I need you to listen."

"Listen to what?" She wound her foot back to kick him again when he spun her in his arms, facing her toward the stage. From her vantage point in the back of the room, she could make out an attractive blonde ascending the stairs of the stage to the mic. It was *her* attractive blonde. Abby swept across the stage to a sea of applause and Sasha stopped squirming.

"I'm going to put you down now, McCray. But you have to promise to stop kicking me. And listen. Can you do that?" Burger's arms around her loosened and her feet touched down on the floor.

She nodded, but once his arms released her, she kicked him as hard as she could in the shin.

"Fuck. Seriously?" Burger huffed. "Just listen, would you?"

Any thoughts Sasha had of leaving vanished when Abby spoke into the mic, her eyes locked with Sasha's. "I'm here to present the Humanitarian Award tonight to my mother, Edie Davenport. But before I tell you about all of Edie's amazing contributions to Boston and her undying support of the arts, I want to tell you about this amazing person that I met. This selfless, brave, infinitely emotional woman taught me how to live and love in a way I'd not experienced before. I'm madly in love with Sasha McCray and I need everyone here to know it."

CHAPTER TWENTY-THREE

As Abby looked out into the audience in front of her, she felt an eerie calm settle in her chest. She'd rehearsed the speech for her mother a dozen times, but this first part was going to be all improvisation. Considering she'd done nothing to emotionally prepare for this moment, the calmness should have been unsettling. But it wasn't. She didn't have to prepare for this part because she was speaking from the heart, probably for the first time ever. It just so happened to be in front of a room full of people and press. No pressure or anything.

She smiled at her mother and Luke. Her mother's words from earlier were fresh in her mind—she'd use that now. They would be her strength; they would be her beacon. Her eyes found Sasha in the back of the room, held in place by Burger just like Samantha had promised. She'd have her chance to try to make amends. But she'd only get one shot at it.

"Thank you for joining us. As I'm sure you are aware, I'm here to present the Humanitarian Award tonight to my mother, Edie Davenport. But before I tell you about all of Edie's amazing contributions to Boston and her undying support of the arts, I want to tell you about this amazing person that I met. This selfless, brave, infinitely emotional woman taught me how to live and love in a way I'd not experienced before. I'm madly in love with Sasha McCray and I need everyone here to know it."

A smattering of applause followed her proclamation, the audience clearly not knowing where she was going. She laughed and nodded.

"I know what you're thinking—who's this Sasha person and why is Abby Rossmore hijacking her mother's spotlight for the evening? But I'm here to assure you that these things are both very closely linked." She exhaled and began.

"I'm an only child. I was raised by two loving and affectionate parents in a world of great privilege and good fortune. But one of the most important things they taught me growing up was to embrace my weaknesses and harness my strengths to help others. There have been times along the way I have faltered. More than once I've taken the easy way out or avoided something that frightened me. But my mother made sure to always help me find my path again. She's a leader, empathetic and compassionate in a way that isn't always typical of someone who heralds from a legacy like our family's. What makes my mother so unique and amazing is that she has been able to utilize her name to improve the lives of just about everyone she comes in contact with. Through her involvement with the Davenport Charitable Foundation and her dedication to Davenport Memorial Hospital, she has revolutionized access to the arts and healthcare, and established numerous grants and scholarships to empower Boston's youth. She is selfless in a way that cannot be learned, cannot be taught. It comes from a place of true goodness. A place in which the health and safety and opportunity for advancement of others must come before oneself.

"Those are the same qualities I found in Sasha. Sasha is, she's...incredible. She's kind and patient and selfless and brave in a way that I have not seen in anyone else but my mother. Which is why at first, it scared me. It scared me to know that someone else out there could have as much influence on me as the incomparable Edie Davenport. She is someone who makes you want to be a better person. She makes you want to live a fuller life. She helps you see the beauty in the darkest and most chaotic moments of life. I am grateful to Sasha for teaching me that my mother's gifts aren't just exclusive to her. They can be found within each of us, if we dare to be vulnerable enough to see them.

"My mother is the recipient for the Humanitarian Award tonight for many, many things that she has done through the work of her foundation and in the name of the Davenport family. We are a proud, dedicated family. But somewhere along the way, I'd forgotten what it meant to be a Davenport. I'd grown so used to running from the great shadow cast by my name that I'd nearly missed acknowledging the most important person in my life. My mother, Edie, is everything to me and more. But it took meeting someone like Sasha to help me remember what was most important—family, giving back, and being brave.

"It is with great honor I present my mother with this award tonight. Mom, you are an inspiration in everything that you do. Thank you for reminding me that love is all there is in life. And as you embark on this new journey"—she nodded toward Luke—"I hope you know how very sincerely and profoundly you have impacted me along the way. Thank you for continuing to be the example by which I set my standards. I love you."

Edie wiped tears from her eyes as she ascended the stage, and Abby let herself live in the moment. She soaked up the standing ovation from the crowd for her mother, the reason they were all there tonight. She'd meant every word she said. She'd be nowhere without her mother and Sasha had helped her be reminded of that.

Edie kissed her cheek and hugged her tightly as she whispered, "Thank you, darling. Now, go get your girl."

Abby didn't have to be told twice. She was off the stage and racing toward the back just in time to see Sasha slip behind the curtain into the still unrevealed exhibition wing. She took a deep breath and ducked in after her.

❖

Sasha's heart felt like it was beating out of her chest. She never would have guessed that this would be her night, hiding in the empty hallway of a museum after Abby Rossmore just announced that she was in love with her to an entire room full of Boston's most influential people. And the *Boston Globe*, she couldn't forget them.

"Sash." Abby's voice sounded behind her. She didn't turn. She didn't think she could face her, not yet.

She sighed and stepped further into the exhibit, willing her heartbeat to slow, her pride at war with her heart.

"Sasha. I'm sorry. I'm sorry I wasn't upfront with you from the beginning. You deserved better than that, you still do. You deserve better than me. And I hate to say that because I want nothing more in this world than for you to turn around and tell me you love me and you forgive me, but I know that these things aren't as easy as that. I know that you needed me to be honest with you when you were nothing but honest with me, and I know that I failed you. I am so, so sorry about that, Sasha. Truly."

Sasha had relived their argument at the hospital. She'd relived that feeling of betrayal over and over again and thought about what she'd said. She thought about what she could have said, what she'd wanted to say and been too angry to organize her thoughts. But all of that started to blur now. All she could hear was the sincerity of Abby's words, the vulnerability of her voice, the way it quivered with emotion. She didn't want to see the look on Abby's face right now, but she didn't think she could live with herself if she didn't turn around.

"Abby." She stopped walking and closed her eyes. She'd felt a myriad of emotions during Abby's speech. How could she not? Abby was saying everything that Sasha had felt when they were together, well, except for all the stuff about Abby's mother. That was new information to her, but the core of it, the heart and soul of it... Sasha loved Abby, and clearly, Abby felt the same. She didn't want to turn her back on that. She turned and opened her eyes.

Abby was close to her, close enough to touch, but she stayed in place, waiting. Sasha waited, too. It felt like forever before she spoke. "Okay."

"Okay?" Abby's eyes were wet and Sasha wanted so badly to cup her face and soothe her in that moment. But she didn't. She stood her ground and let herself collect her thoughts.

"Okay," Sasha repeated. Her mouth felt dry. She licked her lips and Abby's eyes followed her tongue. Her stomach flipped. She'd so missed that look in Abby's eyes, the one that made her feel desired and wanted and…loved. That was what she had seen before but hadn't been able to identify. Abby looked at her with a mix of emotions and feelings, but Sasha could see it clearly now. Abby regarded her with more than affection. She loved her.

Abby shifted in front of her, not moving closer, but not backing away either. Her voice was soft when she asked, "Okay…you accept my apology?"

Sasha considered her answer carefully. Abby was giving her an out. "I do."

It looked as if a weight had been lifted from Abby's shoulders. She stood a little taller, exhaling as if she had been holding her breath, and yet, she stayed in place. Unmoving. Until the dam broke and her tears flowed freely. And Sasha's heart broke for her, her heart broke to see how much it mattered to Abby that she be forgiven. Abby didn't rush to her, didn't fall on her knees and beg or wail. She gave Sasha the chance to decide what she wanted to do next.

"I want to really get to know you though, Abs. I don't want pieces of you or parts of the whole. I want the whole shebang. The good, the bad, the messy. I want the chance to fall in love with all of you, not just the parts you choose to show me. Okay? Can you promise me that you'll be upfront and transparent with me? I don't want a relationship built on secrets."

Abby's tears slowed and she blinked, a small smile on her face. "But you're saying that you aren't opposed to a relationship, right? Or did I imagine that in my ugly cry fog? Because I swear you just said you want a relationship. With me. As in *us*. Together."

Sasha laughed. "I did say that. You didn't imagine it."

"So, I'm really trying to respect your space and not jump you or anything, but can I kiss you now?" Abby looked like she was vibrating on the spot.

Sasha opened her arms and Abby stepped into them, wrapping her arms around Sasha's waist and resting her head at Sasha's shoulder. Abby fit so perfectly here. She'd missed this feeling.

"I believe there was promise of kissing." Abby's lips grazed the underside of Sasha's jaw and she felt all the parts of her warm up, like Abby had reignited a fire within her.

"A promise is a promise." Sasha dipped her head and connected their lips, savoring the taste and feel of Abby's lips against her own. It was incredible how it felt like an eternity since they'd last kissed. A void had been left when she'd pushed Abby out of her life, but she could feel it now, slowly filling back in, kiss by kiss. Like she was rebuilding a fallen wall, except this time it felt more like a gate, one that she wanted to access often. She wanted to let Abby in brick by brick.

Abby leaned back and broke their kiss to ask, "Did you say *shebang*?"

"Uh. Maybe? Why? Is that weird?" Sasha reconnected their lips because she missed them.

Abby smiled against them and added, "It's just, sort of, funny. I know what you meant, and maybe it's because I've missed your touch or your kiss or your everything, but my mind went straight to the gutter. Because, you know, *she...*"

"*Bangs.*" Sasha pulled back and Abby winked at her. "I missed you."

The sincerity from before returned to Abby's expression and she nodded. "Me, too. I meant what I said out there, Sash. I love you. And I want to share more of myself with you. I don't want to compartmentalize my life. Let's start over."

Sasha warmed as Abby repeated herself from before. She loved her. Sasha decided she could hear that forever. "I'd like that."

"Come over to my place. Let me cook for you. It'll be like a first date, a fresh start." Abby dropped her hands and stepped back, putting a little space between them. Sasha missed her closeness immediately.

"It's a date." The faint sound of applause from beyond the curtain could be heard. They both turned toward the noise.

"I should probably head out there, take some pictures or whatnot." Abby looked like she didn't want to go. The feeling was mutual.

"I'm supposed to be at work." Sasha ran her thumb under the bottom of her vest for emphasis.

Abby's eyes tracked the motion. They flicked back up to hers and Abby leaned forward once more for a final kiss. "Nice lipstick, by the way."

"It brought me luck before." Sasha held Abby's hand as they headed toward the curtain. Real life was waiting for them on the other side. She wanted to freeze this moment forever.

"Evidently, it brought me luck, too." Abby paused before leaving. "I'll see you out there?"

Sasha nodded and watched Abby slip under the curtain, out of sight. She never would have expected her night to turn out like this, but she was more than happy it had.

CHAPTER TWENTY-FOUR

The view from Abby's apartment, the penthouse of one of the tallest buildings in Downtown Boston, was unreal. It was the kind of space that Sasha had only seen in movies or those architecture magazines that her mother used to swipe from the dentist from time to time. The entryway led into the living room area that was as big as Sasha's entire apartment. Massive floor-to-ceiling windows ran the length of Abby's condo with not one but two balconies off the living room alone. Sheer curtains and electric shades were controlled by a remote that sat on Abby's designer coffee table which was positioned in front of a grand electric fireplace and an enormous television that had a mirrored finish, doubling as reflective glass.

The light colors and rich white fabrics made everything look custom made and inviting. But Abby's kitchen was what really blew Sasha away. The open concept design had an island that could seat at least six people. Marble-textured granite countertops with a waterfall finish accented crisp white cabinets, with glass fronts and smooth silver hardware. She had a wet bar at the edge of the designated kitchen space that flowed into a dining area. A massive dark wood table occupied the dining space with seating for eight. This home was clearly meant to host. She wondered if Abby ever threw parties here. It would be a shame if she didn't.

All of the furniture Sasha could see was high end and well made, the lighting and color choices clean and perfect. It was a designer's dream home, that was for sure. But even with the glossy surfaces and expensive appliances it still had a very welcoming, homey feel.

"Abby, this place is…" Sasha wasn't sure what to say.

"It's a bit much. I know." Abby stirred the contents of the pot and handed an empty wineglass to Sasha.

Sasha took the glass and poured the wine she'd brought into it, wondering if it was a good enough bottle. From the looks of the wine fridge and rack by the wet bar, she suspected not. "How long have you lived here?"

"About four years." Abby accepted the glass and waited to clink hers with Sasha's before she took a sip. "Mm, this is tasty. Thank you."

Sasha doubted it was the best Abby had ever tasted, but she chose not to dwell on it. "The whole doorman-concierge thing is kind of amazing."

Abby shrugged. "It spoils you. I'm afraid it makes me a little lazy. They'll carry in the groceries and change light bulbs if you want them to." She stopped stirring and looked up, backtracking. "I don't though. I do for myself with everything if I can. But I'll admit it's helpful when I have to move some heavy furniture, to just pick up the phone and all kinds of muscle arrives to save the day…I'm rambling. Sorry."

Sasha thought it was cute. Abby seemed so shy, almost ashamed of her space. "Does it make you uncomfortable, talking about your home?"

Abby looked up at her. "*Uncomfortable* isn't the right word. I'm not naïve to how it looks though. That being said, I live here because I love it and it's a sanctuary to me at the end of the day. But still, it's a bit much."

"You keep saying that." Sasha stepped closer to Abby and stroked her hand. "It's part of you, though. It's a part of your life, one that I want to know more about. I don't want you to be afraid to share it with me."

Abby frowned. "I'm not. Not exactly. It's just, your parents' home, the one you grew up in? It's perfect. It's everything a home should be—warm and inviting and with such rich history and familiarity. No home I have ever lived in has been that—"

"Small?" Sasha was teasing her.

"Well. Yes." Abby laughed. "You should see the monstrosity my mother lives in. She's got a groundskeeper for the groundskeeper."

"I'd like to see it sometime." She meant that. Being around this kind of wealth would take some getting used to but she'd be willing to try. "How is Edie?"

Abby paused. "She's good. She's head over heels for your chief."

"There's something about firefighters...You can't resist them." Sasha leaned against the island as Abby turned off the burner on the stove.

"That's true." Abby stepped into Sasha's personal space and kissed her. Sasha's hands fell to her hips, guiding Abby to the space between her legs. "They're just so *hot*."

"We aim to please." The wine tasted significantly better on Abby's lips. She decided this would be the only way to enjoy wine from now on.

"Oh, you've never denied me any pleasure, that's for sure." Abby's hand slid up into Sasha's hair and she moaned. She liked the direction their evening appeared to be headed.

Abby dragged her thumb over Sasha's bottom lip as she said, "I'm going to step back from you now, because I promised myself I'd make you dinner and that you'd be dessert. Does that sound all right with you?"

Sasha couldn't care less about what was in the pot. The only thing on her mind now was how warm it was where Abby's hips pressed against her own. She let her head drop back as Abby kissed along her neck. "I like this plan."

"Good. Because tonight is all about getting to know you and sharing myself with you." Abby nipped at her jaw.

"What kind of sharing are we talking about?" Sasha slipped her hand under the front of Abby's shirt, tickling the skin as Abby sucked on her pulse point.

"Oh, you know, the biblical kind." Abby was definitely marking her now. She loved it.

"Are you sure dinner can't wait?" Sasha asked. Abby rolled her hips against Sasha's and suddenly Sasha wasn't sure *she* could.

Abby licked the spot she had been sucking and leaned back. "Are you saying you'd rather have a tour of my house than try my grandmother's Bolognese?"

"Does the tour include your bedroom?"

"It can. If you ask nicely." Abby was so, so sexy.

"Please?" Sasha's request was rewarded with Abby's fingers gripping her belt buckle and tugging her away from the island.

"Well, since you're so polite."

Sasha reached to Abby's left and turned off the remaining burners. "Safety first."

"We'll set things ablaze elsewhere—is that what you're saying?" Abby made short work of the belt and soon it was on the island by the forgotten sauce.

"Mm-hmm. I have a feeling we'll be a flaming success."

"These fire references are endless, aren't they?" Abby walked them backward through the kitchen toward the hallway.

Sasha chuckled. "Hazard of dating someone so lit."

Abby rolled her eyes before pressing a searing kiss to Sasha's mouth. "I'm glad you're here."

"I am, too." Sasha slowed the kiss, drawing it out. She didn't want to rush anything tonight. She pulled back, brushing aside a hair on Abby's forehead. She let her fingers linger along her hairline as she spoke. "There's something I didn't tell you at the museum."

"Oh?" Abby's hand paused at her waistband. A look of concern settled on her face.

Sasha cupped her cheek and stared deeply into her eyes. "In the interest of full disclosure, I want to honor what I said to you. I don't want there to be any secrets between us. But I wasn't entirely honest with you that night."

Abby inhaled, closing her eyes briefly as she leaned into Sasha's palm. Her free hand held Sasha's a little firmer against her cheek before she looked back up at Sasha. "Okay. I'm ready. What is it you wanted to tell me?"

Any doubt Sasha had, dissolved in that moment. The moment when Abby was so brave and so vulnerable. It was exactly the kind of thing Sasha had wanted all along: true, honest, scary, feelings. "I love you."

Sasha decided Abby's grin could light up the whole city.

"So, just to be clear, you love me." Abby looped her arms around Sasha's neck and Sasha felt whole in a way she hadn't in weeks.

"I do." Sasha settled her hands on Abby's hips, holding her close, her thumbs tracing the hem of Abby's shirt.

"Whoa, Sash. Let's not get ahead of ourselves." Abby winked and rested her forehead against Sasha's. "No marriage proclamations just yet. You haven't tasted my Bolognese."

Abby's humor was almost as exciting as her lips, or her skin, or her everything else. Almost. But not quite. Sasha thumbed open the button of Abby's pants and pulled them down a little. "I'm sure we'll get there, but there's something more important I'd like to taste first."

Abby let out a low moan and it was the single best thing Sasha had heard all night. "God. I love you."

Correction. *That* was. "I love you, too. Now let me show you how much I missed you."

Abby took her hand and led her to a bed much, much larger than Sasha's childhood twin. But Sasha made sure she stayed close, not willing to let Abby slip away, ever again.

Chapter Twenty-five

A bby had been on cloud nine for so many days in a row now she didn't think she'd ever come back down. Not that she ever wanted to. She was plenty fine up there in her new love high. It seemed like nothing could darken her day. Not a thing.

She looked at the stack of papers she was supposed to review for the foundation, but she had zero motivation. She picked up her phone for the fifth time in the past fifteen minutes and checked to see if Sasha had written back. She hadn't. Abby sighed and pushed her phone away, keeping it in sight just in case her screen lit up with a notification.

It wasn't that she was obsessed or anything, just things were going so well with Sasha, she didn't want to miss a moment. And she hadn't. Since the night Sasha came by her place for dinner, even though they only had dessert—and a lot of it, at that—things had been great. They saw each other often and spoke every day. It was exactly the type of relationship Abby had read about in all those romance novels she'd indulged in over the years but had never experienced for herself. She couldn't get enough of Sasha and she didn't think she wanted to.

But today was a station day and Sasha was at the firehouse. So she was a lot less accessible by phone today, just like all days she played with fires. Abby noticed those days felt the longest. And today was a particularly difficult day to have Sasha be unavailable to talk because tonight, Abby was going to meet Duncan. To say she was nervous was the understatement of the century.

Sasha had assured her over and over that meeting her dad was nothing to be nervous about, but Abby wasn't so sure. She had spent weeks at his bedside with Sasha and Valeria, hearing stories about his life and how much he meant to them. She had seen the look in Sasha's eyes when she whispered in his ear and softly called him her hero before she kissed his cheek. Sasha was always moved to tears in those moments, the quiet, somber moments Abby had felt honored to witness. It had shown Abby a side of Sasha that she didn't know existed. It had reminded her of the frailty of life and allowed her to open herself up to love.

Those weeks had been absolutely fundamental in the bond she'd formed with Sasha. Duncan's medical crisis had brought Sasha into her life in a way she'd never thought possible. The true miracle of it all was that he'd pulled through impossible odds to rejoin his family. Abby still wasn't over the fact that she and Sasha hadn't been in contact when Duncan's health started to improve. She hadn't been there when he was discharged home and Sasha had to have a ramp installed to get him into the house. She wasn't there. And that haunted her. It made her official first meeting with Duncan feel that much more significant. Abby viewed this as her second chance, a fresh start. Meeting Duncan McCray felt like a big step in her budding relationship with Sasha and she didn't want to fuck this up.

"You're going to give yourself wrinkles," her mother said from the doorway of her office. Abby had no idea how long she'd been there. She obviously didn't feel the need to announce herself with a knock like any civilized person.

"I hear there's Botox for such things." She was glad her mother was here. She could use the distraction.

"That's a slippery slope, dear. Luckily for you, I know a guy." Her mother raised an eyebrow in her direction. "Best Botoxer in all of Boston."

Abby pointed to her mother and feigned mock surprise. "Is that what happened? Your forehead hasn't moved in years. I just assumed you charmed the wrinkles away."

"And where do you think you get your charm from, if not from me?" Edie took the seat across from Abby's desk, her posture pristine as she crossed her legs. "You are positively oozing with charm, lovey. You'll be wrinkle free in no time. Feel free to resume that furrowed look from before."

Abby leaned back in her chair and tapped her fingers on the desk. "I'm nervous."

"About what?"

Abby resisted the urge to chew her cuticles. "I'm meeting Sasha's father tonight."

"Oh."

"Oh? *Oh*, I should be worried, or *Oh*, you get it?" Abby's palms were sweating.

"Oh. As in, *Oh, I understand*," Edie supplied with an empathetic expression. "It's scary meeting the family for the first time."

"That's the thing." Abby sighed. "I feel like I already know him. I was completely immersed in the essence of his life for those weeks at the hospital. He was all around us. His love of life and family was celebrated daily, even when he wasn't able to participate. I guess I'm afraid the person I see in my mind won't match the person who sits in front of me."

Edie considered this. "He sounds like a great man."

"If you hear Sasha tell it, he's the greatest." She looked at her phone again—still no texts.

"Is that what's really bothering you?" Edie asked.

Abby was lost. "What?"

"Are you worried that he won't like you?"

Abby swallowed hard. "Well, I wasn't until right now."

Edie cooed. "Abby, please. There's not a thing about you that is unlikeable. Plus, you have all that antiwrinkle charm on your side. You'll do just fine."

Abby hoped her mother was right. Her phone screen lit up and she grabbed for it. Finally.

"You're smiling. Is that Sasha?" Her mother leaned forward to try and see the screen.

Abby covered it reflexively. Their texts had been known to get to inferno level of hotness on long shifts like this one.

"It is." Abby didn't bother trying to conceal her happiness. She'd waited a long time for this.

"You two make a beautiful couple."

"Thanks, Mom." Abby agreed. Seeing their reflection in the mirror with Sasha's arms wrapped around her from behind was one of her favorite things, usually because it led to other *things*. But still. She sighed. "These long shifts are the worst."

"Absence makes the heart grow fonder." Edie gave her an empathetic shrug.

"Whoever said that was clearly celibate and single." Abby poked at the files in front of her. "I have no ambition to adult right now. None."

"What are those?" Edie stifled a yawn.

"Boring." Abby yawned in response—it was contagious. "Some paperwork for the foundation. Evelyn dropped it off."

Edie made a face. "You're on your own with that stuff. I'm allergic to paperwork."

"This is why I handle all of the tedious, nerdy things, isn't it?" Abby opened the top folder and skimmed the first document. She closed the file. Her heart was not in this tonight.

"You handle it because you're much better at it than I am." Edie blew her a kiss as she stood.

"That sounds like a cop-out." Abby stretched in her chair. Her phone pinged again, and she reached for it. Her heart sank when she read it. "Shit. Sasha just canceled. She's picking up an extra half shift."

Edie perched at the edge of Abby's desk. "Okay. It's decided. We're going."

"Going where?" Abby rested her forehead on the desk in defeat.

"Ice cream. When times get tough, we get ice cream." Edie tugged at her arm until she stood up.

"But…there's adulting to do." Abby pointed to the folders weakly. If she wasn't going to see Sasha and get a chance to meet her father, then she should at least get some work done.

Edie pulled her toward the door, grabbing her purse off the chair. "It'll be there tomorrow. There's no guarantee that your favorite mint chip cone from Creedon's will be though."

Although Abby was disappointed she wouldn't be seeing Sasha later, a part of her was a little relieved that she'd have more time before meeting Duncan. Plus, any time she got to spend with her mother one-on-one these days was great. Her mother and Luke were going strong. She wanted to soak up as much mother-daughter time as she could. And if her mother was taking her to Creedon's, then she was definitely buying.

❖

"You're grinning like an idiot. You get laid or something?" Burger disrupted her daydream and she considered homicide.

"A lady never kisses and tells, Burgertime." She leaned back in her chair and rested her feet on the table. She was tired. The last two weeks with Abby had been magical. She'd had a lot of long nights spent getting reacquainted with her, which she wouldn't trade for anything in the world, but her station shifts were clustered together this week and her father's usual full-time caregiver was away on vacation. Her time away from Abby was spent training someone new and trying to calm her father down enough not to fire everyone who wasn't her mother or herself. She was tired. But things were good. So what if she was reliving a particularly fond memory or two while on shift?

"Since when are you such a prude?" Burger chewed with his mouth open and Sasha wondered if she could get her wadded-up gum wrapper in there between bites.

"Since I found out you have a crush on my girlfriend." She had caught him ogling her last week when Abby had stopped by the firehouse for a quick lunch date. Sasha made Casey order him to wash the bathrooms, twice.

Burger's mouth hung open. She could definitely get it in there. No doubt. "That's not…I don't—"

"Burger. It's cool. You have eyes. She's smoking hot. I get it." She rolled the foil tighter between her fingers. She'd need it to be dense to hit the target.

He breathed a sigh of relief. "Okay, cool. I thought you'd be mad. She's super hot."

Sasha launched the gum wrapper at his mouth, but her aim was a little off and she ended up hitting him in the eye instead.

"Ouch! What the hell?" He rubbed his eye and pouted.

"Wrong answer, Burger. That was a test. You failed." She shook her head. "Unbelievable. You have no shame, dude."

He raised his hands in defense. "It's not like I'm a threat or anything. She's clearly head over heels for you. And I assume things are going well, right? Because if they aren't, I'm happy to give her a shoulder to cry—"

"Feel free to stop right there, beefcake. Things are great. Thanks for asking." She looked down at her phone and smiled. Abby sent her the cutest frowning selfie. It was adorable. And heartbreaking because Sasha wanted nothing more than to finish her shift and introduce Abby to her father, but the opportunity for overtime didn't come up very often these days, so she'd jumped at the chance to extend her current shift just a little longer. She was already here, after all.

Normally, she didn't mind picking up an extra shift here or there, but she'd be lying if she said she hadn't been looking forward to tonight. Although she and Abby had seen each other quite a bit over the last few weeks, she'd not had the chance to introduce Abby to her dad. And her father was hounding her constantly about it. It had been entirely a scheduling thing—well, that and the fact that although her father was on the mend, there were still days he wasn't at his best. Those days he needed more sleep and extra help with walking. It was on those days he looked grayer than she liked. The update from her mother earlier warned that today was one of those days. She didn't want Abby to meet her father when he wasn't at his best, whatever that was. So the extra shift opportunity felt serendipitous. At least, that's what she was telling herself.

She stretched in her chair and cracked her neck. Things had been pretty slow around here, and maybe she'd be able to sneak in a nap to recharge. Her phone buzzed again. It was a picture of Abby smiling with her mother, the two of them holding ice cream cones. Abby had included a quick *Wish you were here* text with it. Sasha sighed. She hadn't spent a ton of time with Edie, but the time she had spent with her had been hilarious. Edie was a freaking riot. And on a more personal side, she'd noticed a really nice change in her chief, which she wholly attributed to Edie. Those Davenport girls were something else, she mused.

The photo of Abby and her mother looking so happy gave her a renewed sense of purpose. She was working this shift to help her family, even though it meant she missed out on ice cream with Abby and her mom. Providing for her parents was something that gave her great pride. It gave her a purpose. She wanted to do this to help them. Her father and mother had always gone above and beyond for Sasha her whole life. This was the least she could do. And without her, what would happen to them? She didn't want to think of it.

The firehouse siren bellowed, interrupting her reverie. It was time to get to work. She jumped up from the table and followed the rest of her unit down toward the truck. With practiced ease, she stepped into her hitch and boots, gearing up and climbing into the engine as it pulled out of the station.

"Where are we headed, Lieutenant?" she called toward Casey from the back of the cab, trying to project her voice over the roar of the engine.

"The Woodbourne neighborhood," he called back without turning around.

"Woodbourne?" Sasha's stomach dropped. That was her parents' neighborhood. "Is this a fire or a medical call?"

He turned in his seat. "A little of column A and column B. We have reports of a person in distress with oxygen on the premises. Someone mentioned something about a spark. Also, maybe the smell of gas. So prepare for anything." He directed that last part to everyone in the cab, but to Sasha, it meant something else entirely.

Sasha felt faint. She patted her pockets in search of her cell phone but found nothing. She must have left it on the table in the rec room. Shit.

"You okay, McCray?"

"Do we have an exact address?" She gripped the bench beneath her for stability. Her head felt foggy.

"We're waiting on confirmation. There's a possibility multiple homes are involved." The radio crackled on the dash and he reached for it, redirecting his attention to the dispatch operator on the line. "Go ahead."

From her location in the cab, she couldn't quite make out what dispatch was saying over the engine roar. She leaned forward, nearly falling out of her seat when the truck took a tight turn. Burger's hand was on her shoulder, pinning her against the seat.

"You good?"

Sasha didn't answer. She strained to hear her lieutenant's exchange with dispatch, but she'd missed it. She had to find out where they were going.

"Lieutenant?" Her last attempt to reach him fell on deaf ears. Within seconds, they pulled onto her parents' street, and to her horror, her mother was in the front yard, waving the truck down.

This could not be happening. Not again.

CHAPTER TWENTY-SIX

Ma. You need to calm down. I can't understand you."
She put her hands on her mother's shoulders and tried
to steady her. But it was pointless—her mother was a sobbing,
blubbering mess.

"Sash. This can't be happening, can it?"

She hadn't seen her mother like this, ever. Not even when her
father was hospitalized this last time, when things looked dire, did
her mother appear this distraught. She felt helpless.

"Ma. *Ma.* Chill. Come here." At a loss for what to do, she
reverted to what had made her feel better as a child. She hugged her
mother and tried to soothe up and down her back with her hands.
"Slow down. Say it slow. Tell me what happened."

Her mother hiccuped and gasped, her tears slowing enough for
her to speak. "It's a miracle, Sasha. A miracle."

Sasha exhaled and nodded. Yes, this was a miracle. It was a
freaking miracle that the fire call was for Mr. Dobrowski next door
and not for her father. Her mother was the one who called 911 when
she saw him fall off a ladder outside his house while trying to clean
the gutters, portable oxygen tank and all. She'd been flagging down
the truck for their neighbor and Sasha had never been so relieved.

"I mean, it's physics and stupidity that resulted in Old Man
Dobo hitting the deck, but if you want to call me being on shift a
miracle, then that's cool." She shifted in her jacket. This gear was
heavy when you didn't have the adrenaline of the job pumping
through you.

"That fool? No, that's not what I'm talking about." Her mother shook her head, fresh tears in her eyes. "It's all gone, Sasha. It's all gone."

"Are you feeling okay? Because the paramedics are right outside and I can have them check you out. You're not making much sense." Sasha had left the rest of her squad with her neighbor once she debriefed them on her knowledge of him. They had done a sweep of the property and neutralized any weak oxygen lines and seals. And there were many. Sasha was none too thrilled her neighbor was on oxygen and smoking cigars in the yard like a dumbass in such close proximity to her parents. Old Man Dobo was in deep shit, no matter how you looked at it.

"I'm fine." Her mother slapped at her hand when Sasha tried to check to see if she had a fever. "Listen to me."

"I'm listening to you ramble on like a madwoman." Sasha ducked as her mother swatted at her again. "Okay, okay. I'm listening. What's going on? Why are you crying?"

Her mother took a steadying breath and tried again. "Abby saved us."

"Say what now? Abby? My Abby?" Sasha reached for her radio. Maybe her mother really should be looked at.

"The debt is gone, Sasha. It's gone. All of it. And they are sending a check to pay us back retroactively for everything we've paid out. It's going to save us, Sasha. We won't lose the house now." Her mother was sobbing again, but this time, Sasha recognized happy tears.

"What are you talking about?" That was a lot of information for Sasha to unpack. "What do you mean the debt is gone?"

Her mother sighed with frustration. She reached behind Sasha and pulled out a letter. "The debt is gone. All of the medical debt, all of your father's bills and outstanding copays and equipment costs are gone. And this letter says they are going to help us find support to pay for his new caregivers. It's a miracle."

Sasha took the form but her hand was shaking. The only thing she could make out was Abby's signature, over her name and title. *Abigail Rossmore Davenport, Accountant, Davenport Charitable Foundation.*

"McCray. We gotta go. You ready?" Burger stepped into the open door to her parents' kitchen and thumbed toward the fire truck. "Oh. Hi, ma'am."

"Hi, Aaron. How's your mother?" Her mother wiped away tears as she took back the letter, holding it to her chest.

"Good. She's starting a new knitting group on Wednesday. It's called something like *In a Stitch* or some shi—stuff." Burger blushed.

"Tell her I said hello. Oh, I baked some brownies. Take that plate with the tinfoil back to the station. Make sure you save some for the other guys."

Burger's blush deepened and he nodded, thanking her sheepishly.

Her mother turned back to her and added quietly, "Tell her thank you. No, better yet. Bring her by. I want to thank her myself."

Sasha felt totally blindsided. She had no idea what to say or what even happened.

"McCray?" Burger was fidgeting behind her.

"I'll call you later, Ma. I want to talk about this." She stared at the back of the letter pressed to her mother's chest, trying to make sense of what she had said.

"Fine, fine. Just don't tell your father." Her mother lowered her voice to a whisper. "I don't want him to know we were struggling."

Sasha nodded. "Okay, Ma." She grabbed her helmet and headed for the door, following behind Burger.

The truck ride back was a blur. Sasha's mind was spinning from everything her mother had said. How was any of this possible? What did it mean? This seemed too good to be true. She was eager to get to her phone to text her mother for details. And then…Abby. What would she say to her?

The radio crackled and her lieutenant called back into the cab, "We got another call. We're closest, so we're heading over now. Hydrate. This one's got an active fire. It's a biggie."

Burger handed her a bottle of water from under the bench and she took it without acknowledgment. She looked out the window and mentally prepared for what was next. She'd need all her focus for an actual fire call. So far, tonight had taken a strange and unpredictable turn and suddenly she was dreading what else it might bring.

❖

Abby checked the clock as she paced inside the rec room of the fire station for what seemed like the millionth time. Luke had assured her they were on their way back, but that had been over an hour ago. She was getting worried. Correction, she had been worried for a while. Currently, she was worried *and* nauseous. Both of which seemed to be increasing the more time passed.

She'd grabbed ice cream with her mother and caught a movie but they had gone their separate ways when her mother mentioned that Luke was coming over, and Abby had gagged because that was way too much information. Shortly after midnight, her mother called to ask if she'd heard from Sasha. Evidently there had been a bad fire downtown and multiple fire companies were on the scene. Luke had been called in to help manage the chaos after a few firefighters had gotten hurt, and Edie wanted to make sure Sasha was okay.

Since then, aside from a few texts from Luke and his assurance they were on their way back, there had been radio silence. Sasha wasn't answering her texts and no one in the station could tell her anything.

So she paced and waited for them to get back. It seemed like eternity before the trucks pulled into the station. The sun had been up for hours and Abby was practically delirious. One by one they filed in, some limping, all of them covered in soot and ash with their faces obscured by smudges of dirt. Burger's arm was in a sling and black grime framed his nostrils. He coughed when he tried to say hello to her.

Before she had a chance to ask him about Sasha, she walked in, her jacket singed along the right arm and her face weary. Abby ran up to her.

"Oh, thank God. I've been trying to reach you. Are you okay?" She cupped Sasha's face and did a quick pat down of her body, pulling back when Sasha hissed in pain. "What's wrong?"

Sasha cradled her right arm gingerly with her left. She shrugged off her jacket and exposed a freshly bandaged right forearm. Abby could see it was oozing through the dressing. Her heart broke.

"Oh, Sash." She reached out to take Sasha's hand, but Sasha stepped back.

"Abby. You can't be here." Sasha looked around the rec room and appeared to be embarrassed.

"You didn't call me back. I was worried, Luke said—" Abby couldn't figure out why Sasha was so annoyed. Abby had been an absolute wreck for going on nine hours now. She'd been worried sick over whether Sasha was okay or not.

"Can we not do this right now?" Sasha frowned, her forehead creased with fatigue.

"Do what? Why are you so mad at me?" Abby's temper flared. Sasha was being rude for no reason.

Sasha grabbed Abby's elbow and led her out of the rec room into the quiet hallway space beyond. "Abby, you can't just show up at my work like a worried mother and make a scene."

"I'm not making a scene." She pulled her arm away from Sasha's grasp and huffed. "You're the one dragging me into hallways."

"What did you plan to do, huh, Abby?" Sasha held her injured arm to her chest, her other hand on her hip as she spoke. "Did you plan to swoop in here and save the day, just like that?"

"What are you talking about? I just wanted to make sure you were okay. I figured we could grab breakfast after your shift. What's your problem?" Abby had no idea why Sasha was being so antagonistic.

"My problem? My problem is you people think you can just solve everything by throwing money at it." Sasha's anger was palpable. "First you come in here and humiliate me in front of my crew by babying me after I came back from doing my *job*. Then you're annoyed that I'm not all sunshine and giggles about you interfering in my family's affairs."

Abby was starting to wonder if Sasha had oxygen deprivation. "I have no idea what you're talking about. And who are *you people*? What does that even mean?"

Sasha laughed in her face and Abby recoiled. "You don't get it, do you? This is the job. It's dangerous and scary and sometimes there are more important things happening in my day to day than texting you back at your every whim. You can't show up here after every fire and mother me. I have a mother. She's not you. I get plenty of flak from her about this. That position has been filled—you're off the hook." She scoffed. "But you probably don't get that, huh? That I have to work for a living to pay for things. It must be such a foreign concept to you. You're so used to writing checks and making everything all better—you don't know any other way, do you?"

Abby felt like she'd been punched in the stomach. What was Sasha talking about? What money? Why was this even coming up? "Sasha, clearly you're mad about something but I have no idea what."

Sasha was exasperated, that much was obvious. The feeling was mutual. "When were you going to tell me that you waved your magic pen and all of a sudden all of my family's medical debt was going to disappear? I thought we agreed on no secrets, Abby. That's a pretty big fucking secret."

"Sasha, I don't know—"

"Save it." Sasha threw her hand up in the air, cutting her off. "I saw your signature on the page, *Abigail Rossmore Davenport*, clear as day. I don't need your charity, Abby. I can provide for my family plenty fine without your fucking handouts."

Abby didn't know what to say. She had no idea where any of this had come from. What handout? Sasha didn't give her the chance to ask.

"Maybe it's best if you leave. I have a shift to finish." Sasha turned on her heel and stomped away, leaving Abby with all the questions in the world and no answers in sight.

Chapter Twenty-seven

Sasha's jaw ached from clenching it. She had been lying in her childhood bed, tossing and turning for hours before she gave up entirely, unable to sleep. It was hopeless. All of it.

She sighed and rolled to her side. The smiling faces of her parents and a younger version of herself greeted her. She groaned. This was awful. Nothing about any of this was easy. Everything was always so damn complicated.

Her chest felt heavy. She fought the memories of better times in this bed, so many nights and mornings wrapped up in Abby. Whispered affections and intimacies shared over naked flesh and under cotton sheets. Being in this bed, in this room, with those memories, felt like prison.

She replayed the conversation she'd had with Abby yesterday at the fire house, over and over. She'd been harsh. Mean, even. But for what reason? Because Abby had humiliated her, that's why. But she wasn't upset about her being at the station. In fact, it made her feel very emotional and vulnerable to have someone there who cared for her so deeply they'd wait and pace and panic because she wasn't back yet. She'd never had anyone worry that way, outside of her mother, and it was refreshing to be so loved and cared for. And yet, she'd told Abby it annoyed her. She told her it made her feel small and insignificant. Both were so far from the truth she couldn't imagine why she'd breathed them at all.

But that wasn't true either. As she looked back at her family's photograph she acknowledged she was upset because Abby had done the one thing she had never been able to: financially free her parents. And she wasn't quite sure what to do with those feelings. On the one hand, it was a freedom she doubted she would ever see. They weren't exactly worry free or anything, but they were no longer digging out of debt. They had opportunities and support from the community that they hadn't had before. She'd read and reread the letter, evaluating all the terms and conditions again and again. Before the end of the day yesterday, a social worker showed up from the hospital to help them navigate the home health care system and seek out extra financial support and equipment donations. They had gone from being all alone and piecemealing things, to having a case manager in place who did all the heavy lifting overnight. It was unreal. It was all because of Abby. And Sasha wasn't sure how that made her feel.

Shameful wasn't the right word. No. She felt inadequate. She *did* feel insignificant. She felt useless. For years Sasha had believed she could do her part by helping them make ends meet, even if it was to the detriment of her own life or credit score. She was there to serve. She wanted to be the hero to her father that he had been to her all her life. And now, there was no need to sacrifice. No need to break her back taking every catering job and every extra shift imaginable. Her parents wouldn't need her in that capacity anymore. And she wasn't sure what that meant for her identity.

Sasha swore that the sheets smelled like Abby. That her perfume lingered on her pillow, and every time she moved, more of it drifted into the air. It was all around her and it was killing her.

Her mother knocked at the door. "Pancakes are ready, Sasha. Come down."

She groaned and pulled the Abby-scented pillow over her head, because why not? She might as well suffocate in designer perfume. That'd be an okay way to go, she decided.

After attending the pity party for one for a while longer, she managed to stumble into the kitchen. Her newly bandaged arm throbbing even with the pain medication. She was on injured leave for now, and it would likely be a week or two before she could go back to work. So basically she was just going to be hanging around her parents' house, feeling sorry for herself until work was available to distract her. Fantastic.

Her mother had left a foil-covered plate on the table, and a tall stack of pancakes and some breakfast sausage waited for her.

"I wasn't sure you'd make it down. I was going to feed them to your father." Her mother entered the kitchen and sat next to her at the table. "You look like hell, Sash."

She felt like hell. "Thanks, Ma." She cut into the pancakes and sausage, savoring each bite and pouring extra maple syrup on them as she went. "These are amazing."

"Fresh blueberries from the market. Only the best for my little love." Her mother tapped her on the nose before nodding toward her arm. "How is that today?"

"Better. Not really. It sucks." Sasha shrugged. There was nothing she could do about it but let it heal, she supposed.

Her mother frowned and changed the topic. "Will Abby be coming by today? I'd like to bake her something."

That stung more than the forearm burn. "No. She won't be."

"Tomorrow, maybe?" her mother pressed again.

"No, Ma. Probably not tomorrow. Probably not ever." Sasha chased a blueberry around her plate, trying not to cry at that statement. Abby just gave her so many damn *feelings*.

"What? Why not?" Her mother looked panicked. "Is she okay?"

"She's fine." Sasha considered this. "Well, I think she's fine. I don't really know. We're not talking."

"What do you mean? Of course you're talking. She saved this family, Sasha. She's a miracle worker. But she's more than that— she *is* family." Her mother was adamant about this.

"Ma," she pleaded. She couldn't keep talking about this, or it was going to be a matter of moments before she started crying. She felt so betrayed by Abby, and the last thing she wanted to do was be reminded of all the amazing things Abby had brought to her life. Like, how fantastic she had been at her father's bedside. So selfless. So…loving. It was too much to think about right now.

"Are you not happy, Sasha? This will change our lives. You won't have to work as much, and I can be home more to care for your father if I don't have to have two part-time jobs. We can enjoy our time together. It is the ultimate gift."

"She lied, Ma. She lied about who she was and she lied about helping us out and I just can't face her." Sasha couldn't stop the slow progression of tears that had begun. It felt hopeless to try.

"What are you talking about? What did she lie about?" Her mother looked confused.

Sasha felt confused, too. "Well, about who she was—"

"I thought you already addressed that. I thought that was all behind you when she apologized and professed her love for you in front of all the press in Boston." Her mother pointed to the front page of the Arts and Entertainment section of the paper following that night at the museum. The journalist had made note of Abby's confession in the write-up. Her mother had threatened to frame it. But, for now, it lived on the fridge for everyone to see.

"We did."

"So what's the problem?"

"The problem is she used her vast wealth to give us a handout we didn't even ask for." Sasha's throat ached as she spoke, her emotions at war with themselves.

A look of understanding crossed her mother's face. "Oh, Sasha. You're wrong."

"Ma, I am not. I saw her signature. And when I confronted her about it, she denied it. Right to my face. How can I love someone who lies to me over and over again?" Sasha bit her lip to slow the tremble.

"Okay, I can't explain that. But I can explain the grant." Her mother stroked her left hand and held it. "This didn't come out of nowhere, Sasha. I applied for this."

"Applied for it? What does that mean?"

"The bills were piling up. You were working two full-time jobs, and I was working two part-time jobs and odd jobs, and caring for your father. But it was too much. After one of his doctor appointments at the beginning of the year, I saw a flyer about seeking hospital aid for medical bills. I had to fill out dozens of forms and submit the taxes from the last three years, but I figured I had to try. It was worth the shot." She shrugged. "And then our prayers were answered. We were awarded the money and our hospital debts have been forgiven. This will change our lives, Sasha."

"So you're saying you knew this was a possibility all along?" Sasha couldn't believe what she was hearing.

"Well, yes. I mean, it wasn't a guarantee, like I said. But it was worth trying. I didn't think to mention it to you because I didn't want you to get your hopes up." She sipped her tea. "I figured when a decision was made, I'd tell you then."

Sasha gaped at her. Her mother had been applying for grants and assistance for all this time without her knowing? And if that were true, why didn't Abby just say that to her at the station? She groaned. Probably because she didn't give Abby the chance to get a word in during her temper tantrum. Shit.

"I made a mistake." Sasha dropped her head and sighed. "I'm such a jerk."

"What did you do?" Her mother looked at her with big eyes.

"I told the love of my life to leave. I may have also called her meddlesome, privileged, and out of touch."

"Sasha."

Sasha winced at the tone.

"I know, Ma. I know." She stood up from the table and headed back upstairs to get changed.

"Where are you going now?" her mother called after her.

"To try to win her back." She didn't have a plan, not exactly. But she had to do something. Anything. And she knew exactly who to ask for help.

CHAPTER TWENTY-EIGHT

Samantha rode up the elevator to the sixth floor offices of the Davenport Charitable Foundation with a clear mission. She was there to help Sasha apologize to Abby. And maybe also get lunch with Edie. But that was beside the point.

The doors opened and she stepped out. She smiled, pleased at the amount of natural light streaming through the windows. An admin greeted her in the main reception area.

"Can I help you, miss?" she asked.

"Yes. I'm here to see Abby Rossmore." Samantha flashed her brightest smile.

"Is she expecting you?" The admin looked down at the calendar in front of her with a frown. "I don't see anyone on her schedule."

"I'm just dropping in, no prior scheduled appointment. Just here to say hello and bring good cheer." Samantha hoped her charm would be enough to breach the fortress.

"Oh, okay." She hesitated before her eyes widened. "Hey, are you the matchmaker from the *Improper Bostonian*? The one that makes the—"

"Impossible possible. I am one and the same."

"Cool." She looked a little starstuck and Samantha was touched.

"So, about seeing Abby?"

"Right. Yes. I'll call her and let her know you're here. It's Samantha, right?"

"You got it." She waited by the desk as the admin called back. Abby came out a few moments later, a puzzled expression on her face.

"Samantha. Hi. What brings you by?" Abby looked...tired. And a little sad.

"Lunch with your mother. Can we sit and catch up a bit?" Samantha would rather not do this in the lobby with the admin watching the whole time.

"Oh, sure. Right, yeah. Sorry. My head is not where it should be today." Abby led her back to her office. She motioned for Samantha to join her on the couch by the window, across from her desk. "So, lunch? That sounds fun. Where are you gals going?"

"Somewhere nearby, I imagine. I'm leaving it up to your mother. You know, you're welcome to join us. I'd love to hear all about you and how things are going." She was baiting her.

"There's nothing going on. Trust that." Abby frowned and looked out the window.

"Oh?" Abby wasn't taking the bait fast enough. Samantha decided to help her along a bit. "How's Sasha?"

Abby sucked in a breath, looking wounded. "Sasha and I are... not together right now."

"Oh no." Samantha feigned surprise as she shot off a quick text. "What happened?"

"The short story?" Abby shrugged. "Everything after the night at the museum was perfect but then there was a fire and Sasha got hurt and then there was a grant issued and Sasha thinks I'm a liar. But I'm not. I truly had no idea about that—I don't even remember signing the form. But I found a copy in our records, so clearly, I did. But...I don't know. I didn't mean to hurt her. It's just all so fucked up now."

Samantha leaned back against the couch and looked out the window at the world below. "That's...wow. That's quite a story. What are you going to do?"

"What is there to do? Sasha basically told me she never wanted to see me again. I mean, I guess I can see why. I wasn't exactly honest from the get-go. I know, you warned me. But I guess I'm just not destined to find love."

Samantha was horrified. "Well that's not true at all. Everyone is entitled to love. It's written in the stars." She paused. "Let me ask you a question. If Sasha was here, today, would you want to see her? What would you say to her?"

"I'm not sure." Abby looked defeated.

"Would you listen to her if she had something to say to you?" Samantha tried again.

Abby seemed to consider this. "I would. Maybe. I don't know, she said some pretty harsh stuff to me. I'm still trying to wrap my head around it."

Samantha nodded. "Anger is never the way to communicate." She looked at the window behind them again. "Say, does this window open?"

"What?" Abby looked at her like she was crazy. "Uh, yeah. These are pretty old windows, so they open almost all the way. The newer buildings don't have that option for obvious safety reasons."

"Right. Safety first." Samantha stood and pulled Abby up with her, turning her so Abby's back was toward the window. "Listen, I'm going to give you some advice."

"Okay?"

Samantha stroked up and down Abby's arms for a moment before taking her hands in her own. "We all have histories and complicated pasts. We all make mistakes and have moments of weakness. But we all deserve the chance to be brave and right our wrongs, especially in the name of love."

"Uh, sure." Abby didn't look convinced. "In the name of love. Or whatever."

Samantha smiled. "Not whatever. But I'll leave you two to figure it out. Don't give up on love, Abby. Sometimes you have to look through the window of your soul and find what you really want and need in life. Or in this case, look through the window of your office."

"The window of my—?"

Samantha hugged her and kissed her on the cheek. "I've got to run to lunch with your mother. It was great seeing you. Talk soon."

Samantha slipped out before Abby could ask her anything else, but not before she texted a thumbs up to Sasha. She sure hoped this would work.

❖

Abby decided that was easily the strangest exchange she had ever had with anyone, let alone with Samantha Monteiro-Moss. What was she saying about the window of her office…or was it her soul? A knock drew her attention to the office door. But it was open and there was no one there. She was hearing things. Great. Single, and hearing things.

There was another knock, this time louder.

Still no one at the door. That's it, she was losing her mind. "What the fuck?"

Third knock, this one with a melody. It sounded so close to her. Like it was right behind her. She turned and nearly screamed. Sasha waved to her from the other side of the glass, five stories above the street below, decked out in her full bunker gear, on the top of a very, very tall ladder.

Abby just blinked at her, unsure of what to do.

Sasha was saying something, but she couldn't hear it. Sasha frowned and pointed to the window latch, mouthing the words, "Can you open the window?"

Abby was frozen in place. The window? What the hell was she doing outside the window…to her office. Suddenly Samantha's comments made a lot more sense. She nodded and stepped forward, unlocking the ancient latch and pulling the pane open.

The room filled with the sounds of the city below, and the air was cooler than she expected. She shivered.

Sasha gave her a hesitant smile. "Can I come in?"

"You know, we have doors for these sorts of things." Abby was too bewildered to be annoyed. Mostly she was terrified for Sasha's safety. Of course she could come in. It was a hell of a lot safer in her office than on the top of a swaying ladder.

"Ah, but that wouldn't give me the effect I was hoping for." Sasha braced herself and stepped gingerly through the slim window onto the back of Abby's couch, before she lowered herself to the floor.

Abby didn't dare speak until all of Sasha's limbs were safely contained in her office. "And what effect would that be?"

"The one that convinces you to hear me out and lets me apologize for being an absolute ass. I was going for the shock-you-into-listening-to-me approach." Sasha placed her helmet on the edge of the couch, dusting off a boot print she'd left. "Is it working?"

Abby laughed. "Well, I can't say anyone has ever tried this hard to have a conversation with me. You could have called. Or walked in the front door. That probably would have sufficed."

The wind picked up and the window to Abby's office swung open wider, the ladder swaying in the breeze. Sasha closed the window and the sound of the city was silenced. It was just the two of them now, here, in this moment.

"Yeah, maybe. But when the woman of your dreams makes a grand gesture by announcing that she loves you in front of the entire city of Boston at a fundraiser, you gotta dial up your game to prove you're worth that love."

Sasha stepped forward and gave Abby a small smile. "I love you. And I was wrong and pigheaded and felt a little blindsided, but I don't want to lose what I have with you. I don't want to miss out on anything we could possibly have because of my pride or my fear of inadequacy, or my stubbornness, because the fact is you are the best thing that ever happened to me and I'm willing to fight for that."

Abby didn't know what to say. Part of her wanted to fall into Sasha's arms and get lost in a kiss, but another part of her was still wounded, a little fearful.

When she didn't speak, Sasha continued. "When my mother told me about the grant, I didn't know what to think. I was equal parts elated and distraught. For the longest time, my personal identity in my family had been one of provider. I had it in my mind that it was my job to save them, to provide for them. A part of me was really jealous and jaded that you had been that savior when I couldn't be. I just felt so…worthless. Like I'd spent all my time just spinning my wheels. But I was being selfish and shortsighted. What you did has nothing to do with me and my ego. You saved my parents, Abby, and I am so very, very grateful for that."

Guilt washed over her. Sasha was giving her more credit than she deserved. "Wait, it's not like that, Sasha. I'd love to say this was intentional and planned, if that's what you'd like to hear, but it wasn't. It was a complete and utter fluke. And to be honest, it's best that that's how it worked out. Otherwise it might be seen as favoritism." Abby had panicked once she'd found that paper copy in the files. There was nothing she wanted less than a controversy and for Sasha's family to lose their support.

"I'm not following." Sasha frowned and Abby hoped the truth wouldn't hurt her more.

"I'm the Davenport Foundation's accountant, this is true. And yes, that was my signature on the letter you received. But I didn't knowingly approve your parents' application." She tried to clarify. "Lots of people apply for aid, but it's only issued on a quarterly basis. These things often sit for months until our quarterly meetings— that's why so much of it is retroactive. But I was so distracted this quarter. I missed the board meeting for the first time in forever. I was playing catch up and just signed the forms when they came before me. I had no idea your family was in the mix." Abby sighed. "I would never intentionally hurt you or try to interfere in your family in any way. I so treasure the moments I got to spend with you and your mother. You two really helped me to open up with my own mother, to embrace the meaning of family again in a way I had forgotten. But I didn't help your family to get in your good graces. I had almost nothing to do with it at all. So please don't thank me. I don't deserve it."

Sasha's face was a mix of emotions. Abby wasn't sure what to expect next. She'd been honest. She hadn't meddled with Sasha's family, but she hoped that admission didn't change Sasha's opinion of her. She was reminded of Samantha's advice in that moment. *Choose vulnerability.* She decided to embrace it.

"Sasha, the reason I don't go by my family name is exactly for the reasons you mentioned the other day. I don't want people to see my name before they see me. I don't want them to assume the best or the worst of me by the legacy of my family. I just want a chance to live my life and cast my own shadow outside of the shadow of my name. I was never trying to be deceitful, it's just—"

"That I did exactly what you'd hoped I wouldn't do and pegged you as a selfish, detached rich girl who couldn't possibly understand the troubles of a simple working stiff like myself?"

Sasha's smile was genuine, and Abby relaxed a little more.

"Yeah. Pretty much."

Sasha nodded. "Yup. I'm a total jackass. I accept it." She reached out and took Abby's hand.

"Is that a firefighting term?" Abby intertwined their fingers and stepped into Sasha's embrace.

"Oh, yeah. Totally. I'm a consummate professional." Sasha held her for a moment before pulling back. "Which reminds me. Hold on." She stepped away from Abby to reopen the window and lean out.

"Sasha, please use the door to leave—I'm begging you. I don't think my heart can take you out there again." Abby felt nauseous just thinking about it.

Sasha retrieved something from the ladder and gave someone below a thumbs-up. There was a far-off sound of a motor whirring and the ladder began to retract. Only then did Abby's heart rate begin to normalize.

Sasha closed the window and turned, presenting Abby with a rainbow bouquet like the one from their first date. "It's not the front page of the *Globe*, but it's something. I love you, I want to be with you. Forgive me?"

"You just came through my window like Spider-Man with an overflowing gay bouquet, professing your undying love to me." Abby slid her arms inside of Sasha's jacket, wrapping them around Sasha's waist.

"This is true." Sasha smiled and cupped her jaw.

"I suppose that's as good a reason to forgive you as any." Abby leaned forward and pressed her lips to Sasha's. That familiar spark ignited and everything outside of this moment, these lips on hers, completely slipped her mind. Sasha's tongue teasing at her bottom lip only muddled her brain further. "I feel like this whole firefighting get-up is something we should revisit more often. You know, like, in the bedroom."

Sasha moaned against her lips. "I like how you think."

Abby pulled back, a thought occurring to her. "Do you have to be somewhere right now? Are you on shift?"

Sasha leaned back in, reconnecting their lips. Her hands wandered over Abby's body as she spoke. "Nope. Upside of injured leave. I'm strictly here on the business of seduction and romance. My afternoon is free." Sasha's thumbs massaged along the sides of her breasts and everything felt significantly hotter. "You?"

This was the best news Abby had heard all day. Hands down. Or up, as it were, since Sasha was palming her breasts at the moment. "As my own boss, I'm declaring the workday complete. If your arm is up to it, what do you say to grabbing some food we won't eat and having a bed picnic?"

"Sounds perfect. And I'm feeling no pain." Sasha was unbuttoning Abby's blouse, evidently not interested in waiting. "That door have a lock?"

Abby tried to focus on Sasha's question but her attention was directed to the skirt Sasha was unzipping. "Mm-hmm."

"Great. Let's see how comfy this couch is, you know, as an appetizer to the bed picnic later." Sasha walked her back until her knees hit the couch before she lifted her up in a bridal carry and placed her down with care. Sasha was so strong and sexy it was making her dizzy.

"I love this idea." Abby breathed out slowly as Sasha kissed along her neck.

Sasha pulled back with a smile. "And I love you."

Abby rewarded her with a kiss before gently pushing her toward the door. "Go close that."

"On it."

As Sasha's body weight left her own she grabbed Sasha by the jacket and pulled her back down, running her hand up the tight tank top she had on underneath her gear. "Be quick about it. And lose the jacket. But let's keep the rest of it on for a bit, okay?"

"Of course. I have a feeling it's going to get very, very hot in here. I'd hate to be ill prepared." Sasha was back on top of her in a flash. "Now, where were we?"

"You were just about to teach me the basics of fire safety." All this teasing was making Abby's body feel like it was on fire.

"You seem to me more of the advanced type. Let's accelerate the process a little, no? Strike a match and see if it ignites?" Sasha's mouth was hot against her ear.

Abby decided this was the kind of hands-on training she wanted for the rest of her life. "Definitely."

Epilogue

A nother woman!" her father called out and Abby laughed. "No way. Who would turn that down?"

Abby's response garnered a high five from her father. Sasha rolled her eyes. The two of them were like frat boys.

She was watching them from the doorway to the living room while her mother finished prepping a snack in the kitchen. They were playing couch *Family Feud* and absolutely destroying the contestants on the show. She'd been impressed with Abby's prowess. She was a worthy opponent to her dad.

"It's food. I'm telling you. Food." Abby nodded in confidence.

"You expect me to believe that when they polled one hundred married men and asked them what their wife would never let them bring to bed with them, *food* was higher up on the list than another woman? No way." He shook his head and crossed his arms. "Not a chance."

"Crumbs in the sheets is a divorce-worthy offense, Duncan." Abby waved her finger at him. "It's food. I'll bet you on it."

Her father paused the DVR and turned to face her. "You're on. Name your wager."

Abby tapped her chin in consideration. "If I'm wrong, then Sasha will make dinner every night for two weeks *and* do the dishes."

"Whoa. How did I get dragged into this? No way. Leave me out of it," Sasha protested from the doorway.

"Okay, let's be real, you'd be having Sloppy Joes every day if that were the case. I'll cook six nights of those two weeks to make sure you get some greens," Abby added selflessly.

"I preferred the Sloppy Joe outcome, but I'll compromise." Her father narrowed his eyes at Abby. "And if you're right, which you won't be, but I'll humor you, what then?"

Abby smiled broadly and spread out her arms. "*When* I'm right, you have to tell me about that time Sasha got her head stuck between the spindles of the railing on the stairs and all about how you had to slather her with lard to get her out. Spare no details. I want full embellishments."

"What is this? Why am I the prize for the winning and losing bet here?" Sasha was panicking a little. That stair story was beyond embarrassing. Especially when Abby found out it happened when she was in high school and plenty old enough to know not to try it.

"Deal." Duncan and Abby shook on it without heeding Sasha's input at all. Figured.

He hit play on the DVR and the host called out the answers starting with the lowest scoring one. Another woman was number three, and food was number two.

"You've got to be kidding me." Her father's mouth hung open in surprise as Abby jumped off the couch to do her victory dance.

"Boo-yah. Crumbs in the sheets. Worst. Bed partner. Ever." Abby pretended to hear the roar of the crowd.

"Unbelievable." Her father shook his head in disbelief. Sasha would never admit it, but she thought he was going to win this bet for sure.

"Ha. You're both wrong. The number one answer is going to be a dog." Her mother's voice called from the kitchen and Abby's celebration halted. Her father paused the program again.

"A dog?" Abby looked at Sasha's father and they shook their heads in unison. "No way, people love to sleep with their pets."

"It's dog." Her mother leaned against her in the doorway, holding up a cutting board of cheese and crackers. Sasha went to steal a slice of cheese and her mother slapped her hand away. "Abby gets first pick. She's a guest."

Sasha huffed. *Guest*, her ass. They spent at least one night here a week, most weeks more than that. Abby was no more a guest here than she was.

"All right, all right." Her father surveyed her mother with suspicion. "If Valeria is right, then the wager needs to be adjusted."

"Hey. I won fair and square. You owe me a story." Abby pouted and looked to Sasha for help.

"Oh, I'm not helping you get dirt on me. You're on your own there, babe." Sasha held up her hands in defense.

"Fine. When I win and dog is the answer," her mother supplied with a smile, "Sasha has to cook, do the dishes, *and* do the laundry for the next two weeks. And Abby is responsible for making sure we get vegetables at every meal."

"Again, why am I the wager here?" Sasha looked between the three of them with suspicion. "I smell a conspiracy."

"That's just the dirty laundry piling up for you." Her mother winked as she walked into the living room and handed the snacks to Abby and her father. "Hit play so Sasha can start the light load."

Her father pressed play, and sure enough the number one answer was *wet dog*.

"This is rigged." Sasha gaped as her mother handed her the dish cloth when she walked by.

"I already sorted everything. There's a load in the dryer to be folded. This cloth can go in the next wash." Her mother patted her on the shoulder and walked back to the kitchen, leaving Sasha, her father, and Abby standing shocked in the living room.

"We just got played, didn't we?" Abby looked between Sasha and her father.

Her father mashed a few buttons on the remote and cursed under his breath. "Sneaky woman."

"What?" Sasha took a piece of cheese now that Abby had taken her first piece.

"I record all the episodes of *Family Feud* throughout the day to save some for when you and Abs stop by." Sasha's heart swelled with that adorable admission and even more adorable use of Abby's nickname. "But if you look here, this episode has already been viewed. She totally played us."

"Ma!" Sasha stomped into the kitchen to find her mother doubled over with laughter at the kitchen table. She was wiping away tears and trying to catch her breath.

"You guys are so easy." She barely got the words out between howls of laughter.

"A cheater among us." Abby sighed as she headed into the laundry room off the kitchen.

"Where are you going?" Sasha called out after her.

"A bet is a bet. I'm going to help you fold—otherwise we'll be late for our date." Abby winked at her as she carried the laundry basket back toward the living room.

"Oh, no way in hell am I honoring that bet. First, I didn't shake on it, and second, she clearly cheated. That voids the bet entirely." Sasha had nearly forgotten about their plans later, although she couldn't imagine how that was even possible. She'd been looking forward to this for weeks.

"I'll tell you the stair story if you promise to fold my underwear into those fancy little squares I saw you do with the facecloths." Her father scooted over on the couch to make room for Abby to stack piles next to him.

"You're not helping, Dad." Sasha took a shirt from Abby and folded it in half—she could think of worse things to do with her time than spend it with her love and her parents doing boring household things. Boring was fine by her these days. Well, boring was fine right now. In this moment. But later, she would bet her life that *later* would be anything but boring. She intended to make sure that everyone involved would be a winner.

"This day just keeps getting better and better." Abby giggled and handed Duncan a pair of boxers she had folded into the shape of an envelope. "Good?"

"Yeah, this is cool. Valeria, you gotta see this. What other shapes can you make?"

Her father's excitement was childlike. Sasha loved Abby a little more in that moment.

Abby seemed to consider this. "I can make bath towels into an elephant, and fit jeans, a T-shirt, and underwear into a tube sock to save space when traveling."

"You magical creature, you." Her father patted the seat next to him. "Okay, so, it was a rainy, cold night and Sasha was bored. I mean, what other reason could she have for putting her head between the slats in the railing?"

❖

Abby leaned her hip against the back of her sofa and smiled as her gaze fell on the glass bowl on her kitchen island. That bowl had been made with care. That bowl was the start of the relationship she was celebrating tonight in a very special way. That was her favorite bowl. It had been decided a hundred times over.

In the six months since she and Sasha had gotten together, she had experienced the highest highs of her life. She was reminded of their first time, that incredibly hot first time, every time she put fruit in that bowl. Her favorite bowl.

"You're doing that dreamy-eyed staring thing again." Sasha's arm slid around her waist, then her lips hovered at the skin below Abby's ear.

Abby closed her eyes and purred. "You say that like it's a bad thing."

"Oh, on the contrary." Sasha's breath was hot on the skin under her jaw. "I think it's adorable. And I love it."

"*It*, huh?" Abby leaned back against Sasha's chest and smiled. She could feel that Sasha was wearing her new present.

"You. I love you." Sasha's lips teased at Abby's pulse point and she melted against Sasha a little more, the anniversary gift making its presence known more firmly against the small of her back.

Abby dropped her hand to rest her palm on Sasha's strong, muscular thigh. She was pleasantly surprised to feel Sasha's naked flesh under her touch. No need for pants at this party, it seemed. Her stomach tightened in anticipation.

"What're you wearing?" She didn't turn yet. Instead, she chose to savor the attention Sasha paid to her neck, to her jaw. Those lips were working their magic on her, from the top down. Her sex throbbed and any fleeting thought she had of turning vanished when

Sasha's left hand wrapped across her front and palmed her breast through the nearly sheer tank top she'd changed into when they got home.

Sasha massaged her breast as she spoke. "Only what's important."

Abby struggled to focus when Sasha's hips pressed against her ass. She moaned. "I want to see."

"Soon." Sasha toyed with her nipple as her other hand snaked around Abby's front, pushing her panties down just enough to slip inside.

Abby wondered how soon *soon* was, her body scorching with want as Sasha dipped into her wetness and pressed against her clit before skirting away again.

"You're pretty excited, Abs." Sasha's teasing stopped and she slid one long finger inside her. Her teeth were on Abby's earlobe as she whispered, "So wet, so soon."

Abby shuddered from all the sensations—wet lips, hot tongue, slick fingers, the insistent pressure against her ass. It was fast approaching too much. "I can't help it."

"Because you want it?" Sasha's hand abandoned her breast to glide up her chest and settle at her collarbone, gently caressing the front of her neck as she slid two fingers back inside.

"Fuck. Yes. I want it." Abby dropped her head back and she felt Sasha pull her even closer, her fingers going deeper, spreading slightly, stretching her in that way that would help her get—

"Ready?" Sasha moved her fingers in and out slowly before she pressed the heel of her hand against Abby's clit.

Abby saw stars and wondered if her legs would give out. "Yes. Please."

The hand caressing Abby's neck paused before turning her chin so her lips met Sasha's. Sasha kissed her deeply, her tongue filling Abby's mouth and scrambling her mind. "Bend over the couch for me."

Abby just about died.

Sasha's fingers slipped out of her but before she could voice her complaint, Sasha's hands were on her hips, guiding her panties down her legs to the floor. It was time.

"C'mon Abby. Let me see you. All of you." Without the flimsy barrier of her panties in the way, she could feel the soft yet firm tip of the dildo Sasha teased against the flesh of her ass, before she positioned it against Abby's dripping sex. Sasha rubbed the tip against her swollen lips and encouraged her to flex forward with a gentle hand between her shoulders. "Show me you're ready."

Abby moaned again, the want overpowering her desire to draw this out. She leaned forward on her elbows, balancing herself on the high back of her sofa as Sasha spread her legs with confident, slick fingers.

"You're gorgeous, Abs." Sasha's voice sounded far away and Abby whined as the pressure from the head of the dildo left her opening. Her frustration was short-lived when Sasha's mouth replaced the anniversary gift.

"Oh, Sasha. Yes." Abby's body shuddered and she relaxed onto the sofa cushions, her legs spreading and back arching to give Sasha better access.

Much to Abby's delight, Sasha rewarded her enthusiasm by sucking on her lips and thrusting her tongue inside, licking and humming in that practiced rhythm that she knew drove Abby crazy. It always got Abby to the edge, so fast. It was practically criminal.

"Sasha," Abby warned. She was climbing too quickly. The anticipation of this moment had been building for weeks since their trip to the sex toy shop last month. Sasha had meticulously planned her schedule to ensure that on their six-month anniversary, she would be off. Getting off. Which was exactly what was about to happen to Abby, prematurely, if Sasha kept doing that thing with her tongue.

"All right, baby." Sasha pressed one final kiss to her swollen lips before resuming her prior position.

The skin of Abby's hip burned under the heat of Sasha's steadying hand. But every other sensation was drowned out when she felt the dildo press into her again. This time, Sasha kept it there, spreading Abby's lips with her fingers and coaxing the dildo deeper.

Words escaped her as her body stretched and pulled Sasha's member deeper. All the foreplay and the wetness culminated in this moment, and Abby exhaled into the pleasure of the sensation. Sasha filled her, the feeling of ecstasy locking her in place as Sasha reached a slow but steady rhythm. Abby bent forward a little more, allowing herself to get lost in the delicious feeling of the fullness. "*Sasha.*"

Sasha hummed and Abby knew she was biting her lip in that way she always did when she was focused on giving Abby pleasure. She missed seeing Sasha in that moment. She wanted to come undone looking at her beautiful and masterful mouth.

"Baby." Abby used all of her willpower to slow the seemingly unstoppable orgasm. Every careful but determined thrust from Sasha brought her that much closer to release, stoking the fire that blazed in her core. As badly as Abby wanted to come, she decided she wanted even more to come while under Sasha.

Sasha stroked her side in reply, the soft sensation of a kiss between her shoulder blades warming her in a different way entirely.

Abby tried again, this time clasping the hand Sasha had on her hip. "Baby, I want to see you."

Sasha slowed her rhythm and pulled out just long enough for Abby to turn around and take in Sasha's outfit, or lack thereof. She was wearing a lacy black push-up bra and black boyshorts with an O-ring occupied by that perfect dick they'd chosen together. Her toned stomach glistened with sweat and flexed as she caught her breath. Her dark hair cascaded in long waves across her shoulders. Her eyebrow was raised in that confident and cocky sexiness Abby had grown to love. This was exactly the kind of visual Abby had been hoping to see.

She opened her arms and Sasha stepped into them, lifting her up and carrying her to the other side of the couch. She grabbed Sasha's face and kissed her deeply as Sasha filled her again, resuming the rhythm from before. Abby was right back at the precipice, Sasha's mouth hot against her own, her body trembling under the feeling of Sasha's breasts rubbing against hers.

"Sasha." She was breathless. She wouldn't last long now.

"You're perfect. I love you." Sasha bottomed out on her next thrust and Abby's clit twitched from the contact of the harness, propelling her into the blinding orgasm she'd been waiting for.

Abby cried out and gave in to the tremors provoked by Sasha's repeated thrusts. She felt heat radiate everywhere as her body relaxed in that satiated perfection she couldn't get enough of.

Sasha kissed her sweetly as she slid out, her fingers skating across Abby's opening and teasing at her clit until Abby slapped her away when the sensation became too much to handle.

"I'll never walk again." Abby blinked and stared up at the ceiling. That didn't seem like such a bad prospect at the moment.

Sasha laughed and settled onto her elbow, her body still draped across Abby's. "I'll just have to fireman-carry you everywhere, huh?"

"I could think of worse things." Her gaze settled on Sasha's. Her heartbeat increased at the adoration that shined back at her. She reached out and cupped Sasha's jaw. "I wouldn't mind being that close to you all the time."

"Mm. Me neither." Sasha closed her eyes and rested her head against Abby's palm.

"Happy anniversary, Sash." Abby leaned forward and connected their lips, savoring the warmth and comfort of Sasha's returned affections. She would happily spend the rest of her life sharing moments like these with Sasha.

"Happy anniversary." Sasha nibbled her lips and Abby was reminded that they had some unfinished business to attend to.

She reached between them and grasped the still sticky member, pulling it away from Sasha's body just enough to let it snap back. Sasha moaned in response, her eyes opening in surprise.

Abby massaged Sasha's hips, pushing at the fabric of her boyshorts as she added, "I think it's about time we tried a little role reversal. What do you say, Sash?"

Sasha raised her eyebrow and gave her that sexy, teasing smile that ignited her insides. "Happy anniversary, indeed."

About the Author

Fiona Riley was born and raised in New England where she is a medical professional and part-time professor when she isn't bonding with her laptop over words. She went to college in Boston and never left, starting a small business that takes up all of her free time, much to the dismay of her ever patient and lovely wife. When she pulls herself away from her work, she likes to catch up on the contents of her ever-growing DVR or spend time by the ocean with her favorite people.

Fiona's love for writing started at a young age and blossomed after she was published in a poetry competition at the ripe old age of twelve. She wrote lots of short stories and poetry for many years until it was time for college and a "real job." Fiona found herself with a bachelor's, a doctorate, and a day job, but felt like she had stopped nurturing the one relationship that had always made her feel the most complete: artist, dreamer, writer.

A series of bizarre events afforded her with some unexpected extra time and she found herself reaching for her favorite blue notebook to write, never looking back.

Contact Fiona and check for updates on all her new adventures at:

Twitter: @fionarileyfic
Facebook: "Fiona Riley Fiction"
Website: http://www.fionarileyfiction.com/
Email: fionarileyfiction@gmail.com

Books Available from Bold Strokes Books

Change in Time by Robyn Nyx. Working in the past is hell on your future. The Extractor series: Book Two (978-1-62639-880-1)

Love After Hours by Radclyffe. When Gina Antonelli agrees to renovate Carrie Longmire's new house, she doesn't welcome Carrie's overtures at friendship or her own unexpected attraction. A Rivers Community Novel. (978-1-63555-090-0)

Nantucket Rose by CF Frizzell. Maggie Jordan can't wait to convert an historic Nantucket home into a B&B, but doesn't expect to fall for mariner Ellis Chilton, who has more claim to the house than Maggie realizes. (978-1-63555-056-6)

Picture Perfect by Lisa Moreau. Falling in love wasn't supposed to be part of the stakes for Olive and Gabby, rival photographers in the competition of a lifetime. (978-1-62639-975-4)

Set the Stage by Karis Walsh. Actress Emilie Danvers takes the stage again in Ashland, Oregon, little realizing that landscaper Arden Philips is about to offer her a very personal romantic lead role. (978-1-63555-087-0)

Strike a Match by Fiona Riley. When their attempts at matchmaking fizzle out, firefighter Sasha and reluctant millionairess Abby find themselves turning to each other to strike a perfect match. (978-1-62639-999-0)

The Price of Cash by Ashley Bartlett. Cash Braddock is doing her best to keep her business afloat, stay out of jail, and avoid Detective Kallen. It's not working. (978-1-62639-708-8)

Under Her Wing by Ronica Black. At Angel's Wings Rescue, dogs are usually the ones saved, but when quiet Kassandra Haden meets outspoken owner Jayden Beaumont, the two stubborn women just might end up saving each other. (978-1-63555-077-1)

Underwater Vibes by Mickey Brent. When Hélène, a translator in Brussels, Belgium, meets Sylvie, a young Greek photographer and swim coach, unsettling feelings hijack Hélène's mind and body—even her poems. (978-1-63555-002-3)

A More Perfect Union by Carsen Taite. Major Zoey Granger and DC fixer Rook Daniels risk their reputations for a chance at true love while dealing with a scandal that threatens to rock the military. (978-1-62639-754-5)

Arrival by Gun Brooke. The spaceship *Pathfinder* reaches its passengers' new homeworld where danger lurks in the shadows while Pamas Seclan disembarks and finds unexpected love in young science genius Darmiya Do Voy. (978-1-62639-859-7)

Captain's Choice by VK Powell. Architect Kerstin Anthony's life is going to plan until Bennett Carlyle, the first girl she ever kissed, is assigned to her latest and most important project, a police district substation. (978-1-62639-997-6)

Falling Into Her by Erin Zak. Pam Phillips, widow at the age of forty, meets Kathryn Hawthorne, local Chicago celebrity, and it changes her life forever—in ways she hadn't even considered possible. (978-1-63555-092-4)

Hookin' Up by MJ Williamz. Will Leah get what she needs from casual hookups or will she see the love she desires right in front of her? (978-1-63555-051-1)

King of Thieves by Shea Godfrey. When art thief Casey Marinos meets bounty hunter Finnegan Starkweather, the crimes of the past just might set the stage for a payoff worth more than she ever dreamed possible. (978-1-63555-007-8)

Lucy's Chance by Jackie D. As a serial killer haunts the streets, Lucy tries to stitch up old wounds with her first love in the wake of a small town's rapid descent into chaos. (978-1-63555-027-6)

Right Here, Right Now by Georgia Beers. When Alicia Wright moves into the office next door to Lacey Chamberlain's accounting firm, Lacey is about to find out that sometimes the last person you want is exactly the person you need. (978-1-63555-154-9)

Strictly Need to Know by MB Austin. Covert operator Maji Rios will do whatever she must to complete her mission, but saving a gorgeous stranger from Russian mobsters was not in her plans. (978-1-63555-114-3)

Tailor-Made by Yolanda Wallace. Tailor Grace Henderson doesn't date clients, but when she meets gender-bending model Dakota Lane, she's tempted to throw all the rules out the window. (978-1-63555-081-8)

Time Will Tell by M. Ullrich. With the ability to time travel, Eva Caldwell will have to decide between having it all and erasing it all. (978-1-63555-088-7)

A Date to Die by Anne Laughlin. Someone is killing people close to Detective Kay Adler, who must look to her own troubled past for a suspect. There she finds more than one person seeking revenge against her. (978-1-63555-023-8)

Captured Soul by Laydin Michaels. Can Kadence Munroe save the woman she loves from a twisted killer, or will she lose her to a collector of souls? (978-1-62639-915-0)

Dawn's New Day by TJ Thomas. Can Dawn Oliver and Cam Cooper, two women who have loved and lost, open their hearts to love again? (978-1-63555-072-6)

Definite Possibility by Maggie Cummings. Sam Miller is just out for good times, but Lucy Weston makes her realize happily ever after is a definite possibility. (978-1-62639-909-9)

Eyes Like Those by Melissa Brayden. Isabel Chase and Taylor Andrews struggle between love and ambition from the writers' room on one of Hollywood's hottest TV shows. (978-1-63555-012-2)

Heart's Orders by Jaycie Morrison. Helen Tucker and Tee Owens escape hardscrabble lives to careers in the Women's Army Corps, but more than their hearts are at risk as friendship blossoms into love. (978-1-63555-073-3)

Hiding Out by Kay Bigelow. Treat Dandridge is unaware that her life is in danger from the murderer who is hunting the woman she's falling in love with, Mickey Heiden. (978-1-62639-983-9)

Omnipotence Enough by Sophia Kell Hagin. Can the tiny tool that abducted war veteran Jamie Gwynmorgan accidentally acquires help her escape an unknown enemy to reclaim her stolen life and the woman she deeply loves? (978-1-63555-037-5)

Summer's Cove by Aurora Rey. Emerson Lange moved to Provincetown to live in the moment, but when she meets Darcy Belo and her son Liam, her quest for summer romance becomes a family affair. (978-1-62639-971-6)

The Road to Wings by Julie Tizard. Lieutenant Casey Tompkins, Air Force student pilot, has to fly with the toughest instructor, Captain Kathryn "Hard Ass" Hardesty, fly a supersonic jet, and deal with a growing forbidden attraction. (978-1-62639-988-4)

Beauty and the Boss by Ali Vali. Ellis Renois is at the top of the fashion world, but she never expects her summer assistant Charlotte Hamner to tear her heart and her business apart like sharp scissors through cheap material. (978-1-62639-919-8)

Fury's Choice by Brey Willows. When gods walk amongst humans, can two women find a balance between love and faith? (978-1-62639-869-6)

Lessons in Desire by MJ Williamz. Can a summer love stand a four-month hiatus and still burn hot? (978-1-63555-019-1)

Lightning Chasers by Cass Sellars. For Sydney and Parker, being a couple was never what they had planned. Now they have to fight corruption, murder, and enemies hiding in plain sight just to hold on to each other. Lightning Series, Book Two. (978-1-62639-965-5)

Summer Fling by Jean Copeland. Still jaded from a breakup years earlier, Kate struggles to trust falling in love again when a summer fling with sexy young singer Jordan rocks her off her feet. (978-1-62639-981-5)

Take Me There by Julie Cannon. Adrienne and Sloan know it would be career suicide to mix business with pleasure, however tempting it is. But what's the harm? They're both consenting adults. Who would know? (978-1-62639-917-4)

The Girl Who Wasn't Dead by Samantha Boyette. A year ago, someone tried to kill Jenny Lewis. Tonight she's ready to find out who it was. (978-1-62639-950-1)

Unchained Memories by Dena Blake. Can a woman give herself completely when she's left a piece of herself behind? (978-1-62639-993-8)

Walking Through Shadows by Sheri Lewis Wohl. All Molly wanted to do was go backpacking...in her own century. (978-1-62639-968-6)

A Lamentation of Swans by Valerie Bronwen. Ariel Montgomery returns to Sea Oats to try to save her broken marriage but soon finds herself also fighting to save her own life and catch a murderer. (978-1-62639-828-3)

Freedom to Love by Ronica Black. What happens when the woman who spent her lifetime worrying about caring for her family, finally finds the freedom to love without borders? (978-1-63555-001-6)

House of Fate by Barbara Ann Wright. Two women must throw off the lives they've known as a guardian and an assassin and save two rival houses before their secrets tear the galaxy apart. (978-1-62639-780-4)

Planning for Love by Erin Dutton. Could true love be the one thing that wedding coordinator Faith McKenna didn't plan for? (978-1-62639-954-9)

Sidebar by Carsen Taite. Judge Camille Avery and her clerk, attorney West Fallon, agree on little except their mutual attraction, but can their relationship and their careers survive a headline-grabbing case? (978-1-62639-752-1)

Sweet Boy and Wild One by T. L. Hayes. When Rachel Cole meets soulful singer Bobby Layton at an open mic, she is immediately in thrall. What she soon discovers will rock her world in ways she never imagined. (978-1-62639-963-1)

To Be Determined by Mardi Alexander and Laurie Eichler. Charlie Dickerson escapes her life in the US to rescue Australian wildlife with Pip Atkins, but can they save each other? (978-1-62639-946-4)